NIGHTSCRIPT

VOLUME EIGHT

EDITED BY C.M. Muller

CHTHONIC MATTER | St. Paul, Minnesota

NIGHTSCRIPT: *Volume Eight*

FIRST EDITION

Cover by Barandash Karandashich (via Shutterstock)

Additional proofreading by Chris Mashak

Nightscript is published annually, during grand October.

CHTHONIC MATTER | St. Paul, Minnesota
www.chthonicmatter.wordpress.com

CONTENTS

N IS FOR NIGHT

Steve Rasnic Tem

———◆———

HE HAD LITTLE understanding of human relationships. None of his had lasted long enough for him to acquire any notion of expertise. Yet he believed they were an uneasy balance of truth and pretense. Despite everything, human beings managed to commit and care for each other. The pretense was not only what you said or did to make yourself appealing, but any confidence you had that you understood what someone else wanted or cared about or how they perceived the world in any way. Impossible. No one was a mind reader.

Jeffry never outgrew his fear of the dark. He'd never shared that information with anyone. He was ashamed. It was an embarrassing relic from a frightful childhood. He remembered as a boy lying in bed with the covers over his head listening to every sound. At least as an adult he kept the covers down. How did it help to make things even darker? But he still listened. He still quaked.

He imagined if he were married, he would have a companion for those long dark nights. He came to understand the fantasy promised too much. Everyone takes such journeys alone.

An aging bachelor, he bought the house on Alphabet Row after a significant drop in price. Something was probably wrong with the property, but he could not find it. He had simple needs—he wanted a comfortable place for reading during the day and sleeping safely at night.

The house was set further back than the others on the street. He had no idea why there was this sudden break in uniformity, except it allowed for more trees. Nine large, leafy maples in the front and side yards kept his home permanently in shade during the summer, spring, and early fall. When the leaves fell, he felt buried, and kept the blinds and curtains closed so he wouldn't have to look. The realtor bragged how the numerous windows in the front of the house let in the maximum amount of natural light. But windows which let in light let in dark after the sun went down.

The house was difficult to light at night. It had two stories, although no one looking from the street would have known because of the obscuring trees. Both levels had high ceilings with an unnecessarily steep staircase connecting them. There was no hall light or ceiling fixtures of any kind. Jeffry had to make do with plug-in lamps whose illumination reached barely above head-height. The walls were broad and had too-few outlets. No matter how he positioned the lamps there were always dead spots, broad patches of shadow, and recesses so dark they disappeared.

The night found sanctuary inside his home. After dinner, the ceilings faded into non-existence. The walls were awash in gloom. The interior geometry never appeared normal. The worst were the closets. Wary of their nasty implications, he never opened them after five.

Not that he necessarily deserved light. His had never been a sunny personality, and for someone who was so unsettled by darkness he never bothered to fortify himself with more sun during the day. Since his college years he'd kept largely to himself, and now retired could see little reason to venture out. Sunshine was wasted on him. He had no desire to garden and if the grass died beneath the intense shade of all those trees at least he wouldn't have to mow.

Jeffry understood sunshine to be a kind of medicine, a balm against depression and a source of vitamin D. He made it a practice to sit in a chair in his backyard every morning within the small patch of ground which received direct sun. He closed his eyes and allowed the sun to warm his face and heat his head, almost until they burned. If he got out early enough, he imagined he saw jewels of sunlight nurturing the surrounding plants before blending in with the sky's spreading illumination, a process opposite to what he witnessed in the late afternoon. He didn't take such visions seriously—he was a hermit hiding away in his nonconforming nest, and therefore prone to exaggerated experiences.

Late afternoons the darkness spread from shadows beneath the bushes and trees and drifted down in soft gradients from the sky. If the weather was warm enough the crickets took over and sang the night into full, black bloom.

He had a working fireplace, but he was afraid to use it. What if he fell asleep and some embers tumbled from the grate? But a good fire might be a welcome comfort. The Neanderthals, didn't they require fire to survive? Perhaps not. They were shorter, stockier than modern day humans and much better suited to the European cold. Fire was useful, for cooking, for toolmaking, and for keeping the night at bay.

He familiarized himself with all the sounds his house made, the furnace coming on, the buzz of various bulbs and electrical appliances, the creaking, and the groans of old timbers as they settled and resettled their bargains with gravity, the thumps and the cries and the weeping. He thought if he catalogued these noises, he would feel less alarmed by their presence in the dark. But every stray sound seemed the beginning of a nocturne he'd deal with poorly if heard when half asleep. His own company kept him constantly nervous.

Every evening as bedtime approached, Jeffry practiced certain rituals meant to both distract and calm him. He had his dinner early so a full stomach would not keep him awake. He listened to music on the radio, but he avoided the chat shows and their endless opinions. He read copiously but stopped the last hour before bed to prevent an excess accumulation of language. He double-checked the security of doors and windows, and he took a last look outside, even when it was too dark to see anything. The air under the trees was opaque and inky.

Once the downstairs routine was complete Jeffry turned out the lights and negotiated the steep stairs, never looking back. It occurred to him how the second story would someday become inaccessible because of his aging legs, and he would need to sleep downstairs. Even on the second level the lights failed to reach the corners so any intruders would have numerous places to hide. The upstairs hallway felt narrower at night. Some nights it seemed he could hardly squeeze through. He became less nimble every day. He ran into furniture whose locations appeared to change without warning. Shadows which had once been mere nuisance became obstacles.

Every night he hoped for dreams to sweep him away from worries over the noises and the hidden things meaning him harm. He slept naked because it seemed to make it easier to slip into dream. He kept his clock near, referring to it every time he was startled awake so he would know how many hours he had left to bear.

Every night he heard someone coming up the stairs, someone forcing their way in, someone trying to open a window, someone pounding a door, jiggling a knob, kneeling beside his bed hiding their presence. He didn't know what they wanted—he owned little—

but older people often presented as victims. Thieves and murderers were drawn to the aged like flies to rotten meat.

He needed something new to happen. Even something negative might lead to positive change. He was certain she'd spoken his name. Forgetting his nakedness, he got out of bed and went to the window.

She stood beneath the trees. She looked familiar, but he couldn't remember her name. Was she a neighbor?

Things were wrong with her appearance. She resembled some sort of negative image. The next morning, he remembered getting up in the night but wasn't sure if he'd actually seen her. Perhaps he hadn't left his bed at all. His dreams were numinous, compelling, but incomplete.

IN WINTER, AFTER the trees lost their leaves, Jeffry was surprised by how many branches hid beneath the missing foliage. The complexity of their intermingling limbs seemed an impossibility, as if the sky had fractured.

The biggest change was that he could now see the sidewalk and the street in front, and the people and cars passing by, although they looked much further away than he knew they were. His was the last house on the corner. He'd always heard corner houses were the ones most frequently robbed. In the distance was the M house across Alphabet Row. An elementary school lay beyond. Children were always walking down the Row towards the library. He often heard them, but almost never saw them.

He had not seen the woman under the trees again, although he looked for her every night. He hadn't decided whether she'd been there, but the possibility nagged him, and the search became part of his routine. Every morning he lay in bed, staring at the ceiling, listening. The sounds he heard were not that different from the ones he heard at night—creaking and breathing and footsteps on the stairs—yet they seemed less ominous in daylight. In fact, there

were far more sounds to sort through: traffic on a distant highway, children on the school playground, people on the sidewalk
out front, the noise from neighboring yards. None of it particularly
sinister.

When Jeffry eventually climbed out of bed, he did so gingerly,
as if not to awaken whatever might be sleeping in his house. A
nonsensical notion, but it persisted. His feet were numb in the
morning, not quite ready for the floor. Once he put on his shoes
they felt better, but his footsteps made too much noise.

He wasted an hour or two each day sitting by the large front
window, watching. There wasn't much traffic. Many people preferred to walk. A number carried book bags as they made their
way to and from the old library. As much as Jeffry was intrigued
by the building and the books which might be found there, he
hadn't yet worked up the nerve to go.

A few couples walked by, the younger ones holding hands.
They didn't understand what was in store for them. The older
people appeared to walk together but separately, intent on their
own missions. Many of the pedestrians were women. He paid
special attention to them, looking for some resemblance to the
female apparition who'd lingered beneath the trees, but it was difficult to draw comparisons with these quite real women under the
harsh glare of daylight.

Now and then, one would pause on the sidewalk and glance his
way. It was some distance, so he wasn't afraid of being seen, but if
they smiled, he felt foolishly encouraged. He assumed many locals
never saw his house when the trees had their full complement of
leaves, and so were curious what the place looked like. As far as he
could tell his was much like the other houses, at least the few two-
story ones. The houses on this street were lettered rather than
numbered—he'd never seen such an arrangement before. But he
didn't know what his house letter was—that character was long
gone, and for some reason it wasn't on the deed. All his paper-

work referred to an outdated lot number. When he called for grocery deliveries, he referred to it as "the house on the corner with all the trees out front" and they knew which one he meant.

Perhaps that explained why he never received any mail. He had a cell phone but used online grocery lists and text messages to order food, and seemed to have been spared the unwanted sales calls which plagued the modern world.

None of this seemed entirely natural. He couldn't always distinguish his days from a pointless, languorous dream. He was eager to see the woman under the trees again, no matter if she were real or not.

Despite his fears his life was best at night. Even when he woke up in the middle of the night, terrified, at least he felt something. His breath quickened and his heart beat with urgency. It also seemed his thoughts were far more interesting between nine PM and dawn. Ideas and perceptions came in such a flood he couldn't keep track. He'd leave notes to read the next day, but most were illegible.

One night in midwinter he peered out his bedroom window and saw the woman moving across his front yard. She had a paler look, and moved among the trees haphazardly, as if a long twist of newspaper caught in the wind. He might have thought she was no more than a bit of trash, but he heard the fretful sounds she made, distressed weeping, and moans of disappointment. Twice the twisted debris turned its face to look at him as if wanting something.

He threw on his bathrobe and raced down the stairs, risking catastrophe. The open front door made him stop. Had someone gotten inside or—as unlikely as it seemed—had she come from inside his house? He went out into the yard in his bare feet. The rough frozen ground felt like broken glass. He had trouble breathing, his chest seizing with a fierce cold pain. He stayed out as long as he dared, but he did not find her.

He turned on all the lights when he got back inside and searched the house. He found no traces of a break-in, or indications of any kind that another person had been in his home. He left the lights on, unable to sleep the rest of the night. There seemed to be several possibilities, but none appealed.

The rest of that evening and all the next day Jeffry spent looking out his windows from various angles, thinking an optical illusion involving distortions in the glass and accidental geometries might be involved. His neck was sore from straining to see what wasn't there. When he grew exhausted, he searched his problematic closets on the off chance the woman might be living in one. He discovered items he did not recognize but assumed they'd been left by the previous owner: old china, men's leather gloves, a hairbrush, an old hatchet head, a spade with a cracked blade, and a rope studded with hard, blood-stained knots. Perhaps these things had been hers. Had he overheard her mumbled prayers or was that his imagination?

During the next few weeks Jeffry suffered from extended bouts of narcolepsy, unable to stay awake for days, so numb with worry over what the night might bring he could not keep his eyes open. He would wake up in the dark not knowing where he was, having lost hours, in a chair or on the couch and more than a few times lying on the floor. The experience was humiliating. For safety he began spending most of his time in his bedroom, lying down on the bed at the first sign of somnolence or even a noticeable period of inattention.

He stopped having dreams, or perhaps his waking experiences were his dreams and those periods of dead unconsciousness his newly awakened life.

One day he woke up to numerous sharp objects littering the bedroom floor: fragmented metal and broken glass, pins and needles and knife blades and jagged bone.

Another morning his pajama sleeve was nailed to the headboard. That same morning, he could not feel his nose. When he examined his face in the mirror, he saw that his nose was there, but it had been nibbled on, altering its shape. Dried blood caked his nose, cheeks, and chin. After this event Jeffry couldn't smell anything after dark. Either his nose had been ruined, or the scents themselves had translated into something else.

His life had departed any sense of a consistent narrative. His clock had stopped running. He had no idea how long ago. Not that these human-conceived numerals had any meaningful relationship to time. If it felt like nine AM when he woke up, it was nine AM. Surely somewhere on this vast world it was nine o'clock something.

After the narcolepsy passed, he noticed he could stay awake for days. He sat cross-legged on his bed and stared out the window through the trees and to the street and houses beyond and the neighborhoods beyond and even the skies and fields beyond the city. He couldn't remember having been able to see so much before. He used a small hand mirror to examine his eyes. The pupils were hard to catch the way they kept darting around, anxious to witness everything. It felt as if they were two untamed creatures over which he could no longer claim ownership.

Black ink began to drip from one pupil and then from the other. The ink streamed down—he was literally weeping ink—over his chest and over his bed, flooding the floor and pouring out the window until nature itself disappeared into the endlessly spilling ink. Night had arrived again, and with nothing left to see Jeffry fell back asleep and slept for days or maybe even longer, it was hard to say with his clock stopped.

When he awakened again, he could not open his eyes without nausea. He had reached the nadir of his season, it seemed, when he understood he could feel no worse, and could look forward to a climb back into normalcy.

He practiced opening his eyes slowly until he could keep them open without getting sick. He mustered enough determination to put his clothes and shoes on, thinking that increased his chances of having a normal day.

Outside his window a noirish quiet had settled in. It appeared to be late afternoon, the air looking heavily polluted, but he decided it was only fine bits of darkness, the first suggestions of evening. There appeared to be more black silhouettes of trees than the nine he owned, or at least more limbs, multiplying as the darkness deepened.

He crouched on the floor by the window, at first self-conscious being seen from the yard or the street. He considered turning out the bedroom light, but he heard the front door open, and saw her rushing out into the yard, arms stretched overhead in dismay, a sound like wind pushing in front of her, but he grasped immediately she was making that soft howl.

He got downstairs as quickly as his stiff legs would allow, but this time he slipped into a coat and woven cap. She was still making a mournful noise, and it was certain to draw the neighbors, and the idea of meeting them under such circumstances disturbed him more than the less than substantial female standing in his yard.

"What can I . . . " He paused, the sound of his own voice unsettling. He couldn't remember the last time he'd heard it. The figure fell silent and moved deeper into the trees.

He couldn't tell what she was pointing at, so he stood beside her, and it was difficult to focus on anything but the way the minimal light from his window lit her form, reflecting an eye, a bit of her open mouth, shining through most of her torso so he saw more ground than belly, more tree trunk than leg. Then there were the bruises: dead black splotches on her face, neck, and shoulders where no light shone through. He shouldn't have stared, but he hadn't been this close to anyone, and certainly not a woman, in more than a year, so he had to force himself to look at the exposed roots of the first tree, where a fragment of discolored hip bone lay revealed, much like a piece of stone, but he had no doubts what it was. Nearby lay scattered finger and toe bones like worn pebbles—he couldn't remember their names—and above a limb penetrated a section of yellowed sternum with a few attached ribs, and an entire mandible wedged into a fork further up the tree which would have to remain because he had no way of getting it down.

Because that was what she wanted wasn't it? All this evidence brought inside, all this dirty laundry, so the neighbors wouldn't see, and ask their nosy questions, and call the police.

JEFFRY HAD NEVER seen such a snowstorm, a hard wind, and blinding white blasts lasting for days. The storm made him near-sighted. He couldn't see anything beyond their trees, beyond their yard.

The wind died down, and seeing how the white clung to almost everything, so bright it hurt the eyes, Jeffry considered how the landscape looked like a reverse night. No human beings, no creatures of any kind were in evidence. He might have been staring at an expansive still life. The neighborhood had become a necropolis. He remained inside, cozy within the nest they'd made.

He was a novice at this. He didn't know what he was doing. He followed her lead.

He did not know her name. He supposed he could call the realtor who sold him the house or do a little research at the local library, but he didn't think it mattered. She had lost her reticence. She often sat at the table with him at meals. He set a place for her with one of those cracked china plates from the closet. It was a ridiculous thing to do he supposed, but she did sit there and stare at the plate as if recalling past meals. She spent most of her time wandering the house, floating up and down those stairs. Sometimes it looked more like falling—was that how she'd met her death?

Sometimes she lay in bed with him. They did nothing untoward. He felt her tickling his nape as if seeking entrance into his skull, but he could have told her she was already there. Touching her left his fingertips numb.

Had she killed an abusive husband? That's what the few details he had would suggest. But it was an interpretation from too few facts. Human beings made up stories out of a need to know, but it did not mean they had acquired any degree of truth.

Other people looking at his story might pity him, might think his personal narrative a sorry excuse for a life. But did they know their lovers any better? Were their lovers any more real? Like everyone else he lived at the nexus of now and yesterday and only imagined what he knew.

Dust continued to accumulate. Spiderwebs filled the corners. The front steps overgrew with nettles and rabbitbrush. Neither had a knack for housework it seemed. Night and day blended into long stretches of sepia.

He wondered if she would let him know when he died. He might not recognize it otherwise.

I CAME BACK

Christi Nogle

———— ◆ ————

I CAME BACK. That's one thing no one can take away. When Jaimie got really sick, I came back and loved her the way she always wanted me to. I took care of everything. Our daughter Olivia was a drama queen the whole time. Who could blame her, really, but still. I'd been gone three years, tops—with visits of course. I'd never gone a full year without laying eyes on her, but I guess time draws out when you're a teenager.

Olivia didn't even trust me to drive her to her after-school things. She kept whining at Jaimie to do it up until she just physically could not do it.

Now it's all different. We're just a few months out from our trip to Florida. All Jaimie wanted was for everyone to meet at her folks' for a big drunken potluck, all the family and all her friends from elementary on up. I never knew she had so many friends or so many cousins. And Olivia was like a movie star to all of them.

They kept going on about how pretty and sweet she was, which made her smug, and they gorged her with food. They wanted to keep her.

But I was back. I came back, and I said the two of us would go back to our lives, thanks for your concern.

Now when she's not needed, she stays in her bedroom drawing, reading, doing homework. She gets up and does her chores, makes dinner, makes nice. Just a few months past it, and she's a whole lot better. We've gotten into a routine.

WORK SUCKS. I'm trying to get on full-time, but they keep jerking me around. I've always taken a lot of pride in my work, and now, desperate as I am, I'm volunteering for everything, fixing everybody else's messes. You'd think that would be enough, but it isn't. I've got to keep buddying up to Roy and Chase, going out for a few beers every night or they'll start to think . . . I don't know what they'll think. Or I'll get pushed even farther out, I suppose.

I call Olivia. Is she OK having dinner on her own again? She is. She'll set me a plate in the fridge.

IN THE GROCERY store, Olivia puts a sack of fun-size candy bars in the cart. It must be a five-pound sack.

"*Huh*-uh," I say. "Put it back. You don't need to be eating candy."

She flushes. She knows I'm not supposed to ever mention her weight. "It's for the trick-or-treaters," she says.

"They can get it somewhere else," I say, and I lead her past the candy stacks with an arm around her shoulder. I feel how tense that makes her.

"Or maybe we won't even be home. Who knows? Halloween is still a few weeks off. Maybe we'll be at a party."

It's when we're driving home in the truck, after ten minutes of silence, that she says, "We always stayed home and passed out candy. She wasn't strong enough to go out, and we liked seeing all the little kids. They were so cute."

"Olivia," I say.

She looks at me, says, "We didn't get to do it last year because she was so sick, but every year before that . . . " and her voice hitches. She turns her face to the side window and cries without making a sound.

OLIVIA CAME DOWN with a cold. I think it's because she worries so much. I picked her up some chunky soup and orange juice and Seven-Up, and she was a little grateful for a change. She looked up at me with sleepy eyes and said a genuine "Thank you, Dad."

Roy's wife had anniversary plans, so the guys didn't go out at all. I sat on the couch next to Olivia, watching cheesy horror movies while she rolled in and out of sleep. It was nice. And now she's in her bed, and she should be sleeping it off, but she's not. She's coughing up stuff and going silent for just ten or fifteen minutes, then launching into another coughing fit.

I go back out for something to help her get back to sleep.

I TEXT OLIVIA every time I get the chance. If we had insurance, if things weren't so bad at work, I'd have taken her to the doc-in-the-box this morning. I'll do it tomorrow if she's no better.

"You OK?" I say.

"OK," she says.

"Need anything? Plenty of pop still?"

"I'm OK," she says, but it's like half an hour later.

Olivia hasn't cleared the coffee table when I get home. She's deep asleep with a hot sweaty forehead, her body all burritoed up in that plushy Korean blanket we got at the state fair.

I fall asleep in the recliner, and there's a time deep in the night when I wake because she's moaning. I sit beside her, slide her glass of water close.

"Feeling better? You slept a long time," I say.

"I dreamed Mom was here. I didn't want to wake up," she rasps.

"What's wrong with your voice?" She sounds like the frogman in that old song.

"Something in my . . . " she says and tries to clear her throat.

"Gargle and spit it back in the glass," I say, and she does.

"That helps," she says. I pet her head.

"Mom wanted to make all these different things. She never had time and then she was too sick," she says, and then she starts telling me her dream, which was all about her and her mom working on crafts and making them all come out right like Jaimie never had the time or the energy to do for real. They made something in the yard like a nativity. They made something purple and red. I don't think she's told me one of her dreams since she was, what? Four or five years old.

Being so sick has made her like a baby again, and I get guilty thinking how nice she is like this, how much I've missed her being sweet like this.

"It's a good dream. You dream some more," I say, and I take the glass into the kitchen, pour it down the drain. The water she spit back looks like skim milk.

IT FEELS ALMOST like a dream when I come upon her in the bathroom in the early morning. There's a pile of balled tissues and a thin trail of blood and snot in the sink. Olivia's leaned over it all, half-sitting on the vanity top. She's angling into the light, reaching in with something metal.

"Stop that," I say. The tweezers are in her hand, then the tweezers are in my hand, and she's begging me to look, just look.

It looks like a big pearl far back in her throat.

"I promise not to gag. Just do it," she says, and I am doing it. Careful, careful, like that OPERATION game, careful not to touch her. So sure it's a pearl, I expect it to slip away from the steel, but it grasps there like hard taffy or soft plastic, and gently I pull. It catches and releases in her throat, catches again and falls out into the sink, a pearly white object the size and shape of a lawn grub.

Olivia goes in under the faucet, fills her mouth from her hand. She's swishing, gargling.

"What *is* that? How'd you swallow it?" I say.

She spits pale pink water, wipes her mouth, holds the thing up in wonder. "I didn't swallow anything."

"We need to go to the hospital," I say.

"I think it *grew* in me," she says, and is she laughing?

I take her up in my arms and I'm going to the door, going to put her in the car and come back in for my keys, but she's looking at me, laughing. She's so light and her arm so strong around my neck.

"Don't be stupid. I'm all right. Dad, I'm all *right*."

She is. Her eyes are clear now, her voice clear and beautiful. I lower her feet to the floor.

I'm rattled, though. I go out back for a cigarette, and when I get back in, Olivia's already cleaned up the bathroom.

I WISH I WAS young again. A couple of weeks bedridden and every ounce of baby fat is off of her. She's come back brighter, stronger. She draws stares in the grocery store.

She puts two of the big candy sacks in the cart and doesn't look back to see what I think of that. I smile to myself to see how bold she's gotten.

OLIVIA LOOKS LIKE some sixties sitcom girl in a black turtleneck with her clean hair falling loose down her back. She stands in the doorway clutching a ton of candy in a papier-mâché bowl that she and her mom made. It's ridged like a pumpkin but painted metallic red and purple with glitter and jewels crusting the edges.

When Olivia took me down to the craft room in the basement this morning, she showed me a whole lot of the crap that Jaimie and she had made over the years, and of course she could see as well as I could how badly done it all was. She isn't that stupid.

There's a pride in her, though, and a low-level rage under that, and over top of that a desperate hope. She stands at the doorway until full dark. I'm just inside, watching TV, but even I can hear the little kids going by in packs on the other side of the street.

"They'll be coming this way soon," she says. "You going to come help?"

But they don't come this way. It gets darker, and Olivia brings in a kitchen chair so she has a view out front. A couple of teenagers come, and I tell her it's time to turn off the light.

She doesn't cry like I think she might. Before bed, she puts a lot of the candy into tiny Ziploc bags for my lunches and then takes the purple bowl out onto the porch. In the morning, the rest of the candy's gone and the bowl is smashed. She decides it goes in the recycling and not the trash because it's mostly paper.

I WAS REFLECTIVE for a while after Olivia got sick, after she got better. It isn't my natural way to be, and I soon got back to going out with Chase and Roy and not thinking. Yes, I got back to usual soon enough, but there were a couple of weeks there where I couldn't sleep, and I guess I was thinking about Jaimie.

I thought she was probably why the little kids' parents didn't bring them around this year. The year before, when she was so bad, how scary she must have looked, how the neighbors must have avoided her.

Jaimie always wanted to be some sort of an artist. She said she never had the time—and I'm sure that's true—but she never had talent or grit either. She'd fart around with something for an hour or two and forget about it.

She never could follow through on things. Wasn't that her problem? Half-assed everything. Not just the crafts but, too, the "exercise room" with the second-hand machines she never used.

And wasn't part of the problem, too, the laughing she and

Olivia did—in the kitchen making dinner, in Olivia's room when they got her ready for bed, and especially down in the basement. They were always laughing together in another room. I knew it wasn't so, but still I could never get over the feeling they were laughing at *me*. And maybe that was part of why I left in the first place, that jealous feeling, that paranoia.

I couldn't stop feeling that way, but I could sure enough leave.

Olivia and I went down to the craft room a couple of times while I was in that reflective place and she was feeling so good. I think we both had a mind to try to make this work. Find something to do together, something to have in common. We looked through some of the craft books and rifled through the bins of materials. We fiddled around with some of the projects Jamie had left half done, but we never really finished anything. It was sad to me to be in that little white room with all the masses of paint tubes and sparkly gew-gaws.

I didn't want to make a sock doll. I didn't want to make a thread painting.

"What is this?" I said, holding up a curve of cold plastic, or was it stone?

"I thought it belonged down here," Olivia said, looking at it, not meeting my eyes. "After all, I made it."

I didn't get what she meant at first, but when I did, I couldn't put it down fast enough. The thing is, I didn't remember it being that big when she coughed it up. I didn't remember it being half that big.

IT WAS AN IMPORTANT winter for Olivia. Her life seemed like something out of a teen movie. She had several dances and the talent show, a long Christmas back in Florida—they bought her ticket and wouldn't take no for an answer. For the dances—I couldn't get over this—her grandma would send her a couple hundred dollars for a dress each time, with the agreement that

Olivia would send pictures.

Olivia was ravenous, constantly eating, but growing more beautiful by the day. I swear she grew three inches. She made more friends, really quality girls. Boys started to come around by then too, always as part of a group. I teased her about their little hairdos and their funny-looking clothes, and she would just blush and turn away.

Some of the kids had their licenses already. In the spring, she had a couple of them drive her to Fred Meyer to get flats of annuals, and they planted them in all the flowerpots one Saturday when I was out.

When I got home, I said something about the flowers before I thought to stop myself—it *was* a waste of time and money but still, commenting on it was not the smartest move on my part. She got pissed and snapped back that it was her own money, from her grandma, and then I got a little pissed too, I guess, because before long we were screaming at each other. She was saying why not just let her go and be with her own family and I could trash Mom's house like I wanted and we'd all be happy.

She went out and pulled a bunch of the flowers out of their pots and stomped off somewhere.

The old lady across the street was watering her bushes and looking my way, so I replanted the flowers with bare hands and went over to let her know it was just hormones making the girl act out like that. She laughed and told me all about how her own girls acted back in the day.

I NOTICED ONE day when Olivia was out, a fancy jewelry box stood on her bedside table. It looked like it was made of that brightly colored art clay that you bake. Fomo? I could see it was handmade, but it was just precious. All these rainbow-colored flowers made out of layer after layer of clay. My first thought was maybe Olivia had an admirer—one of those arty boys or maybe even a girlfriend—but the more I looked, the more I thought it couldn't have been made by a kid. I lifted it off the table and was surprised to see it had a cord. I thought it must have a music player or light in it or something, but when I opened it, there was nothing inside but some rings and a pair of Black Hills Gold earrings that I'd bought Jaimie long before we were married. The cord wasn't an electrical cord after all, just a tough strip of white plastic, and it didn't come out of the electrical socket. It came out from between the floorboards.

I put the earrings in my pocket and went on about whatever I was doing, but I must have known.

That thing was already putting out its flowers, then, in early spring. I knew—I had to have—but what I did, instead of going down to the basement, was to put those earrings in my pocket and go out with Roy. At the end of the night I said I'd found the earrings in a bathroom at work and did he think his wife would like them?

That thing was growing all that time, and I just ignored it, just kept working and going out and microwaving my plate of dinner, falling asleep watching TV, doing it again.

The thought would come that I ought to leave the house, but I couldn't do that. I couldn't leave Olivia again.

Pearls began rising in the grass like mushrooms that summer. I'd stub my toe on them on the way to the truck and then just push them down with the ball of my foot, tuck the grass back around them.

OLIVIA MOWS THE YARD now. She rakes the first fallen leaves.

I can't stand to be out there. The thing hasn't moved in the way I thought it would.

You can still stand at the top of the basement stairs and not see it. You don't see it until you climb down four or five steps and then you can see it eating away at the door frame of the craft room and dripping its white foam down to the floor. It's taken that whole room and the door to the room, but it isn't moving into the exercise room.

I suppose it hasn't gone into the laundry. The clothes still keep getting washed, after all.

It must be moving into the crawl space and up through the floorboards into the rooms upstairs instead—and further into the lawn.

I look out front where Olivia weed-eats around a sculpture coming up in the yard. I think it will be a skeleton when it's finished, and she'll string it with the orange and purple lights she bought. The little kids won't be able to stay away when the yard's all done.

My first thought in the morning and last at night: *I'm not getting on full time.* I'm never getting on full time anywhere in this town. We ought to go. *I* ought to just go.

On my way to the bathroom, I catch Olivia in her room talking with it. It makes me want to vomit. Some of that thing in the basement, in the crawlspace—some of it has taken the form of a girl and lies on the bed beside her—commiserating, laughing—in her room now filled with marvels.

The thing eats glitter and paint and art clay, sequins and pipe cleaners, silk flowers and seed beads. The thing eats Swarovski crystals. It eats scrapbooking papers and craft books, scissors and needles. It eats wood and concrete and dirt and the laminate of table tops, the heavy metal and plastic and rubber of an exercise machine. It eats and pukes it all back as marvels. Sculptures and scrollwork and floral decorations crowding Olivia's room, all tied into the floorboards by tough white tendons and threads.

It *flowers*, I once thought, and it's flowering now as a girl just like Olivia but with wavy black hair like Jaimie's. I see the back of her, see Olivia seeing me, and she smiles at me as the girl fades to white and melts off the bed. Olivia keeps staring at me as the thing sucks back through the floorboards until it's just a piece of chewed gum on the floor, and the gum grows into a little cartoon hand that reaches up and slams the door closed.

IT'S NOT THAT I didn't try. When it was still small, I went down to the craft room. It was stuck to the table then and the size of a dinner plate. I stabbed it, the knife sinking as if into cold taffy but never piercing. I poured drain cleaner on it. I tried. When it was the size of a large dog, I saw how deeply its tendrils reached into the art bins and how they reached up toward the floors of our rooms, and I tried to cut the individual cords, but while they would bend, they would not cut.

I took a torch to the side of it, and it bubbled there but would not blacken. Iridescent glitter poured out of the melted wet side. A foam crept down the side—its blood, its spit. I took a knife to the wet part, which I thought had weakened, but the knife stuck there and would not pull out. The white crawled slowly up the side of the knife. I knew it would take the knife, and if I did not let go, it would take me too. I let go.

It kept growing no matter what I tried.

The whole time, Olivia worked against me. I knew she'd been pushing the exercise machines and storage bins over to it so it could reach them, so it could feed.

She is never alone now. She always has something to do and somewhere to go with her friends, or she has friends in her room whispering and laughing so that there is never a time to take her aside and speak.

The maniac energy, the overflowing of life in her! She does all the house work and makes A's in school and keeps up with clubs and dances—the whole messy calendar, does it all. She does all the shopping now, too. She stays up late, laughing. I think, well. I don't know for sure, but I think she has a love life. I think she has a . . . some kind of following.

I think that thing *was* a pearl, after all, at least when it started. Something of her fused around it, gave it life.

I keep turning back to work as though it will redeem me, but more and more, I look to the truck and think of where the few hundred dollars I've managed to save might take me. This house is not mine. It never was.

On Halloween, I'm late getting done with work. I have a date for the first time in years, a date with Chase's sister who got divorced not too long ago. We're going to dinner and then there'll be dancing at the bar with Chase and Roy and their wives. A regular triple date. I feel stupid to be this excited, but there you have it. There's only half an hour to shower and get into my cowboy costume, but when I pull into the driveway, the dread comes over me.

The yard is all done now, a copse of skeletons to the left of the door strung with lights and loops of black and orange roses. They're more beautiful than anything you can buy. I don't see little kids out yet, but there are people moving slowly on the sidewalk and cars slowing to gawk, and the old lady from across the street calls out that it looks great.

To the right of the door, three witches stir a cauldron that bubbles up dry ice smoke. Their skin is pearly green and violet, their bodies alluring and faces grotesque in silent laughter. I stop and watch their motion, which is like the motion of animatronic figures in its repetition but not in its fluidity. No, they move like living things.

Bats and spiders hang from all the trees on tough black cords, and inside the open door there is an enormous bowl filled with candy. This bowl is the perfected version of the one that got smashed last year. It's metallic purple like the papier-mâché one, ridged and bejeweled like that one, but it's the version that can never be smashed.

Spiderwebs frame the porch. They're moving, slowly crawling.

I can't believe I am moving toward the door still. I should turn around. I have no place here.

Except it's still my girl who sprawls on the couch inside. I see her through the window. She is dressed like a witch with whited skin, black cherry lips, blue-black hair flowing down like water.

"Tell me that's a wig," I say, soon as I'm through the door.

"*Huh*-uh," she says. "I changed it this morning."

I am a little surprised—of course I am—that she would do this without permission, but there's nothing more important now than the shower. I make a sound, a sigh or a scoff, and move past her. I shower in the bathroom, which is still free from any influence of the thing, and I move off to my room, which is also free from any . . . *flowers,* though it's cold in here. Olivia's opened every window in the house.

I have a kitchen chair by the side of my bed where I sit to finish drying myself. I pull on Halloween boxers and a pair of jeans. I can't pull my foot up to put on the socks, though. One of its white cords has me by the toe.

It has me around the waist. I'm stuck fast to the chair and I'm screaming until it has me, gentle as a shushing hand, around the mouth.

THE LITTLE KIDS don't come to the door. I hear them chatter along on the other side of the street and their parents saying, "Say thank you." I catch a few admiring words about our display, but no one comes to the door.

An hour gone by, my phone rings from where I left it in the bathroom. I hear it smash against the sink or the tub, and it doesn't ring again. I can't move, but the thing loosens each time I need a deep breath. It has me. That much is clear. I do not fight.

I wish I could say that I wonder whether Olivia knows it has me. I wish I could say that I wonder if that person out there is even her. It is her, and she knows and doesn't care. Or maybe she told it to take me.

I came back, but coming back was not enough. I ought to have done more, but what more could I have done?

An hour more has gone by now. I think that Roy or Chase or even the date might come to check on me. It's a small town, after all. It wouldn't take a few minutes. I imagine them cramming into Chase's truck to bring me to the bar. That's what your friends would do in high school; it's what Olivia's friends would do.

I hope they don't come, and I hope they do. I imagine Roy saving me, the date saving me, the thing killing everyone. I imagine that last one a hundred ways.

There's no light on in my room, and it's getting truly dark now. I hear the voices of older kids out on their own and teenagers on their way to parties and then the stranger teenagers in groups of one coming right up to the door, saying "trick or treat" in their bored monotone. I could grunt or scrape the chair. They might hear me through the open window. I don't make a sound, though. I listen to Olivia tell them to take as many candies as they like, and then she clicks across the floor and turns on some creepy organ music. She turns it up loud, and only once it's been on a while do I make out the sounds of more people moving in the room.

I've stopped struggling by the time my door opens. Two of the skeletons have come in from the yard. They've come for me, to bring me to the party! White cords lead from their ankles, but the extension cord must not have been long enough because their string of lights have gone out. They grasp the front chair legs and make a terrible screeching sound dragging me across the floorboards.

All of the yard-witches are in the living room mingling with Olivia's friends, and the rest of the skeletons are here, and here too are other marvels that look like people dressed as griffins and dragons and unicorns, fantastical cats and bears and werewolves, lean dancers and bird-people, all of them looking carved from pearly ivory-colored plastic. They all dance and sway to music that shifts and changes. They're talking too loud over the music and talking over each other and laughing, laughing.

The skeletons take handfuls of candy and pour it into their bony mouths, and it scatters out over the floor. Olivia's girlfriends hoot and screech. The witches start raiding the kitchen, breaking dishes.

I will Olivia to stop. I can't speak, but with my eyes I will it. I cry.

I am looking her in the eye. The room has cleared somewhat. I am looking her in the eye and her black-red mouth is wide, laughing a high shrill cackling laugh. *I made all of this.*

The first screams come from across the street.

Still laughing, Olivia moves the slit in her skirt as if to show off her shoes. What she's really revealing is the white cord leading out of her ankle. She points a clawed fingernail to show me where it loops around the room and where it disappears into the floor.

THE MYTHOLOGIZATION OF TYMBER PRESCOTT IN FIVE SELECTED PHOTOS

Luciano Marano

———— ✦ ————

IT HELPS THAT she's dead now, because we never thought of her as a real person anyway. She was an aspiration, the avatar of something we wanted or wanted to be. An attractive algorithm with a pretty face and keen sense of style, designed to be irresistible and sell us stuff. She was basically a brand, like any other. At least we no longer have to feel conflicted about what happened to her—the few of us who did, that is.

Her objectification was an achievement of sorts. She was everything to everyone, inscrutable but endlessly appealing. Mona Lisa in fair trade fashion. The girl next door with eyes full of unspoken promises, more followers than the Dalai Lama, and liked by absolutely everyone.

A true influencer, she made it easier for us with every post.

Tymber Prescott always looked good. She knew exactly what she wanted, was happier than we could ever understand. She was certainly not alive in the same way as lesser humans like us—people with desperate hopes and bitter disappointments, shame, regret, and secret thoughts we could never share.

Her perfection haunted us.

Her destruction obsessed us.

Now, her feed fascinates for very different reasons.

Influence: the capacity to have an effect on the character, development, or behavior of someone or something; or the effect itself.

1. COTTAGECORE CUTIE

Vibrant in a pink thermal shirt and white overalls against the crumbling interior of a ruined cabin, it was exactly this sense of personality—cute, cocky, perfectly posed—that shot Tymber from zero to 40,000 followers in her first year on the app.

Hands jammed in pockets, blonde hair flowing from beneath a black watch cap, Tymber laughs at us, rocking back playfully on her heels. She is incongruously at ease in such a place. You want to warn her away. It somehow doesn't feel right that she should be there, that anybody should. How much of that reaction is due to our knowledge of subsequent events is impossible to say. Still, the place is eerie.

Scorch marks on the splintered wall behind her seem less than random, an unsettling pattern of darker blacks beneath the char of some long ago fire. A stain, or perhaps weirdly intricate growth of mold, sends seeking tendrils upward from the ground beneath Tymber's tan boots. A moldering blanket of leaves and bristling patches of brown grass. Here and there small round beads of shiny black stone glint in the weak rays of light coming through what we imagine are holes in whatever remains of the sagging structure's roof. High on the wall, underneath the mold, a vague design of scratches can be seen. Curling lines within a circle, seemingly too deliberate to be the work of weather or wildlife.

Likely taken by Oliver Perkins, noted lifestyle photographer, the picture is the last of several Tymber posted from a weekend trip to a rural section of the Olympic Peninsula, where she and other models, influencers, and photographers from the Seattle area rented a house for a collaborative working weekend.

Investigators subsequently ascertained Tymber and Oliver went for a walk around noon and returned later than expected, nearly causing the group to miss their intended ferry back to the city. Others in the party said the pair were behaving strangely when they got back: "Like they were high or something," said one witness. In the case of Oliver, known to be a regular drinker and frequent user of drugs, this was not unusual. Tymber, however, did not often imbibe, and at least one witness expressed concern for her.

Searches of the area conducted after Tymber's death located no cabin. Oliver, of course, could not be asked about the image, as he was found dead just two weeks after the trip. Authorities assert he fell and struck his head in the kitchen of his Ballard apartment and bled to death while intoxicated by a combination of codeine and alcohol.

Initial evidence seemed to suggest another person was present at the time, but the investigation was ultimately inconclusive.

2. SWEATY & READY

Tymber's athleticism was often a secondary aspect of her influencer persona. However, seeing her in workout clothes and holding a kettlebell, muscles flexed, we are reminded she initially rose to fame as a fitness model.

Wearing gray tights, white sneakers, a black sports bra, Tymber's hair is pulled loosely back in a playful pink band. She is standing beside a wall of windows in a large room with padded floors. The light is warm and clear. She is turned partially away from us, looking over her shoulder with a mysterious smile that is part challenge, part invitation. She wears no makeup or jewelry beyond a small gold stud in the visible ear. She is lightly sweating, as if, having just completed a warmup, she is ready to begin exercising in earnest.

On the skin of her shoulder is an area of discoloration. It might be a bruise, though it's almost perfectly symmetrical. The outline of the shape is more prominent, easier to spot. And within the circle are faint lines which seem to curl inward as if part of an intricate design.

Her eyes, previously a startlingly light green, appear different now, darker. A shade of brown so deep as to be almost black.

3. #NOTHAPPY

Her expression is difficult to decipher. Tymber sits on the floor just inside a pair of slim white doors, one open to reveal a small balcony rimmed by ornate blue ironwork outside. The light is dull and gray, threatening rain. She sits on a plush rug in faded jeans and billowy yellow sweater. Her legs are not fully visible. The nails on the fingers we can see, on the hand not holding her phone, are unpainted, though the skin beneath each is lightly blue.

Again, she wears no makeup. The dark circles beneath her eyes are obvious. She is smiling, but it has the feel of habit rather than true expression. Despite the apparent chill of the day and open door, there is a thin sheen of sweat on Tymber's forehead. It is not difficult to imagine she will soon begin to cry. The image has the feel of a haphazard selfie more than staged photograph meant for posting. And yet, post it she did, without hashtags or explanation.

The location of the room where the picture was taken remains unknown. When asked later, Tymber's friends and associates were unable, or unwilling, to provide authorities with any additional information.

In the wake of this post, and several likewise melancholic and ambiguous selfies shared shortly after, Tymber's number of followers leapt astronomically.

4. The Infamous Mirror Image

Easily the most famous of her series of bizarre selfies, this picture is unquestionably more responsible than any other for the disturbing rumors that surround the influencer's sudden grisly and mysterious death just six days after it was posted.

She'd been avoiding friends, investigators later ascertained. She hadn't been seen in public for weeks. Essentially, Tymber did not exist beyond her increasingly strange postings to various social media platforms.

Here, Tymber leans forward, face close to the bathroom mirror. The hand of her raised arm is out of frame, likely braced against the wall, while the other holds a phone near her shoulder, lens forward. Though shirtless, Tymber's hair, wild and tangled, clearly unwashed, is long enough to obscure her breasts. She is terribly pale, and looks even more so against the uniformly white tile of the bathroom. Despite the light source above the unseen mirror, her eyes appear entirely black.

There is a trickle of what may be blood coming down Tymber's forehead from somewhere within her hair, though the viscous liquid seems too thick and dark. She is very thin, with much of the lean muscle on display in previous photos seemingly wasted away. On her concave belly and bony hips can be seen a forest of harsh red scratches, the sort which may have been inflicted by the claws of a large cat or perhaps her own fingernails—those we can see have grown long and ragged. The waistband and visible portion of her light blue briefs look soiled.

Most disturbing of all, however, is her expression. Tymber's mouth hangs open, her discolored tongue lolling to one side, much longer than it should be. Milky drool slicks her chin. And although the edges of her cracked and bleeding lips are pulled slightly upward, as if in a smile, the young woman appears at the same time to be screaming. Looking back now, one cannot help but wonder if she was perhaps calling for help.

The image has received more likes and comments than any other Tymber ever posted. It has been shared countless times and remains a popular meme.

5. #WHOISWITHME?

Her feet, bare and dirty. The last photo posted to Tymber's feed, barely two hours before she was found dead. One imagines she was sitting with her knees up and apart, soles pressed nearly together.

Her skin is cut, deeply in places, and blood flows through the frosting of filth smeared across her soles. Dark blue veins bulge in small patches on her ankles and portion of her calves we can see. Her toenails are black. Several have split apart and blood oozes from the ravaged tips of her toes. A small shard of glass can be seen, distractingly shiny amidst so much darkness, piercing Tymber's left heel.

She had clearly been walking without shoes, but for how long? And where? What is the meaning of her final hashtag? A siren call to would-be imitators? Encouragement to follow in the troubled icon's suicidal footsteps? Or is it simply the honest and desperate final question posed by a terrified young woman who was—or at least believed she was—in the thrall of some inexplicable influence?

These are just a few of the many questions that plague those who seek answers to the question of what truly happened to Tymber Prescott.

According to law enforcement, not long after posting the image, the 24-year-old influencer leapt to her death from the top floor of a commercial parking structure in the Seattle's downtown business district.

She has since been the focus of several investigations, both written features and broadcast TV specials alike, along with countless YouTube videos done with widely varying levels of respect and production quality.

To this day, there are those who insist Tymber committed suicide while under the control of a supernatural force. Others argue it was true demonic possession, using her story to warn non-believers of the dangers of godless glory and vapid idolatry.

Most balk at such notions, however, maintaining Tymber was simply the victim of an undiagnosed, but decidedly non-supernatural, mental illness, nothing more.

Admittedly, members of the latter camp struggle to explain the state of her apartment.

In Tymber's home police allegedly found extensive writings carved into walls, written in numerous languages, none of them English and not one of which Tymber was known to speak. Also, several advanced mathematical equations were scrawled in human blood and excrement on her living room floor, apparently solved. Experts remain in disagreement as to the technical accuracy of her solutions, the math being of a reportedly highly experimental and theoretical variety, perhaps unprovable. But none of them can explain how a C-average student who hadn't completed a single hour of college instruction could manage even as much as she did.

And rumors persist of more macabre findings in the apartment—bottles filled with urine; dozens of watches, all broken; a mound of dead birds in one closet; bones that appeared to have been gnawed; and, perhaps most disturbing of all, several articles of shredded children's clothing.

No officials involved with the case have cooperated with outside investigators or journalists. Several, in fact, have died premature and mysterious deaths themselves, a fact which only strengthens the resolve of those insisting the ultimate cause of Tymber's condition to be supernatural.

Meanwhile, Tymber herself lives on after death, in a way.

Ascendancy: Occupation of a position of great power, dominance, or absolute influence.

HER PHOTOS ARE a ubiquitous presence on social media. She remains a popular choice for those seeking a Halloween costume both sexy and scary. The strange symbol on her shoulder is a tattoo favored by rising influencers and celebrity personalities. Her likeness has even been found painted on buildings in various cities around the world. A kind of new secular saint, Tymber's visage seems to mark scenes of similar, likewise unexplained, suicides. Of which, for whatever reason, there are many of late. And more happening all the time.

North American government health officials have persistently stopped short of calling the recent spike of suicides among young people an epidemic. Tech company representatives continue to be reticent to discuss the appearance among posts made by the deceased those including Tymber's now-infamous hashtag—#whoiswithme? Such posts are now typically flagged, if not removed, by company moderators, though critics and parent groups insist such action to be an insufficient response. Industry experts are in disagreement as to the connection, if any, between the proliferation of such content and national suicide trends, and free speech advocates rush to decry such censorship as both unnecessary and unethical. The debate rages on.

Meanwhile, independent research and multiple surveys conducted by mental health advocacy groups in the United States and Canada claim an indisputable correlation between these otherwise unexplained deaths and posts containing the image and/or famous last words of Tymber Prescott.

Of course, such evidence in no way proves those deaths are the result of a widening instance of some sort of mass possession, the work of supernatural or demonic forces, as many claim (some religious groups have gone so far as to encourage their members to avoid the internet altogether). But neither does it establish the existence of a lethal copycat craze among impressionable young people either, a kind of "lethal viral challenge" as mainstream media outlets and some prominent psychologists insist.

All that's certain is the continuing presence of Tymber Prescott, inscrutable and enigmatic as ever. Her story is somehow aspirational and simultaneously cautionary. What exactly about this figure continues to resonate with so many is a mystery.

Only her influence is beyond question.

HOMECOMING

Joshua Rex

———— ◆ ————

DALTON STOOD ON the Arrivals level of Clinton International airport watching a thin line of cars stopping and then starting off, picking up and moving on again like bees gathering pollen. Beyond the ring road and the fortress-grey parking garage was the interstate, sewn like a seam between the spring fields. Looking past the cars over the vast flat emptiness surmounted by the theatric swirl of white/grey clouds spiked with evening sun leavened Dalton. Coming home had never felt like this. For the majority of his forty years he had found the mostly blank landscape as bleak and featureless as deep space—a space that, he'd decided as a teenager, was one he would wind up buried in if he did not make a plan to get out. Now, the sweet verdure of May grass and wild flowers unfurled not only in the quiet fields out there but in his barren internal landscape, long overcast by smog and cacophony and marked by the steady dissolution of the inchoate magic of youth.

He had decided to take this rare trip to his home state after a serendipitous unearthing of long-buried sentiment. It had been a playlist started at random in his car during the gridlock of his three hour commute that had instigated the dismantling of his supposed contented professional and personal adult existence. The songs were those from his childhood—radio pop music of little lyrical profundity, though imbued with the zeitgeist of his youth. The recollections and sense impressions cached in those pieces were so rich, so saturated with his feelings and perceptions of that time (a time laden with decidedly more hope and aspirations for the future than the present) that he found himself weeping in a way he forgot he could. It was a clarity of vision that had slowly and imperceptibly become occluded by the responsibilities of adulthood (work, bills, money management) as well as by its dubious pleasures (sex, alcohol, shopping). With the portal re-opened, the light and lucidity of Dalton's early period illuminated the squalor of the current stage of his life (the city, the highway; his cheap suit, his rusting car). This stage was as much a metaphorical platform as it was an era—one upon which he had been doing little more the past two decades than play acting at "becoming successful" in film and television. The dream, and the talent, had been pure in his childhood, but he'd failed to develop the requisite discipline (hindered, perhaps, by a lifelong proclivity for depression) that would prepare him for the manifold industry pitfalls, i.e. the struggle to emerge above the mediocre hordes and their pernicious, soulless ambition.

But the songs had drawn back the drab and decadent tapestry, revealing the scintillating landscape of his early days. Somehow it was all there—all those seemingly interminable seasons preserved as if in a sealed chamber in his memory, without even the yellowed edges or crusting of verdigris. The music had been the precise key.

Dalton's mother pulled up in the anticipated pre-owned maroon sedan—the same car she'd been driving since the divorce settlement.

She was a small woman thinned by Crohn's disease, with murky eyes and the coiffed fluff and bangs of thirty years ago. She had the coarsely-sanded drawl of a life-long smoker, and the department store wardrobe of a career receptionist with the same small town doctor's office (Dr. Akins, Chiropractor). Her embrace was warm, though overly firm, as if Dalton were leaving rather than arriving, already trying to pull away from her and reestablish that substantial (and intentional) calculable distance. She didn't drive far due to osteoarthritis from a prior injury in one hip, so Dalton got behind the wheel, steered toward the highway and took the onramp heading west.

He was stunned by the mostly empty road, the pace of the scarce traffic, the unnerving quietude of the scene through the windshield. That quiet seemed to permeate the car, and though he and his mother chatted continuously, he felt it omnipresent in the small pauses—there and waiting to cover everything like dust in an abandoned house. It had the ability to do this here. Despite his flowery feelings and sentimental reminiscences of his hometown during the preceding months, Dalton recalled this aspect of the place now as well—the deceptive no-movement character of time here; the silent and invisible flutter of hourglass wings which beat, nevertheless, hummingbird-quick.

"How's Darren? He hasn't called in a while. Do you see him much?" Dalton asked.

"Monday through Friday. Alyssa gets off the bus at my house and he picks her up around five," his mother replied. She paused, lips pressed together. "He told me not to tell you. He and Alyssa are staying over tonight. They're so excited to see you!"

"Oh, great," Dalton said, sounding more dismal than he'd intended. Darren was a drinker and would want to split a case of Old Steeds, and though Dalton was certainly no teetotaler, clarity during this visit was paramount. He needed to be porous and alert to his formative surroundings. Dalton had hoped to drive around once his mother went to bed (invariably at 8:30) to take them in. Instead he'd be up until after midnight with his brother, talking about old times and comparing them to the disappointing present—and later, when they were both well-sauced, the hellish shared crucible of their upbringing. But there had been genuine cheer in his mother's blowing of the surprise—this woman, for whom cheer had not been doled out in spadefuls—which Dalton had no intention of tempering.

Forty miles on, the settings of his youth began to appear. First, the single runway of chain stores in the neighboring city. Next, the fruit farm with its decrepit and weather-scoured market. Then the reedy marsh near the bridge which spanned the bay. Before the bridge was an exit; Dalton took it. His mother, interrupting her own anecdote about Dalton's niece which involved a bathroom accident at a supermarket, said: "Where are we going?"

"I'm curious what the old neighborhood looks like."

His mother stared at him.

"We used to live here. Remember, Ma?"

"Yes, but you were so small . . . I didn't think you'd have any memory of it."

Dalton smirked. "I was seven. That's old enough."

He started down a curving road which led along the bay, passing the village's handful of stores and taverns. They were all changed, and his mother was right: he had only rudimentary impressions of this stretch. Some, however, were quite strong, and as he regarded them a bloom of warm nostalgia opened within him. He was standing in the general store in front of a rotating tower of VHS tapes; he smelled warm wood and groceries; he was opening a package of shredded bubble gum and sucking on a faceted red candy gem ring. "Hey Ma, remember when you won that ham from the store's Christmas raffle?"

"I *do* remember that. I can't believe you do!" his mother said with a chuckle. She continued on with the bathroom emergency story as Dalton signaled left and began winding through the narrow, tree-shadowed roads, plucking out a fossil image here (a boy who'd had a seriously deformed face who had lived in a grey metal-sided house on the corner), and a nebulous impression there (Pharaohs and animal-headed gods when he looked at a monument in the park . . . had he been reading about Egypt?). Two of the songs on Dalton's playlist had been infused specifically with the feeling of this place, and he was stunned to discover that the current sites aligned closely with the pictures of the past in his mind. The scenes were physically intact, as it were, though with an uneasy museum-like stillness. The house of his best friend at the time, for instance, was *exactly* as Dalton remembered it: same decaying race car in the driveway, same cracked blue vinyl siding, same back deck of treated lumber and even the same charcoal grill and cheap set of patio furniture. Dalton recalled racing Match-box cars along the wooden porch railings—railings which were now grotesquely warped and curling up at the ends. The grill and patio set were as corroded as things dredged from the bottom of the ocean. But they were *there*, and Dalton found himself regarding them affectionately as if they themselves were old friends.

Perpendicular from the backyard was his house—the mid-century brick Ranch. The front lawn had been decorated for Easter by its current inhabitants, and the house itself appeared remarkably clean and un-shadowed compared with the snapshot of it in his memory. There, it was draped with shadow like a pall. It took Dalton a moment, but at last he noticed why.

"They cut down the willow tree!" he cried, glancing at his mother. He realized, feeling somewhat shameful about it, that she had finished the bathroom story a while ago with neither acknowledgment nor comment from him. Now she was staring past him at the house with disturbing intensity, as if she were watching something violent occurring amidst the grinning bunny signs and scatter of multicolored plastic eggs. Dalton gazed into the black casements as the car rolled past at the pace of a funeral cortège. Something began to coalesce in the central pane of the bay window: his father's face, hard and rectangular like a roughly hewn block of wood. The narrowed eyes were like chisel gouges, the etched nasolabial folds bracketing that perpetual scowl. Dalton turned away before the face could solidify and become animated in grim replay.

His mother lit a cigarette, her hands knobby and palsied as she flicked the lighter. She cracked the passenger window and kept her eyes there as Dalton drove to the village exit and turned onto the ramp leading to the bridge. The water was rose-colored and stunk of algae blooms. Seagulls hovered like floating bits of ash in the flame-colored ether. As Dalton watched them he felt the familiar mantle of despondency threatening to snuff out the blush of nostalgia. Desperately, he took out his phone and queued up the playlist. But the old car didn't have an auxiliary plug so he turned on the radio and began scrolling through the stations until he found a song from the same period. It wasn't one from the list, but was equally abundant with images. It was a summer song. Dalton smelled mosquito repellent; was riding in the bed of his father's pickup down one of the old farm roads; was on the beach sitting in a folding chair watching the Fourth of July fireworks; tasted sugary ice pops in long plastic sheaths. Oh there was much, still so much to be culled, so many joyful fragments yet to unearth from his native clay.

The exit for his mother's house was the second past the bridge. As they approached it Dalton said: "Ma, you care if we take a little drive?"

"I got some stuff from the store earlier, if that's where you were thinking of heading."

"Actually, I wanted to see what's going on in town."

His mother was silent a moment. "Your brother and Alyssa are waiting for us. Keeping dinner warm. I made your meatloaf and scalloped potatoes."

"This won't take long," Dalton said. He drove two exits further, signaled toward the off ramp and started down the long straight stretch of macadam that led through the fields south of town. Dalton was surprised to find that they were still fields at all—still cultivated, still "undeveloped." In fact, there was more space than he remembered; the drive-in movie screen, blank as the wing of a dead and drifting satellite for over a generation, had been razed. A Folk Victorian farmhouse and accompanying barn which he had watched decompose like an exposed corpse over the course of his school days had been dismantled and interred. Other changes: the veterinarian's office on the corner of Old Timber Road, where his father had ostensibly taken the family dog to be put to sleep when Dalton was ten, had been replaced with a rib restaurant. The local grocery store had razed and rebuilt on the same lot. Beside it was the hotel where Dalton had drank his first beer and woken with his first hangover. Bad memories. Inglorious cul-de-sacs.

As they passed beneath the band of highway preceding town the fractured sun-stripped signage of the forsaken stage of his youth stretched before him like the set of a play that hadn't been produced in decades. Scuffed and curling paint. Flaking shingles. Plazas half occupied, the closed businesses offsetting the open ones like a jaw with missing teeth. Skeletal pylons. Sheets of plywood covering the credit union windows. A roped-off parking lot where the grand hotel (circa 1880) once stood. A hamlet of sagging houses and unadorned yards. New fast food restaurants with neon signs bright as litter strewn in virgin wilderness.

"Not as exciting as what you're used to, huh?" his mother said with a clotted laugh.

"It's better," Dalton said. Ruined or not, he didn't care. What mattered to him was that most of the place was original, had been touched by the singular radiance of those past suns. He did not look at his mother, knowing the confounded expression she'd be wearing. He did not feel like explaining himself. As they passed the town beach and the expanse of tarnished silver lake, one of the songs from the playlist came on the radio—a ballad about the futility of pretending that all is well. An inadvertent hitching breath, the prelude to a sob, caught in his throat.

"Are you all right, Dalton?"

Dalton blinked rapidly, cleared his throat. "Yeah. Fine." But the emotion had been frighteningly powerful, almost unrestrainable. Then he wondered: *Why should I restrain it?* Wasn't there a fundamental part of him that wanted to show/share these feelings with his mother? Or, were the sentiments too distant for two people so long separated, both geographically and personally, for them to reflect with the intimacy of shared experience? Though they were startlingly clear for Dalton, he began to understand that for his mother, whose entire story had taken place in the town and its environs, his childhood was merely a series of chapters in a single, harrowing novel. In contrast, his own life seemed more a collection of disparate flash fiction pieces—stops and starts and radical shifts in setting and mood with scores of diverse characters. *Of course* the days of his early youth weren't as fertile for her as they seemed to him. For her it had been the same errands with a slight variation of places, the same seasonal routines, the same set of family members to visit (now minus the few lost). The summers for her were only "endless" in the way they are for a working parent with two young children and a useless, nightmare of a husband. Speaking of summer, there was the ice cream stand shaped like a soft serve cone beside the baseball diamond. It was the field were Dalton's team of outcast grade schoolers had won consecutive little league championships. Dalton tuned into one of the diagonal spaces off the four-lane road and put the car in park.

"I'm going to take a quick walk," he said.

"Oh honey . . . can't we do this tomorrow?"

"I'll just be a minute."

His mother lit another cigarette and flipped open her phone, most likely to let Darren know what was taking so long. Dalton got out. He could hear that old music playing in the car, growing fainter as he walked. The backstop fence was high and rusted like the bow of a sunken ship. There were metal bleachers behind the dugouts along the first and third base lines. Dalton stepped into the home dugout, recalling the sound of the crunching gravel under his cleats, the feeling of the polyester pants and stirrup socks, the foam and mesh cap. Of running out onto the field with his team with his glove on his hand to cheers and applause. *They sure don't do that during your commute to work,* Dalton thought, stepping onto the dirt infield.

He stood at the pitcher's rubber, then crossed the forty-six feet to home plate. He squatted behind it like he'd done when he was a catcher, and stared beyond the arcing outfield fence at the red line of sunset, like a laceration on the horizon. He realized he hadn't squatted here since the last pitch of the last championship game twenty-eight years earlier. In this stance he could still feel the mask, the chest and shin protectors, the clam-shaped glove thrust outward toward the pitcher, framing one corner of the plate. It was almost as if the two moments were superimposed. Dalton wondered: if he closed his eyes would he hear his teammates and his coach shouting position adjustments? Was time travel not really travel at all but an instantaneous switching, like a mental quantum leap, between events which grew increasingly distant yet ran parallel forever? Dalton tried, pinching his eyes shut, but no game noise came, no smell of leather and chalk or the aftershave of the umpire behind him. He opened them again and looked at his budget size-eleven loafers scrunched in the reddish dust. He reached down and scooped up some of it, letting it sift through his fingers. It had once seemed hallowed, this dirt, this field—a fertile seedbed of potential and glory. Now it seemed to him like grave dirt. He looked over his shoulder at his mother in the passenger seat of the parked car. Her face was angled down and seemed to float, illuminated by the bluish-white cell phone light. Dalton turned back to the field, kissed his fingers and touched home plate as if it were the lid of a coffin, and rose wincing, his knees cracking simultaneously.

He drove the long way through the old downtown, passing the post office and library—two mainstays which brightened him to find unaltered. They passed the towering stone courthouse and the defunct, vine strangled Export Wing and Nut factory. As they approached the Three Bells Tavern, Dalton found himself scanning the gloomy rear lot for the orange and white pickup with the rust-eaten wheel wells. The truck had been scrap for nearly two decades, and yet part of him still expected to see it backed into the space beside the dumpster that it had occupied most days during Dalton's youth and young adulthood.

"That place is looking dingier and shittier than ever," Dalton scoffed. "Is it still the busiest dive in town?"

"I never come this way," his mother said quietly. Which was curious, Dalton thought, as it was the most direct way to Dr. Akins's office from her house. Just past it, Dalton saw his former high school.

"You know, I'm surprised you'd want to come this way," his mother said.

Dalton noted the barb in her tone—a mounting impatience and frustration. Smiling slightly, he said: "Why's that, Ma?"

"The arrest. I know it *used* to bother you . . . "

Looking at the school's parapeted stone façade, Dalton saw himself being led by two officers out the front doors toward the cruiser parked along the curb. He hadn't killed him, though he'd thought he had, *wished* he'd had at the time. At the court hearing three weeks later Dalton had been happy to see the old son of a bitch limping and covered in soot-black bruises. He'd hoped they'd last the same seventeen years that Dalton had been made to wear them. Dalton had been prudent in his decision to take action while still a minor: during the subsequent trial his age, coupled with the revelations of abuse, saved him from what would have been a lengthy federal prison sentence. Instead, he'd served six months in county jail and two years' probation. The day after the latter ended he'd gotten on a plane for the west coast. He had returned a half-dozen or so times since, though not three years ago for the funeral.

"I'm over all that . . . I mean, that's over," Dalton said, though as he piloted the car out of town and back through the dusk-smothered fields he seemed in his reminisces to be traveling into dark country as well, away from the evocative place that the playlist songs had gilded, ormolu-like. That shimmering façade was peeling now, flaking and falling around Dalton faster than he could press it back into place.

At the familiar V in the road he stayed straight instead of bearing right, passing the picket-fenced graveyard that hadn't seen a burial in seventy-five years; passing the junkyard over which he'd glimpsed Halley's Comet (that burning white tail still streaked across his memory); passing the convenient store behind which he'd first gotten high. The large tracts of farmland here were tilled though unsown, and stuck with billboards that read "Development Opportunity" and "Future Site of—." Dalton wondered whether it was because the farmers had sold out, or because the land itself had gone fallow—drained at last of all its miracle-producing minerals. A mere foundation now, inert as concrete, for strip malls and modular homes.

A road was approaching, line-less and straight and flanked by ditches like slashes in the earth. Dalton signaled right.

"Dalton. Please," his mother said.

"Aren't you curious, Ma?"

"*Please*. Let's go home."

Dalton turned sharply. "Sure thing."

The house was the same shape and shade: skull-white siding,

the roof a palate knife slash of black. The acreage had been divided, so the house no longer stood alone on the denuded plot like it did in Dalton's memory. Dark swells of bushes were clustered on either side of the structure like malignant growths. A single yellow porch light glowed will-o'-the-wisp-like in the deepening gloom.

With his mother ice-silent beside him, Dalton put the car in park and got out. He crossed the road without looking (there was no traffic on the abandoned thoroughfares of the past, only tolls) and stopped at the edge of the ditch. He hadn't lived in the place in twenty years. The landscaping had been altered, the shutters painted, the front door replaced. And yet he regarded it now as if it were the face of his father—bloodshot windows, its gaping entry a mouth bellowing articulated fury and the malty vomit stench of Old Steed beer. Dalton dared it to speak. He was strong now, able to defend himself, to confront whatever came out—even his mother's hideous pleas or his brother's terrified brays. It could no longer circumscribe his will.

When the sound came, it was not from the house but behind him—a soft, vanquished weeping. He thought it was his mother, and felt a sudden intense remorse for bringing her here. Dalton looked back at the car. His mother was on the phone—presumably with Darren—and though she was indeed crying it was not she whom Dalton was hearing. What he heard was coming from *outside* the car. And it was familiar, wasn't it—a strain that echoed inside him with more well-deep resonance than any of the playlist songs.

Dalton crossed in front of the car, the headlights distending his shadow up the road like a rubber streak. He saw the figure lying in a few inches of shit-colored water at the bottom of the ditch. It was a young boy, maybe ten, maybe twelve. He wore an oversized white T-shirt speckled with holes and a pair of ratty black jean shorts. His hair was the same color as the water and his skin was fish-belly white and nearly translucent. His limbs, bruise-blackened by the leather strap and length of chain and the wide-jawed crescent wrench, were folded in like a dying insect.

"My god!" Dalton gasped. He took a few steps forward and then stopped as the boy began whimpering again. The abject misery of the sound turned Dalton's bones to eggshell, consumed the tenuous sunlit veil he'd spread over the town like tissue paper touched by flame. Dalton slid down the slanted edge of the ditch, his shoes sinking into the cold slime, and lifted the boy out. He was light, like a cardboard cutout. He began to bray; the sound was long and eviscerating and ran the length of Dalton internally like a blade. "It's all right," he stammered. He wanted to hold the boy close but intuited that he would collapse, or worse, come apart like a doll in Dalton's embrace. Dalton glanced at the house as he carried the boy to the car, noting the trampoline, the basket-ball hoop, the desiccated tree house and thought: *How could it have happened again? How could it be the dominion of nightmare twice?* He got the back door open and placed the boy on the smoke-stinking upholstery of the backseat.

His mother began to scream.

"It's okay," Dalton said, alternately to the boy and to his mother. "You're safe now, you're okay." His mother had dropped the phone. From where it lay on the passenger-side floorboard Dalton could hear Darren shouting, *"What's going on? Ma? What's happening?"* Dalton slammed the back door, got behind the wheel again and floored the accelerator. The dark fields raced past as they had all those times when battered blood-raw he'd pedaled his bike fast as his legs could pump, a bleating moan rising in his throat, wishing that he could ride far and forever. In the end he had, hadn't he? As far as he could—all the way west . . .

"Dalton . . . " his mother said.

Dalton had one hand clasped over his mouth. He dropped it and shouted: "I know. *I know.* But we couldn't *leave* him there, Ma."

"Honey, look at him. Don't you—"

"We have to help him!"

"Dalton, please. *Look at him*," she replied beseechingly.

Dalton sniffled, shook his head, his eyes on the windshield where the headlights barely penetrated the rapidly condensing gloom. When they reached the driveway Dalton pulled in crooked, threw the gearshift in park and then gently scooped the kid from the backseat. The boy seemed to be slowly deflating, his body flaccid and oddly flattened in places. With his mother wailing behind him, Dalton carried the boy up the front steps. He was met at the door by a paunchier, balder version of Darren. Alyssa peered around her father. She was grinning, dressed in a pearlescent fairy costume. Behind them, strung across the doorway between the wood-paneled living room and kitchen was a chain of sheets of construction paper which read "Welcome Home Uncle Dalton!"

Darren's expression was one of revulsion and terror when he saw the figure in his older brother's arms. Alyssa, reaching for an embrace, quickly drew back as well, as if her uncle were holding a dog that had just been run down in the street.

"Alyssa, go to Gram's room," Darren said sharply. For a moment the girl didn't move, not until the boy belched up a soupy drool of brown water. Alyssa flashed Dalton a final, frantic look before disappearing down the hall, her nylon wings fluttering behind her.

Dalton moved along the opposite end of the house, toward the guest room which had once been his high school bedroom. There, he laid the kid on the flannel bedspread and knelt before him. The boy opened his eyes. They were the milk-white and ash of a burned-out light bulb. He opened his mouth, and Dalton opened his mouth. The screams, when they came, were in perfect pitch—an octave separated by little more than a stave of years.

THE ABANDONED

Jo Kaplan

———— ◆ ————

MRS. HARLOW WAS STANDING at the kitchen sink when she saw the delivery truck go past a second time. She disliked delivery trucks—they were big and noisy, unsuitably vulgar on this quiet suburban street—so she noted it the second time with a bit more ire than she would have noted, say, a bicyclist coming around again, or the mailman.

She didn't know *why* she should be so annoyed by the sight of the ungainly brown truck but that it was so out of place, and out of place twice now, and she disliked things that were out of place. She disliked when Mr. Harlow absentmindedly put away the coffee in the wrong cupboard—even though she should have been grateful that he had half a mind to put anything away, at all.

There was a smooth order to her days, each one overlapping the next like a rolling tide. She had gotten so used to the comfortable boredom of marriage. Days duplicated and triplicated, and it was only when an obscene intrusion jarred her from complacency that she remembered herself, felt that creeping unrest—and had to calm herself by remembering that she always kept an escape hatch. One of these days, she just might use it.

She poured the last of the coffee into a filter and waited for the pot to burble, cueing Mr. Harlow to come tromping down the stairs still buttoning his trousers. She turned on the television for the inane babble of morning news because Mr. Harlow liked the white noise. Yesterday, they had been talking about a death caused by some kind of illegal cheese in Italy. The day before that, a virus in Kenya. Today they were talking about scientists at the laboratory upstate who had split something very small with a very strange name. Not the atom; Mrs. Harlow was sure we'd already done that, and anyway, it would've made an awful explosion if they had.

Hearing her husband's footsteps creaking down the stairs, she fixed on a smile. "Good morning, *Mr.* Harlow," she said, as she had nearly every morning since they had married five years ago—but it was a funny thing, really, because he had *always* been Mr. Harlow, married or not. It was only she who had changed.

"Morning *Mrs.* Harlow," he replied with an absentminded kiss for her cheek. She remembered their nuptials, how delighted she had been by her new identity, how she had told him while they lay tangled in bedsheets, *Call me Mrs. Harlow.* And he did, softly, and it sent a tingle down her spine.

She imagined what he might do if he came down the stairs one morning and found her lounging on the sofa with her slippered feet propped on the ottoman, with only a grunt of "Morning, Ed." And maybe she'd be smoking a cigarette, too. When she was finished smoking it, maybe she would put it out in his eye.

She scolded herself for the thought—and then scolded herself twice, for even though it was an intrusive thought, it brought her less disgust than that delivery truck going by a second time. She wondered what happens to an eye when it dies by the tip of a lit cigarette.

They drank their coffee without speaking. Mrs. Harlow made a mental list of chores to be done: the floor needed a sweep, the garbage was beginning to smell, the electric bill wanted paying, and she had a hair appointment this afternoon. The list consumed her. She wondered when it had happened that her whole identity could be reduced to a list of chores, and a kind of suffocating nausea rose in her throat. She sipped her coffee to swallow it down, the TV buzzing in her ears.

"—revolutionary, the idea of parallel worlds. As an example, say, have you ever had déjà vu? The mind makes patterns—"

She thought of the small bag she had hidden away in the closet, packed with spare clothes. A certain ease filled her, so palpable that Mr. Harlow looked up with a frown. "What are you so happy about?"

"Nothing, hun." She glanced at the clock. "You'd better go or you'll be late."

Checking his watch, Mr. Harlow cursed under his breath. "What would I do without you?" He left on the table his cold mug with brown dregs at the bottom, which would stain. Looking at the mug made Mrs. Harlow want to scream. "Should we try again tonight?" he asked. "We're at the right time in your cycle, aren't we?"

She kept her smile fixed. "Next week is better."

"Well, all right."

He left, and then it was just her, alone at the kitchen table with his forgotten mug of coffee. She dumped its remains in the sink, then took the wet filter and coffee grounds to the trashcan. The automatic lid closed with a robotic hiss. She sat down again, but she could still smell the garbage. And the floors needed a sweep. The pile of bills watched her from the counter.

Outside, the rumble of a large truck announced itself as it motored down the quiet little street.

"—say, have you ever had déjà vu?—"

EVERY SO OFTEN, Mrs. Harlow went into their bedroom when Mr. Harlow wasn't home and took out her bag. She had to get on her hands and knees to pull it from the back of the closet. She opened it up, just to check—yes, there were her shirts, rolled up tightly, a dress, one pair of pants, some underwear, and a thick wad of cash. It was all that would fit comfortably, except for—wait, what was she forgetting? Oh yes, her toothbrush.

But she needed that each morning and night, so she had decided that it would only mean she was serious when she finally packed her toothbrush away. Then there would be no turning back.

First she took care of the chores. When she was finished, she rummaged in the refrigerator for something to eat, pushing the container of strawberries to the back where they might hopefully rot. She disliked strawberries, but they were Mr. Harlow's favorite, so she pretended to like them. It was easier to smile and pretend than make an argument out of it, just like it was easier to smile and pretend that she wanted very much to have a child, and hide her birth control pills in a small container that had once held vitamins.

All else in the fridge was more of *his* food—roast beef, the only sandwich meat he liked; carrots, something they could both agree on at least; and several different kinds of jams, which Mr. Harlow spread on almost everything, as he had a terrible sweet tooth. Mrs. Harlow had admonished him more than once that if he kept on eating as he did, he was going to have to get more cavities filled, but he couldn't seem to help himself. Like a child, she thought scornfully. Extra sugar in his coffee, extra jam on his toast, fruits always dipped in honey, and he only liked his carrots roasted in maple syrup or brown sugar.

When it was time for her haircut, she walked into town. It was one of those lovely spring days, ripe with sun and just enough cool breezes to keep summer at bay and electrify the air with its strange energy. As soon as she stepped outside, she felt light and free.

In town, she stopped as a customer exited the bakery and brought out the aroma of fresh pastries, so she went inside and said hello to the man behind the counter, Mr. Barber, who was not a barber but a baker. Mr. Barber asked if she would like an apple fritter, which he had just made, and Mrs. Harlow thought to herself, why not? If Mr. Harlow would continue to eat as much sugar as he liked, why not indulge herself too?

Mrs. Harlow was not known for indulging herself; the more Mr. Harlow let his belly expand, the more stringent his wife grew with her own dieting, as if she could counterbalance him somehow. But it grew so tiresome, all this self-restraint. And for what?

There was something in the air, maybe, that made her say yes.

She thought of the bag in her closet and realized, with a sudden bright certainty, that she was going to go through with it, after all. Tonight she would pack her toothbrush.

"You seem different today," remarked Mr. Barber.

"I'm just pleased at what a nice day it's turned out to be, after all that rain," she said, reminding herself not to seem so strange. She should act as if it were any other ordinary day, and so she sobered.

When he asked if she would like anything else, she hesitated over the danishes and croissants. Seeing her indecision, Mr. Barber pulled out a tray and put it under her nose. "How about a strawberry turnover?"

The scent rose up and she turned away, faint. Strawberries, following her even here! Suddenly the cloying smell of the bakery was too much, and she felt the sticky sweetness of the fritter unpleasantly in her mouth. "No thank you," she said stiffly. "I *despise* strawberries."

And, saying it, she felt better, more herself. With a nod to Mr. Barber, who looked at her strangely, as if he had never seen her before, she left the bakery.

How wonderful it felt to tell the truth! All the time she tried to placate others in the interest of civility, but all of that placating grew tiresome, and made her feel as if she were changing her skin like a jacket.

High above, a pair of twin airplanes cut tiny parallel lines in the sky. A dog barked, and then barked again. Mrs. Harlow forgot, suddenly, what she was doing in town. She had been here so many times, for so many different purposes, that she couldn't decide which one was for today. The post office? No, she had left the unpaid bills at home. The grocery? Well, then she would have taken the car, wouldn't she?

She wandered past the park, which held a little playground, and saw a child standing beneath the monkey bars. "Shouldn't you be in school?" she called out, prompting the child to turn and run beneath the slide. Mrs. Harlow shook her head and remembered, abruptly, why she was in town. It's always like that, isn't it? Just when you start to think about something else . . .

But she wondered where the child's parents were, and when she turned back to find them and admonish them for letting that little girl play hooky, she found the child standing beneath the monkey bars, staring at her. And Mrs. Harlow felt somewhat faint at the sight, for why should the child be there, alone, standing in the park like that, with her inscrutable child's eyes flouting social decorum, staring even when it was rude? Seeing she was watched, the child turned and ran off to duck into the shadows beneath the slide.

Mrs. Harlow continued down the sidewalk without looking back. Perhaps the girl had a twin. And perhaps they were home-schooled, and they didn't get out much, so they had come out on this fine day to play. That seemed reasonable. There must be a hundred children like her. There must be a hundred little towns like this one, in a hundred different places all across the country.

"HOW WOULD YOU like it?" asked Betty Friedman once Mrs. Harlow was seated in the salon chair, shampooed and draped with a black gown. She frowned into the mirror at herself, at the same shoulder-length haircut she had kept for years, because Mr. Harlow liked her hair that length, not too long and not too short.

"Just a trim," she said, as she always did, but as Betty readied her scissors, Mrs. Harlow let out a yelp. "Wait! No."

"Are you all right?"

"Cut it all off," Mrs. Harlow declared. "Cut it off, short. Very short."

Betty hesitated, looking at her as if she did not know her, even though Mrs. Harlow had been getting her hair cut here for years. "Are you sure?"

"Do I look unsure of myself?"

Betty shook her head and shrugged. "Something in the air today."

As long tendrils of hair fell to the floor to curl like snakes, Mrs. Harlow felt the thrill of the shears and the abandoned locks. Betty was uncommonly quiet, forgoing their usual tepid conversation as she snipped.

When it was finished, Betty handed her a mirror looking nervous, and when Mrs. Harlow saw herself she found a stranger staring back with hair buzzed nearly to the sides of her head and coiffed sharply in front. It was the least feminine she'd ever looked. "Well!" she said.

"If you don't like it—"

"Oh, shut *up*, Betty." She got out her purse to pay, leaving behind a stunned silence. She had never spoken to her hairstylist like that before, but something had come over her after seeing herself in the mirror. She realized that now *she* was out of place. She didn't belong here, not anymore. And now that she knew she would go through with it, really and truly, there were no longer any repercussions to what she did in this town. As she handed over the payment, she said, "Your haircut could use a little updating, you know. Keep it as boring as your conversation, and no one will trust you to give *them* a decent look." She smiled at the stylist's shock. "Goodbye, Betty."

Not wanting to pass by the playground a second time, she took the long way home. This route brought her past a little dive bar that her husband occasionally patronized, and while she never would have considered being seen here in the afternoon, she decided to go in. The bar was dim and earthy-smelling, with an old tube television in the corner of the ceiling offering its flashes of light and color. Two men sat at a table, but they paid her no mind. She seated herself on a stool and waited for the bartender, Theodore Carnacky, to approach. When he did, his gaze was blank, unrecognizing. "Help you, ma'am?"

"Whiskey, neat."

He poured. She thought about saying, *Mr. Carnacky, we've known each other for ten years, don't you recognize me?* But instead she decided to enjoy the anonymity. Today, she was someone else. She sipped her whiskey, glanced up at the TV, and frowned. More news, more scientists. "Can't you change that?"

Theodore took up the remote and switched to a channel that would ordinarily have daytime programming on, but there, too, she saw only talking heads and images of the upstate lab surrounded by large black cars, a helicopter whiffling overhead. "It's all they're talking about," he said.

"You know what I dislike about the news?" she said, leaning forward like a regular barfly. "It never has anything to do with us. What do *we* care about some scientists upstate, doing their silly little experiments? How does that affect *our* lives?"

"It's all they're talking about," he said again.

The two men at their table turned to stare at her, and Mrs. Harlow didn't like their looks. She hurriedly finished her whiskey, paid, and left.

When she got home, she decided to throw out all the sweets. The chocolates in the cabinet, the jam in the fridge, the strawberries—all of it.

Then, satisfied, she started dinner, and as it cooked she went out for an evening stroll in the cooling dusk, feeling the breeze on her bare neck and ears, and quite invigorated by it.

She waved to the neighbor as she passed. At first, Mrs. Beasley seemed not to recognize her, and did not wave back but merely stared. Unsettled by that blank look, Mrs. Harlow called out hello, so that her neighbor would recognize her voice. "You look different," said Mrs. Beasley.

When she came back around the block, she saw her husband's car in the driveway; her gait slowed, but she knew she must go back inside, because dinner was in the oven and her bag was up in the closet, and her toothbrush was still in the bathroom, and it was getting dark besides.

As she came in, she called out, "Oh darling, I'm *ho-o-ome!*" the way she always did when she arrived knowing Mr. Harlow was there. Her little joke, a riff on the traditional *honey-I'm-home* call of the man making his gallant return from work. The reversal had tickled her at one point.

She closed the door and set her keys on the table. While they ate, Mr. Harlow kept looking at her shrewdly, as if he could tell something was different but couldn't put his finger on what. She had a half a mind to take the cast-iron skillet and slap that shrewd look from his face, slap it into a strawberry jam.

At long last, he said, "Where have all the sweets gone?"

Mrs. Harlow tilted her head. "What sweets?"

"All the sweets I keep around for dessert. It seems they've vanished."

"Oh, well," she said as she set her dirty dishes in the dishwasher, eyeing the cast iron skillet cooling on the stove with regret. "I'll go to the grocery store tomorrow."

When they settled into bed and shut off the light, Mr. Harlow said, "You're different today."

"Am I?"

SHE ROSE BEFORE her husband, as usual, and, knowing that there was no coffee to brew, she decided to get on with it. Her heart beat rapidly. Sliding open the closet door with perfect silence, she fished out her bag, remembering to grab her toothbrush from the bathroom. Then she went downstairs, opened the front door to another sunny day, and walked straight out of the house.

Mrs. Beasley was out in her bathrobe picking up the paper from the end of her driveway. Once again, she stared vacantly at Mrs. Harlow—a dead, unseeing look. How strange, thought Mrs. Harlow as she offered a small unreturned wave.

She boarded a bus in town that went to the train station, and from there, she took a train into the city, where no one knew her. Tall buildings walled in the streets with elegant storefronts and upscale coffeeshops, and strangers buzzed down wide sidewalks, looking past her, *through* her, not seeing her and not knowing who she was. She might as well not even exist. She might as well be a ghost.

How easy it was, she thought, to abandon a life.

She checked into a hotel using her maiden name, and then she sat alone in the room, laughing and wondering what on earth she was going to do now.

What would Mr. Harlow be thinking? What had it been like for him to wake this morning without her there, to find that she was not in the kitchen with the coffee, to call out to her and hear no response? The imprint of her, lingering on the air—the question, perhaps, of whether she had ever really existed at all—the desolation of her absence must have filled him with dread.

Over the following days, she sat in the hotel room watching television and reading the news, searching for missing persons reports, thinking surely he would have reported her by now. Everyone loved a good mystery. News of murder and kidnapping and disappearances always traveled. But she flipped through channels with frustration, finding nothing, just as if she had never existed in the first place. The only thing anyone wanted to talk about was science and scientists. Well, who needed it?

When she went out into the city, she wore sunglasses and hats to disguise herself, even though she needed no disguise; but she wasn't supposed to be here, she was a missing person, and none of them knew it. She walked down the crowded streets, bustling with strangers, a stranger herself. She imagined herself a different person each time she walked out the door of her hotel, and she bought a small new wardrobe to match this urban persona, which incidentally matched her short, chic haircut. She bought herself a black blazer, a pair of slim jeans, some high-heeled fashion boots. Several times people bumped into her without so much as an *excuse me*, and she wanted to stop and tell them who she was before realizing she didn't know who she was. What was her name, again?

She had the first inkling that the city wasn't for her not when she heard those bar-hopping university students loudly bashing some of her preferred politicians, nor when she stepped into a hole-in-the-wall restaurant and felt uneasy that she was the only white person there (though she had at least the decency to scold herself for this feeling)—no, it was while walking down the street in falling twilight, careful not to step in the dirty puddles that had gathered in the sidewalk's dips. She looked up in time to catch the briefest glimpse of the man walking briskly past her in the opposite direction. At the sight of him she stumbled, her foot landing in one of those grayish puddles she had been trying to avoid, and she turned to watch the back of his receding head.

What had made her stumble was that she could have sworn, even in that brief glimpse, that the man who had passed her *had no face.*

Her stomach lurched as she tried to comprehend the smooth flesh pulled taut over the shape of a face where none was—neither eye nor orifice.

But it *couldn't* be. Even some unusual deformity wouldn't allow such a thing to live as if with a caul over its head. Desperate to prove herself wrong, she hurried back the way she'd come.

He was far ahead of her, his legs much longer than hers. She pushed through pockets of city folks out enjoying the evening, trying to keep the back of his head—with its nondescript brown hair cut just like Mr. Harlow's—in her sight. Around sharp corners, into dim alleyways, and down dizzying streets she followed him, never quite catching up. And the man never once turned around to reveal his face. "Hello!" she tried calling out, not knowing what she would say if he turned. "Excuse me!"

But he never turned.

At last, tired and aching with frustration, she had to stop. The man vanished around another corner and was gone. Though she tried to get her bearings, she did not recognize this place. The buildings here were dingy brick, windows broken and badly-patched, and she saw two homeless men in the alley, their faces obscured by identical bushy beards. Backing away, she tried a different direction, but her panic only deepened.

She was lost.

When she went around another corner, she found herself returned to that same dismal alley, and tears of frustration prickled her eyes. The two homeless men looked up, and she couldn't tell one from the other, supposing that all homeless men must look alike, but their eyes seemed to gleam like the tip of a burning cigarette, and when they opened their mouths they exhaled something like smoke. Irrationally, she thought, *Something is in the air*, and fled, unaccountably horrified by the sight of that smoky substance leaking from their gaping maws.

After several more turns she found herself surrounded once more by strangers, but by then she almost wished again for the desolation of that lonesome alley. There were too many people crowding her in on all sides, jostling her this way and that, forcing her to drift along in the tide. She tried to stop, to steer the other way, but she had no control over where the crowd led her. When she looked up, she thought for one terrifying moment that all the people around her had no faces. She lowered her eyes and tried to convince herself that it was only her panic playing tricks on her mind.

At long last, the surging crowd spat her out and she recognized the bank up ahead; she could find her way back to the hotel from here. Trying not to look at the strangers around her, she followed her feet to familiar ground, and when she made it back to her room, she collapsed on the bed, laughing, until her laughter turned to something else.

After that, she almost thought of herself as a city person. Maybe all city people have such an experience—an initiation of sorts. She'd made it out the other side of that terrible crowd, hadn't she? And so, she stayed. She walked the streets and tried to ignore the dwindling cash at her disposal. She didn't see the faceless man again.

One evening, she bought a pack of cigarettes and smoked them, one by one, on the sidewalk in front of the hotel. She flicked the butts into the street, aware that it was wrong but not quite caring. The city air had a hazy, dreamy quality to it, some combination of exhaust fumes and pollution, and she felt nothing about adding to the filth of her environment. A young couple strolled past, deep in heated debate, and she knew at once they were talking about the scientists. They were all talking about the scientists, and no one was talking about missing persons.

"Well I, for one, think it's all a bunch of bunk," she chimed in, startling the couple who turned to look her up and down. She blew smoke carelessly into the air.

"You wouldn't," said the woman sharply, "if you had seen what they brought into the world. Educate yourself."

The way she phrased it made Mrs. Harlow laugh. What they brought into the world? As if they had given birth.

"I've been too preoccupied to pay attention to matters that don't concern me," she said. "I've just left my husband."

"Good for you," said the man without a trace of sincerity.

The woman frowned. "It concerns all of us."

"Not me."

"One day, it will concern you, and what will you do when no one cares?"

She had no response for that. The couple hurried on, away from her secondhand smoke.

The cigarettes made her sick; the charm of being no one in the city started to wear off. All these meaningless conversations with strangers, and no one knew who she was. She didn't even know who she was anymore, or where she had come from. A small town somewhere, perhaps, or maybe upstate. She had visions of the lab, smoke pouring out of a tear in the fabric of the air beyond which lay a vast and all-encompassing mirror. None of it seemed real. She hadn't been Mrs. Harlow in all this time, not really, and she wondered who Mrs. Harlow was, now.

She was just a stranger, related to no one, meaningless to all. The thought sent a burst of panic through her.

Meaningless even to Mr. Harlow, apparently. How was it that he had not come looking for her? It had been weeks now; he must be worried sick. Or had he given her up for dead? Perhaps he was too angry. Who was brewing his coffee? Who was sweeping his floors? She imagined he must be living in squalor and misery. Maybe, now that she had been gone, he would understand who she really was and what she did for him, and he would love her again, like he did before.

HOW STRANGE IT FELT to stand in front of her house again! She had returned the way she'd gone: by train and bus, all the while wondering what it would be like to come home. Would it be different, on the inside? Would it be derelict? Was she returning to a haunted house? She imagined herself as a ghost, haunting her own home—or the outline of her absence, still haunting where she had left imprints of herself. *Oh, don't be silly*, she thought. It wasn't as if the house had been abandoned for years. Only it felt like just that, it felt as if it *had* been abandoned, because she hadn't been in it.

Meekly, carrying her bursting bag filled with new clothes over her arm, she started up the driveway. It was Saturday. His car was there, and he would be home; her heart beat nervously, excitedly. What would he look like? Had he shaved, or had he allowed a stubble of remorse to reclaim chin? Would he grovel at her feet? Would he yell? Would he give her a black eye?

She had left her keys, of course, thinking she would never come back, but luckily when she tried the door she found it unlocked. Quietly, she let herself inside, locking the door behind her out of habit, for one never knows what strangers will decide to steal into one's home, and if the city had taught her anything, it was the fear of strangers. Her husband never thought of these things, of course. There were lots of things he never had to think about, because Mrs. Harlow thought them for him.

A spiderweb dangled from the corner of the ceiling, and she thought for a moment that the house *was* abandoned. But of course it wasn't; her husband's car was in the driveway.

Was this how the hall had always been set up? She could swear the painting of the lighthouse had been a foot or so to the left, and the table beside the door just a few inches shorter. So strange, how the familiar had become unfamiliar. Wondering, in a moment of panic, whether this was the right house at all or if she had only stepped into a house that looked nearly identical, in a completely different but nearly identical town, she crept down the dim hallway.

But it must be her house after all, for she found him in the living room. She said, "Hello," meaningfully, to the man who sat on the sofa holding a book from which he hardly looked up.

"Oh, hello," he said, flipping the page.

She stood there, rooted to the spot, amazed at his nonchalance. "What do you mean by that?"

Now he looked up. "What do I mean by what?"

"What do you mean by that—*hello?*"

"Just what I said." He frowned at her. "Are you all right?"

"I mean—haven't you noticed? You must have noticed, by god, it's been a month!"

"Noticed what?"

And now Mrs. Harlow felt an irrational desperation, a hot swell of anxiety, rising within her. "I've been gone for a month, and here you are, greeting me as if I've never left!"

"Gone for a month?" he said, amused. He put the book down and stood up, shaking his head and smiling. "Don't you think I would have noticed if you'd been gone for a month? What's this all about?"

"Well . . . well . . . " She couldn't figure it. What did he mean? "I don't understand," she said. "I left a month ago, and I've been in the city ever since. I promise you, I've been gone!"

"Are you feeling well?" he asked, concern in his voice, and she had the notion that he wasn't her husband at all but some imposter who only looked the same, and that was why he was behaving this way. A sliver of a smile crept over his face, like a crescent moon. "Or is this some sort of joke? I mean, you haven't been gone. You've been here the whole time."

She wanted to scream, but all she could do was stand there pitifully, shaking her head and opening her mouth wider and wider, so wide she thought her jaw would crack off and fall to the floor, leave her faceless.

"Now, don't upset yourself," said Mr. Harlow, taking her hands in his. "It's just your hormones." He placed the flat of his palm against her belly, and, discomfited by the gesture, she backed away from his touch. "Why don't you just relax. Better for you, better for the baby."

"What baby?" she cried.

"What baby!" he said, astonished.

"I am not pregnant," she said, backing away from him in horror.

"I'm not!" Dropping her bag, she fell to her knees and starting flinging clothes from it, trying to find her little bottle of pills. "See!" She found the vial and rattled it, but of course all Mr. Harlow saw was a bottle of vitamins. "I couldn't be pregnant. I haven't— I haven't even *been* here!"

Mr. Harlow only looked at her. "But you have."

She put a hand to her belly, knowing there was nothing growing inside of her, but wondering fearfully, irrationally, *what have you brought into the world?*

On the verge of weeping, Mrs. Harlow looked up at her husband and said, "But I've only just gotten home. Where do you think I've been, just now?"

"You went to the grocery store, not half an hour ago, to pick up more strawberries. *You* know. For the pie? Pregnancy cravings, you said."

Mrs. Harlow shook her head so hard that her hair, growing out again to its proper length as if returning her to whom she had once been, fell over her eyes. "I hate strawberries."

"Come on, don't lie," he said. "This isn't you. You're not yourself."

"I *am*," she insisted. "I *am* myself."

But the more she insisted, the more he began to back away cautiously, until at last he said, "You're not my wife."

"I *am* your wife—"

He shook his head, his hands raised almost defensively. "Oh my god. It's true, isn't it? They said it could happen."

"What?" she asked. "What?"

"You're from the lab, aren't you? You've come from upstate. From that awful thing they did—"

"I'm *not*."

But the more she insisted, the less sure she was of what she was even saying. She could see it in his face and knew she was not convincing him any more than she was convincing herself. It was a look she'd never seen him wear but which she recognized as one *she* had worn when looking out at that ugly, rambling delivery truck with disgust.

She was breathing heavily now, each exhalation imparting a smoky quality to the air, as if she had brought the pollution of the city with her in her mouth, or as if some residue of those cigarettes still lingered inside of her, which she hadn't finished expelling. She put a hand over her mouth, hoping whatever was inside of her would not leak out between her fingers.

From down the hall, she heard the sound of a key rattling in a lock, and then the front door creaking on its old unhappy hinges. As it swung open, it admitted the sounds of the street beyond, the birds shrilling and a neighbor's dog barking, and with these sounds came, too, the sickly sweet aroma of strawberries. There was the jingle of keys dropping onto the table, and the door slamming shut, entombing them here, together.

Then they heard a voice, so very like Mrs. Harlow's, call out, "Oh darling, I'm *ho-o-ome!*"

Kindling

M.C. St. John

———◆———

IN THE VILLAGE that summer the men killed many witches.

With Ann Meechum they tied stones to her ankles and threw her in the lake. If she floated, the rules went, she was evil. If she sunk to the bottom, she was innocent. In the end, she bobbed back up to the surface, but she did not move.

Then there was Theodora Bump, who had a wine-colored birthmark across her brow. Ned Beecher, the local carpenter, claimed it was an evil mark. He claimed too that she be hanged, along with her tabby cat, Asanath. What was good for the witch was good for the familiar.

The all-male town council approved the building of the gallows, much to Ned Beecher's delight. The gallows he built was straight and true. Theodora's feet swung plum to the ground, as did Asanath's paws. Afterward, the men drank hot mulled cider with cinnamon and cloves.

Sarah Lawry was another on the list. No one knew the exact reason why, but the gossip had most of the truth wrapped up in its whisperings. Supposedly, Pastor Merrick found Sarah naked in the Lawry's horse barn. Sarah begged him to lie down in the hay like the animals they were. She spoke in tongues with her request.

What went without mention was why Pastor Merrick was in the Lawry's horse barn past midnight in the first place. No matter. The work of the devil, regardless of where it occurred, must be rooted out.

They crushed Sarah Lawry between two slabs of granite. Once cleaned, the stones were used to build Pastor Merrick's fireplace in his rectory.

On and on that summer the witches were killed.

But with each killing and subsequent celebration, things began happening in the village, strange and disturbing signs that had not been witnessed before. Corn wilted in the fields and apples rotted in the orchards. Cows gave sour milk. Dogs barked at shadows. Children muttered and moaned from nightmares.

By autumn, the truth was plain as the harvest moon hanging in the sky. There was another witch, one more powerful than all the others so far.

The men turned their murderous gaze to the edge of the forest, to the mossy hut that blended in with trees, only a soft curl of smoke rising from its chimney. Of course, the worst witch lived there. With all of the gossip, public executions, and mulled cider, the men had overlooked the quiet yet obvious choice.

They finally came for me.

I answered before they knocked, flinging open the door. They startled easily, these men. They had their fears, and they did not hide them well. "I am the one you are looking for," I said.

"Witch! Witch!"

"John Yancey Langford, you need not shout."

"How do you know my middle name?" The young man christened Yancey glanced sideways at the others. Some were snickering, most of them his fellow fisherman. His face turned scarlet. "I have not told a soul."

"Because I am a witch, you dummons. In how many more ways must you state it?"

Pastor Merrick came forward. "You have brought ruin to this village. For righteousness to prevail, we shall smite you like we have the others." He held up his good book as a talisman. Expecting me to weep and drop to my knees. To beg for forgiveness, for mercy.

But I was not like the others. I stood firm and met his gaze. "That would be unwise." My tone made him flinch. He almost dropped his Bible.

Ned Beecher ended up saving him. The carpenter squinted with one gimlet eye, sizing me up as he would a plank of warped wood.

"Who are you to tell us what is wise?" He paused for dramatic effect, to let the most dim-witted men of the lot catch up with his logic. He eventually received it with a rumble of grunts and curses thrown my way. "We are clever enough to know what you are. And we are perfecting the ways to rid your filth from our village."

"Perfecting? You killed those poor women, *your* people, friends and neighbors, in hot and hateful blood. They were innocent. Every one of them. I know it for a fact. The only thing you are perfecting is your own road to hell."

Ned roared with laughter. With a beefy elbow he nudged Pastor Merrick. "Do you hear it? The witch preaches to us about fire and brimstone. The world is truly a backwards place."

"One in need of saving," Pastor Merrick said.

The pastor clenched his jaw. He thought about Sarah Lawry, how the granite slabs ground her to blood and sinew. Her punishment for refusing him. I knew the truth, had known it the day I saw Sarah from my window during her public trial. Her raw terror was a bolt of lightning, harsh and searing to my senses.

Now I saw the pastor's guilt, a flash in the murk of anger and shame that swirled inside his skull. He hated himself for what he had done, but he hated others more in order to shield himself from his sins. He needed this hate to survive.

Every man crowded close to my door was lit in a similar way. I could see it with my powers, could see it all too clearly. Their heads were cheap tin lanterns with crude shapes punched in their shades. When they glowed fiercely, as they did now, their ugly thoughts radiated. They crossed over the faces of the others, this shadow show of the mob. They found safety and solace in the darkness they cast together.

If I hadn't been so angry, I would have felt sorry for them. But I was angry. The time for apologies had vanished with Anne Meechum's body, which did eventually sink to the bottom of the lake. I had been idle for too long. I deserved what was coming, accepted it with seething delight. These men would finally get what they wanted.

Ned Beecher was lit with the fire of the pulpit. "Aye father, indeed, this world needs saving. No man should be cut down by the sharp words of a creature such as this, let alone belittled because of his Christian name. Do you not fancy such a world, John Langford?"

"I do, I do!" the lad outed as Yancey shouted. "No man should ever be judged by what they are named, only by what they do." More savage chants rose from the crowd. An ugly smile crawled across Yancey's lips and settled there. "What we do as good men is purge the wicked."

"Until when?"

I stepped from the doorway and drew myself up tall. Again, the men leaned back. The flames in their heads sputtered with fear, and for a moment I relished reprimanding this patch of idiotic jack-o-lanterns.

"Until there is no more wickedness? Why, that would be impossible. To you, wickedness lies in unmarried women, the supposedly marked, the hags. You can rid of them easily, as I have witnessed. But what if there are no more wicked women? What then?"

Another step into the crowd. I felt my throat constrict, the way Theodora Bump's did when the noose had cinched round her windpipe. But I kept talking.

"You will find more wickedness. No, not more. *New* wickedness. It will lie in the men you do not like, the next batch of colonists from across the ocean, the serfs, the servants, the slaves. Eventually, you will find it in each other, in the very men with which you surround yourselves. If you had your way, you would destroy everyone for the sake of wickedness and still not find the truly wicked."

"And who might they be?" Yancey said. "The truly wicked?"

I saw behind his words to his earnestness, his mindless thoughts. No sarcasm, no wit. He had no idea. He was truly curious.

My response was to laugh. A high, lovely cackle that could have been mistaken for a scream. I wiped away happy tears with the crooks of my fingers. It felt so good to laugh in their faces, to laugh at the end drawing near.

When I caught my breath, I had his answer. "You will never know. I pity you for it."

"I can think of a way to shut you up."

This gruff comment came from Gregory Samson, the blacksmith. He rubbed his thick, blistered hands together. He grinned through his soot-stained beard. "We have not tried what they do so well in Salem."

"The best witch hunters in the country," Ned Beecher said. "Nay, the world."

Pastor Merrick unclenched his jaws. He stared down at the book in his hands as if he had discovered it for the first time. "It is fitting to purge with fire what came here from the flaming pit. As it is written, so it shall be."

"Amen," Gregory Samson said. "I will get my coals."

"I have a gallows beam for a stake," Ned Beecher said.

Yancey turned his bedeviling smirk my way. "The rest of us will take you."

The fisherman had brought rope with them. Yancey took pleasure in wrenching my hands behind my back and binding my wrists. He shoved me into the arms of other men, the cobbler, the constable, the butcher. The village council was accounted for to do their civic duty. They threw taunts, spat, and yanked my ropes. I faltered in my steps but did not fall.

A man to my left pinched my earlobe. "Move along, witch. Can't be late for your lesson. Setting an example for the others is all you're good for."

He meant what he said. Throughout the village, the pale faces of women and children peered out from half-open doors and parted window curtains. Some were terrified. Others, like the old women, were tired and downtrodden. They had watched the same ritual play itself out too many times before.

True to his word, Ned Beecher had his gallows beam erected in the village square. Other men helped him secure it, and still others hauled the kindling from behind Gregory Samson's smithy. They built a neat ring around the stake. One small break served as my path to the middle. Yancey led me by the arm, as if we were a couple entering the hall of a harvest dance.

"I am a forgiving man." He circled rope around my waist and the stake in a fisherman's knot. "I want you to know I hold no grudge. You have made the ultimate sacrifice of your soul for witchcraft. There is no need to burden you further with my grievances."

"I will give you one last chance," I said. "You are stupid like the councilmen, but you are young. You can change if you choose. Call this off."

"Why would I do such a thing?"

"To save yourself."

"I already am. From you." Yancey cinched the knot. "Mr. Beecher, the witch is bound."

"Very good. Then we are ready to commence. Father, will you do the honors?"

"Yes," Pastor Merrick said. He opened his Bible and addressed the crowd, which now had grown from the mob of men to the whole village. "Now, a passage from Deuteronomy, where Moses warns of the evils of divination . . . "

As the pastor recited scripture, Ned Beecher led the men in piling the last of the wood. He had the audacity to drop me a wink. Then he joined Gregory Samson, who had filled a large iron bucket with coals from his forge. Gregory handed Ned a short-handled shovel. The blacksmith held his bellows.

" . . . and so sayeth the lord." Pastor Merrick shut the book and frowned at me. "Have you any last words?"

"I will for you later."

"Blasphemy."

"For whom?" I addressed the crowd, focusing on the silent women. "Remember what happened here. I tried my best to stay out of the affairs of these men, and look where I ended up. They found their witch today, but they will find another tomorrow. Remember it can happen to you. It *will* happen to you. Unless—"

"Enough," Ned Beecher said. "Save your talk for the devil."

With a piggish grunt, he threw out a spadeful of burning coals. The dry wood caught in an instant. The fire turned the brambles to a burning lace. Gregory Samson opened his bellows and sent a blast of air to feed the flames.

The sparks caught the hem of my dress. The gray threads seared, then blackened. Soon they blazed into flowers of red and orange and yellow, the petals turning to ash that set fire to new blossoms, higher and higher.

I drew fire into my lungs.

My eyes turned to burning coals.

The marrow blackened in my bones.

Finally the ropes binding me withered to ash.

I was free.

In a cloud of embers, I rose above the fire and soared over the village square. I watched the crowd from every angle, every perspective. Each spark was me, and in each spark were eyes, a mind, a heartbeat. I could taste the cool autumn air. I could hear the crackling of the fire, and the gruff mutterings of the men. They watched what they thought was the rest of me burn.

The men had no idea I was high above them.

And now the wind moved me on its currents, combing through my particles, smoothing them down to near nothing, to a fine smoke.

The men had no idea I was all around them.

A soft inhale was all it took. Through the lips I was inside, coursing down the throat, filling the lungs, riding the bloodstream. Nerve endings crackled and came to life. I was the filament and the fire. Another body for hearing and touching. For feeling a heartbeat, for tasting a familiar bitterness.

With new eyes, I observed the crowd.

I saw Berenice Merrick, the pastor's wife. Mary Samson and Henrietta Beecher. And through their eyes they saw me as Eliza Meechum, Ann's surviving daughter. They nodded to me; I nodded back. We looked to the others and sent out a gentle message. Breathe deeply, my sisters, and see me. See us.

All of those pale, placid faces. All of those dark, shining eyes.

The soft gray smoke slipped through the crowd, and I awoke in another body, drew breath with another set of lungs. More women, more girls. Wives, sisters, aunts, grandmothers, cousins, nieces, widows.

Dozens of hearts beating wildly beneath their black and gray cloaks and tight dresses, then slowing, finding partners, finding the group, and then beating in unison.

I listened to ten thousand silent thoughts and fears. I calmed them with the truth. With what we could do. And soon we all saw each other, the excitement lighting across every formerly frightened face.

We can make sure this time that everything will change.

We all took a deep breath. Yes, if we worked together. We nodded as the heads of flowers when rustled by the same strong wind.

It was Gregory Samson who declared the deed done. He nodded with satisfaction at the cooling ash. "Aye, the best way to kill a witch. Nothing more than what one sweeps from the hearthstones, eh Father?"

A troubled smile touched Pastor Merrick's lips. The mention of his rectory fireplace troubled him, especially in front of his wife. As always, he recovered himself with scripture. "From dust they shall return," he said. "God willing, there will be no more wickedness for this reaping season."

"It will certainly be a warning to any creature who dares," Ned Beecher said. "Thanks to the council, Henrietta and I will sleep well tonight. Won't we, my dear?"

"Aye," I said. "We will."

"The same can be said for us," Gregory Samson said. He placed his rough hand on my waist and gave me a squeeze. "After we have supper. Mary is making a lovely kidney pie."

I smiled at him. His beard reeked of char. "It is Gregory's favorite," I said with Mary's voice. "He deserves a good meal for what he has done here."

"There should be plenty to go around. Would anyone like to join us? Father?"

Pastor Merrick opened his mouth, but I cut him off. "Oh, we should not intrude," I said. "After such an eventful day, we should all go home and take care of ourselves."

"Berneice is right," the pastor said, nodding to me, his wife. "God helps those who do, after all."

The crowd dispersed. Each of us took our men by the hand, or spoke with a soft word of pride, or coaxed with the thought of a meal, and led them to our houses and huts and shops. There, we would build fires of our own and feed the flames until the windows glowed a rosy red. The entire village would look like embers burning with a strange, hypnotic light. And when our men, sated and tired, nodded off, by the same light each of us would rise and . . .

"Papa," I said. "May we go home?"

John Meechum gently took my small hand in his. It was with that same tenderness he had tied the first stones to my mother's ankles before she was cast in the lake. "Yes, Eliza. It is getting late. I need to tuck you into bed."

"Will you read me a bedtime story?"

"I can. What would you like to hear?"

"Little Red Riding Hood," I said. We walked through the mud back home. The smell of smoke was strong in the air. I heard my other hearts quicken as doors opened and closed throughout the village, our thoughts turning to serving many last meals. "I want to hear about the Big Bad Wolf dressed up as the nice old grandmother."

"I thought that part frightened you."

"Not anymore." Smiling, I squeezed his hand. "I have changed."

The Drums of Baron Ridge

John Garland Wells

———— ◆ ————

I WAS ON THE VERGE of being fired when the "last chance" assignment came across my desk. Nursing the peak of a hangover from my temples, I scanned the provided details.

```
To: Humbert Godofrey
From: Upstairs

Fluff piece. Drummers. Baron Ridge. Leave
today. Last chance.
```

As busy as they were, they sure did have a way with words, in a Hemingway kind of manner. I crumpled the assignment into a messy square and shoved it in my pocket. I had little doubt that the fluff piece would be my last at the magazine. The chaos of my office reflected this nonchalant acceptance. I had lost whatever lust for reporting I once had at least a decade prior; the rest of the time had only been running on fumes, killing time until the inevitable. And now, the inevitable was a final hurrah in Baron Ridge getting plastered and talking to bar folk about what . . . drummers? Whatever. An end with a whimper is still an ending.

An hour later, I was on a train headed from the city to the surrounding rural depots. Baron Ridge was one of the last stops on the route, a secluded little village that had long been seen as a sign that one was completely lost and needed to turn back towards the direction of the civilized. Nevertheless, one thing remained a fundamental truth—the ridges that grew larger and larger as one ventured further rural were a sight of almost mystical beauty, their roves a faint teleporter to more ancient and unknowable times. Baron Ridge itself was settled on one of the more majestic of these ridges, overlooking a steep dropoff that led to the enormous valleys marking the edge of the territory. All that stood across the valley was dense wilderness.

Earlier in my career, I had made a slight name for myself by turning in reports of various traditions, superstitions, festivals, and such by the settlers on the ridges, those that had rejected the modern comforts of the city. Once they had fascinated me to no end, though that had dulled to a middling interest at best. Still, it made sense they would send me on that assignment before pulling the proverbial trigger.

After falling asleep to the throb of a migraine, I awoke to a conductor ushering me to get off the train at the stop. I looked out the window and saw the depot was nothing more than a wooden shack and concrete platform. I had certainly arrived in Baron Ridge. I gathered my briefcase and exited the train. Immediately, I was met with a gust of air much chillier than the lower-elevation city streets. It had been many years since I had visited Baron Ridge, but I had a sense not a single thing had changed since my last visit.

I approached the single employee monitoring a stall where she was selling train tickets.

"Excuse me, but is The Blind Pig still open in town?"

The girl nodded affirmatively.

"Same location?"

Another nod.

I thanked her for her time and started the long walk to town.

FOUR WHISKEY SOURS later and I was starting to become restless as I listened to an elderly man ramble on about some bizarre incident in a barn he remembered from childhood. I could feel my impatience fermenting the good drunk into something more bitter.

The elder was still going when a slightly younger man approached him with a friendly hand on the shoulder, causing the old man to cease his rambling immediately.

"Can't you see you're boring the poor man, Febus? He's clearly trying to drink in peace. Furthermore, I speak for the rest of us when I say I can't stand to hear that damn barn story one more single time."

The old man, Febus I guess, sunk into his frame and sauntered off to the corner to sulk. The man playing savior sat down in his place and held out a bill to the bartender.

"Let me pick up your tab, friend," the man said to me.

I waved him off, but it was too late; the bartender had already taken the bill. "Sorry about him. He's always been a talker, but it's gotten worse with age."

"It's no bother. I was lost in my thoughts anyways."

The man extended his hand to shake. "I'll let you get back to it, but welcome to Baron Ridge. My name is Jonah. Just let me know if you have any questions."

I sloppily returned his shake. "Humbert. I'm a reporter from the city."

His eyes widened. "A reporter? What brings a reporter from the city all the way out here?"

I sipped the last of the whiskey sour and signaled for the bartender to bring me another one. "Off the record, I'm here to drink and kill time until they fire me. On the record, I'm here to write a story about something to do with drummers."

Now he all-but-fell into a state of shock, he appeared nearly star-struck.

"Where are you staying?" he asked.

"I hadn't thought that far ahead. A hotel, presumably. Maybe this bar."

"Stay with me and my family. Not only will you get your story, but I suspect you will be promoted, not fired."

"You assume that's something I want, 'friend.'"

"I'm the reason you're here. I sent out a request for someone to come to every one of the papers and magazines in the city. You're the only one who came."

"Why?"

"Please, you must stay with us, tonight they will come, and you will want to be with safe people when they begin."

I was thoroughly confused, but I was too drunk to refuse the offer of a warm bed and there still remained a buried flame of curiosity regarding the whole affair.

I followed him out of the bar and through town until we arrived at a small house nestled at the corner of a neighborhood. The place was hardly bigger than a shack, though once I was inside, I had to commend Jonah and his family on making the place into a cozy home, a place that would serve well in the nostalgic memories of his sons.

"Humbert, this is my wife Terry. She's making coffee if you would like a cup. This here, is my youngest son Peter," he said, motioning to the sullen smaller boy. The older boy stood up and came over to shake my hand. He was lanky, gaunt even, and he refused to make eye contact. "Welcome to our home, sir. My name is Percy." I shook his hand and shot him a polite smile, which I seriously doubt he noticed.

Their mother, who was both plain and pretty in an unorthodox kind of way, made me a cup of coffee and disappeared into the living room with the two boys, leaving just Jonah and me at the small breakfast nook.

"So what's this drumming business all about, Jonah? I'm starting to feel a pre-hangover migraine coming on, and I'm thinking a good night's rest on your couch or guest bed would be just the right ticket."

"Humbert, you underestimate your own assignment. I assure you that you have never seen or heard anything like it."

My drunken mind was trying to remember what he had said at the bar, and in the order that he had said it. "Jonah, am I in danger in Baron Ridge?"

He leaned back in his chair and rubbed the side of his mug nervously with his thumb. "Not in any direct danger, no. It's just that . . . well, to be blunt with you . . . this drumming that you're here to report on, it's a town tradition that is very important to everyone that lives here, and I fear that your unsupervised presence might serve as an unnecessary, and indeed, a potentially dangerous distraction."

"I feel like I should be insulted right now, but I can't quite figure out why," I mumbled.

He let out a long sigh. "Listen, friend, what I'm trying to say is that, if you stay through the weekend, through the parade and the ceremony, you will see things that you've never imagined could happen. It's just that there are some that might wish that you didn't see them, understand? So with me and my family, you'll have more of a chance of flying under the radar. Story or not, you'll have something to report."

It then began to occur to me that the man was deeply frightened of something, his esoteric description belaying not suspicious malice, but rather a scared and anxious last-ditch cry for outside help. It was obvious that he wanted me, as representative of the modern world and authorities, to witness something, something he found himself unable to speak of directly. There is something deeply unsettling about witnessing a member of one's own community become paralyzed with fear to the point of indirectly betraying that community's trust in favor of exposing a secret. In my younger days, I had carved a niche out of goading these informants out of the rough and aiding them in giving up the secrets, secrets I then turned into borderline tabloid fodder.

But this, this was a whole different kind of secret. I could see it in Jonah's eyes as he spoke, even taste it in the coffee.

I looked around the tiny home. "All right, Jonah. I don't know what it is you're convinced I need to see but simultaneously can't say what it is. Something's got you spooked, and that's got my interest piqued. I'll stick around for the weekend."

He breathed a sigh of relief.

"So when does it start?" I asked.

He looked at the clock above the sink, 9:45. "Fifteen minutes. Come, let's go watch on the porch."

I followed Jonah through the living room and out onto a small porch deck that overlooked the main road. Terry and the boys sat in rocking chairs, sipping coffee in silence. Not one of the three had said a word to me since I had entered. They, too, seemed shaken by something they knew that I could not yet know.

The rest of the town matched their silence. The only sound that could be heard was the slight churning of the trees across the valley. Jonah looked at his watch.

"They've no doubt crossed the ridge. They'll be starting their walk now. In just a moment, they'll start to play. You'll hear them."

Looking down the other street, leading into the neighborhood, I could see the vague silhouettes of other families gathered stoically on their porches, mothers, and children rocking back and forth, fathers eyeing their wrists.

I was about to go back inside for a refill when I thought I heard a soft noise in the distance. I turned around and walked to the edge of the porch. Sure enough, there was a light tapping noise coming from the far end of the main road. All down the row of houses, the children left their chairs and went to the edge of the porches to see the source of the tapping, which was growing exponentially louder.

I looked over to Jonah; his face was focused but held in a grave expression, eyes fixed on the road.

Just then, appearing at the edge of sight came a line of young men carrying torches, enormous and bright things that threatened to burn the retina. They marched in sync to a cadence emitting from a block of drummers just behind them, beating out a war-like rhythm in perfect form. Each one of the fifty or so drummers wore a mask, each one different in design, each one more regal and terrifying than the one adjacent. On sight alone, it was preposterous and humorous. However, paired with the sheer confidence and force of the percussion, the experience was intimidating, holistically disarming. So loud were the beats that there was no room for a single coherent thought.

Trailing just behind the drummers was a boy, no more than fourteen, carrying a snare drum with a rip through the center. As the convoy made a turn and began to come up the neighborhood, the boy took his broken instrument and displayed it through a series of bizarre jerks and twists to each one of the townspeople on the porches. As he passed by us, I could see he had no teeth, his mouth twisted into a gnarly half-smile that was grotesque and impossible to look away from. I could already see the phrasings I could use to bring his likeness to the readers.

The parade continued up through the street. At the point where all the drummers were reaching musical peak, the entire house shook behind us, threatening to tumble down beneath the power of the sounds, tribal and organized, universal and obscure. I struggled to keep my eyes still as they rattled through climax after climax, playing out with such visceral energy that it seemed they would cease to exist if their everything wasn't infused with each stroke.

Achieving new heights of volume, the drummers continued to play through endless combinations of war rhythms as they circled back up the street and paraded back, giving everyone one final tremored look at their obfuscated faces, their impossibly precise motions, perfect synchronicity, total commitment. Though they must have all been just young people, they became a unit there that night, a unit that brought with it intense awe and unbridled horror.

Eventually, the drummers disappeared down the valley, their preciseness never wavering even in the face of the treacherous descent and succeeding ascent back to the wilderness where they originated. Terry and the kids went back inside. Jonah packed a pipe and began to puff at it as I continued to stare into the darkness. Finally, he came and put his hand on my back.

"Tomorrow will be worse. The third door on the left is yours. Sleep well, friend," he said before leaving me in a cloud of stale pipe smoke.

THE NEXT DAY I woke up to the sounds of eggs and bacon being cooked. In the kitchen I found Terry at the stove, her hands trembling terribly, and Jonah sitting at the nook with his sons.

"Good morning, Humbert. Terry is making you breakfast. I figure after we eat, you and I can go on the porch and discuss last night at a bit greater length."

I sat down and ate breakfast with the family as they tried to maintain some semblance of small talk between them. Whatever information that burdened them the night before seemed to be practically eating away at them all, registering in clanky forks, nervous bottom-of-the-bowl scraping, and various verbal tics ("Ummm," "yeah . . . ," etc.). Only Jonah seemed invested in keeping up appearances. He primarily led the stream of boring school and work-related lines of questioning to keep what little momentum the conversation had going. Suffice to say, the meal ended in complete silence.

As Terry cleaned up, Jonah and I adjourned outside. For the first time on an assignment since almost ten-years before, I brought my tape recorder and notepad with me for the interview.

"What the hell was that last night?"

Jonah puffed on his pipe and sipped at a glass of red wine. "That was a demonstration of sorts. It's an ancient tradition that is as old as Baron Ridge itself. It was established by the first settlers of this place. The idea was that all the town could come together in something as essential to nature as rhythm. It was a way to bind us as a whole. You will see the full extent of this tonight, but I think it's important to understand that when we first settled Baron Ridge, there were ten families, each one with a patriarch who was attempting to flee from some kind of city-related prosecution. Each of these men understood that something had to be able to keep us together, a sacrifice that everyone partook in and agreed in its significance. The drumming is a show of unity, yes, and a demonstration of skill, also yes, but it is a symbol of the pact they made, the process by which that drumming is achieved, the *sound* of the drums. Tell me, Humbert, have you ever heard drums *sound* like that?"

"I've never heard or seen anything quite like that in my life."

"And why? You've seen parades before. There was something terrifying about it, right? Something that beckoned a feeling out of you that has never been beckoned, yes?"

I nodded.

"It's all in the sound. There is not a single drum on earth that sounds like that."

"Why did you ask for someone to come? Why are you afraid?"

"Well, to be honest, I am afraid because even though I believe abstractly in the pact, I am a selfish man. And I see things, and you will see things, that are perhaps too etched into the past. I have reached a point in my life that I knew was coming, but wished would not."

"Please try to stop speaking in riddles."

"I don't mean to. It's just . . . the pact requires that I give up the life I have here to become a part of the parade. The pact is in my blood, my ancestor agreed to its terms, and I have to play my part in the grander scheme of things to ensure that my family can continue to live in peace here, away from the dangers and tribulations of the city. No offense to you, of course. We don't live on the ridges so we can renounce the progress of time. It's just that we can abide by a strong bond here. I have no doubt that the full arm of Modernity will reach us at some point, but that point is not today, so . . . I must hold up my end of a very old bargain. Commitment is the name of the game if one wishes to keep an idea alive, Humbert. I'm willing to be a part of that, but the selfish side of me thinks that it is time for an outside opinion."

I stopped the tape recorder. I was even more confused and irritated than I had been when the interview had started. Jonah stood up and dumped out his ash.

"I've got to go to town to prepare some things for later. Dinner will be at 7:30. The ceremony will start at 9:00 tonight. Terry or the boys will see to anything you might need in the meantime."

He left, and for the second time, I was standing dumbfounded on his porch.

JONAH RETURNED AROUND 6:30. After he greeted me, Terry and Peter, he went and got Percy out of his room. The kid, no more than 17, still kept his gaze to the ground, hands in his pockets. As they walked back through the house, and out onto the porch, I was able to eavesdrop on what was said.

"We need to go to the shed and practice one more time. I need to make sure you know exactly what you're doing. You cannot afford to make a mistake, son," Jonah said, his voice firm but supportive.

"I understand, but really I don't want to do this," Percy responded, voice trembling.

Jonah exhaled. "Nobody ever has. You have to, though. For everyone's sake. Meet me in the shed. I must speak with Humbert."

I could hear the boy walking away as Jonah re-entered the home and asked me to join him. When we got outside, his demeanor let me know that something very heavy was indeed on his mind.

"Humbert, I need to make a confession to you. I'm afraid it was actually my son Percy that sent the letters out to the magazines, including yours. He is afraid and had a foolish notion that he might be able to opt out of his responsibilities by way of you. I support you being here and writing about what you see. It is nothing that I or any other member of the community feels ashamed of. On the contrary, I would say it is a great source of pride for many.

"I need you to understand that what you're going to witness tonight will not make sense to you. It will likely appall you. I cannot make you write one thing, or not write another thing, but please be kind to us."

I looked at him and gave him a slight nod to say that I understood and would agree to tread lightly when finalizing the hypothetical story.

Jonah nodded back and began walking off in the direction of the small shed next to the house. Before he went in, he turned back to me. "And one more thing, friend. Please, for your own safety and the safety of my wife and children, do not try to stop anything. What is going to happen has been happening since the first settlers on the ridge, and it will continue long after."

AFTER FINISHING THEIR mysterious practice, Jonah and his son returned inside where we all ate dinner together. The mood was heavy with a silent pressure that pushed down harder and harder with every passing moment. Nobody uttered a sound, and the meal seemed to pass eternally slow. Once everyone had finished, the family all adjourned to the master bedroom for some interaction I was not privy to, nor did I particularly want to be. Though I did not feel the presence of immediate danger, I couldn't escape the notion that I was on the verge of a point-of-no-return, and that whatever I was about to be a voyeur of would leave a permanent cerebral mark.

Around 8:45 we all went out onto the porch and waited until we saw the glow of the lanterns followed by the singular sounds of those drums, their masked players marching in perfect unison to their hellish meter. However, instead of parading up and down the streets, the drummers dispersed into a large circle, marking time with their heels as soon as they reached their individual positions in the shape. As they faced each other, they began playing louder, their sound a ferocious wave of pure rhythm that roused the most core and feral aspects of one's self.

The families that had watched the night before from the safety of their porches now went together down the street and to the side of the drummers' circle. I followed Jonah and his family to a spot near the front of the crowd and got my first up-close experience with the thunderous music being produced by the strange masked young people; it rattled the skeleton.

Once the entire community had gathered to the side of the drummers, they stopped and put their arms and sticks down to their side. A well-dressed and older gentleman from the crowd stepped forward and was allowed into the middle of the circle where he turned and addressed the rest of the citizens.

"As the mayor of Baron Ridge, it is now time for our annual induction ceremony. As it has been every year since our ancestors first came to this ridge, we must give something of ourselves so that we may be able to keep their memory and meaning alive. They settled here and forged a life for all the generations that have come thus far, and will continue to come, and prosper here in this community. We must remind ourselves every year so that we can continue to live off of the land and forge our bloodlines."

The mayor motioned around to all of the drummers. "Here are the sons, and here are their fathers. When it came the time for our forebearers to pass on, it was their sons that managed to come up with a solution, a tradition, to keep them in our world so that we may never forget, so that they may continue to participate in the community. It was the sons that took their fathers and made symbols of their bodies. And it was their sons who did the same and so on until the sons began to leave, began to abandon this place, our ridge. Times had sped their minds up to where patience of death could not be afforded. So it was then that the fathers created the ceremony. Jonah and Percy, would you please come forward?"

From behind me, Jonah strode to the middle of the circle next to the mayor, his son shuffling along behind him. The mayor stood between them and patted them both on the back. I could not help but notice that he carried himself much more like a priest than he did a local politician. Then again, I suppose there isn't much of a distinction between the two.

"Jonah, as you are aware, the tradition set out for us dictates that every year, a living paternal member of one of the ten original families must give himself over to his son, to become a tool for him, and indeed all sons, to remember the sacrifice of the community, the ancestors, the sons and fathers past. It is through this demonstration for our pride that you and your son will be eternally bound to this place through the symbol you will create together. What you will do tonight will continue a legacy of commitment to our land and our lineages. Do you understand what is being required and asked of you tonight?"

Jonah held his head high and looked into the eyes of the crowd. "I do."

Percy seemed to be looking around as well, but for an easy exit, a hole in the formation to bolt through and vanish into the valley. The mayor put both arms on Percy's shoulders to steady him and prevent his leaving.

"Percy, do not be a coward. You have lived here your entire life, and you have seen this ceremony and its benefits seventeen times. You have seen the other sons and their fathers, the noble ways in which they lent themselves to this. You must understand the meaning, the importance. Do you understand that? Can you perform the task that's being asked and required of you tonight?"

Percy was trembling all over, his legs seeming to melt and give way beneath him. It was only after the mayor had grabbed Percy's head and forced him to look into his eyes that the boy was able to steady himself and nod. "I . . . I do."

The mayor turned back to face us. "Now we must begin," he said as he raised a hand and gave a signal to what appeared to be the captain of the esoteric drum corp. The drummer began to tap out a tempo, and after sixteen counts the entire troupe launched into a minimal cadence as the mayor was joined by four men that looked to be around Jonah's age.

Jonah removed his shirt and handed it to one of the men. He then allowed one man on each side of him to grab his arm and hold him in place, as though bracing him for something. The other man and the mayor took Percy and positioned him just behind his father's bare back. The man holding the shirt slung it across his shoulder and brushed back his overcoat, revealing a long blade, which he unsheathed and handed to Percy. The mayor whispered something into Percy's ear.

"Percy, now you become a member of the most elite echelon of Baron Ridge. Now you and your father can take your place among these distinguished archivists of our history. You may begin at your leisure."

Percy took the blade and seemed to be frozen, paralyzed in the moment, crumbling beneath the sheer weight of it all. His father was breathing heavier with each inhale, the full scope of the imminent dawning on him exponentially as the tension grew. Finally, Jonah turned around and looked at his son.

"You must do it, Percy. I'll always be with you after this moment. I love you. Now do it."

He turned back around and let out a long exhale as his son stepped up and placed the edge of the blade against the nape of his father's neck. With a grunt and a tug downwards, Percy began to slice, flaying his father's skin from his back in large and smooth motions. Jonah tried to restrain himself but was eventually unable to stifle the yelps of unimaginable pain as his entire back was stripped away from him. As the pieces fell, the mayor and the men collected them and gently deposited them on a large pile of ice on a table.

I grew nauseous and felt a need to intervene in some way, to call them all barbaric and make them see the archaic torture they were performing. I wanted to. But I didn't. I would be stopped before even getting close to the circle. Besides, I was nothing more than an alcoholic washed-up tabloid loser. All I could do was watch and remember.

Once the skin had been completely removed from Jonah's back, Percy dropped the blade and fell to the ground, tremoring uncontrollably. Jonah, who had been released from the hands of the two men, also fell to the ground. It was disturbingly clear by the ocean of blood pooling around him, as well as the way his body was twitching and contorting, that he was in the throes of shock, a precursor to an even worse death by blood loss. He would be dead in minutes at most.

Percy sat staring into the wound he had created, the muscles, veins, and arteries all severed in some ghastly way, chunks of his father's skin lay scattered in places they shouldn't have been within the wound, and spurts of blood were mixing with dust and mud from when he had fallen. The poor man lay on display in a fit of torment, coughing up mucus and bloody vomit as the shock and holistic pain made one final assault across his body before allowing him to drift into unconsciousness. And there, as a whole town watched, as they did every twelve months, their friend and neighbor Jonah died in complete agony.

The four men each took a quadrant and lifted the body. Percy was allowed to kiss his father's forehead before the body was taken away to an unknown location. The mayor whispered again into Percy's ear, and the boy then walked to the edge of the circle and stood in between two of the masked players. I could only assume they too had performed the heinous act that Percy just had. It seemed Percy had been inducted.

"Would Mr. Xander Henlock please join me for the dedication," the mayor said.

The strange-looking boy with the broken drum that I had seen following behind the parade the previous night emerged from the circle and took his place with his damaged instrument next to the mayor, who took the drum from the boy. He then walked to the table holding the ice with Jonah's skin on it and picked something up. At first, I was unable to determine what it was he was holding; in hindsight, it should have been obvious.

"Last year we gathered here for the ceremony. Young Xander's noble and brave father stood where Jonah stood. And just as Jonah was brave in the face of his ultimate responsibility, so too was the senior Henlock. His contribution was collected, stored, treated, and prepared for tonight, and now the moment has arrived."

He placed the drum on the table and began stretching the hide across the top, fashioning it into a new drumhead. At last, the full concept was revealed to me in sickening fashion as the mayor returned the newly repaired instrument to the boy, who then strapped the thing to his chest and began to rattle off a crisp series of paradiddles.

"Jesus Christ," I muttered.

"Now, Xander, head of the family of Henlocks, take your place among the other beacons of history," the mayor said, handing the kid a mask.

Xander complied with glee and took his place alongside his fellow drummers, each one cradling their drums, their fathers, their generational sagas.

"Next year, we will gather for the parade and to witness Mr. Percy receive his dedication. Goodnight to you all and thank you for doing what you do to make Baron Ridge the singular oasis that it is." And with that, the mayor signaled for the captain to start up again. A celebratory cadence followed, accompanied by the drummers moving into their parade block and beginning a march back down the streets towards the valley.

The crowd began to disperse as they grew farther away, but I waited. I stayed until I could no longer hear the drums and until poor lanky Percy, shuffling behind with a broken drum of his own, was no longer in sight.

```
To: Upstairs
From: Humbert Godofrey

No fluff piece possible. No drummers in
Baron Ridge. I quit.
```

SOPHIE ANNE

Harrison Demchick

————•◆•————

SOPHIE ANNE SPROUTED from the Honey Tree on a sunny Saturday in mid-September at around half past noon. Ava was all giggles and glows when it happened. Devin had forgotten she could be that happy.

The bark of the Honey Tree was smooth and plastic, colored in shades of brown, green, and purple, with dozens of wide-eyed, felt-formed faces stuffed into the doll-sized holes carved in-between the gnarls and the branches. Cast underneath the glow of violet lights and lent gravitas by the dramatic music piped in from somewhere beneath the rolling artificial fog, the acne-pocked sixteen year old calling herself Ranger Jane plucked Ava's new doll straight from the tree and held her bulbous, fat-fingered body in the air for all the gathered children to see.

Ranger Jane asked Ava for her name. "Sophie Anne!" Ava shouted. She didn't know how Ava had come up with the name, but

Devin had delivered it dutifully to the woman at the ivy-covered front desk they called the Honey Tree Forest Ranger Station. Ava had also specified that her Honey Tree Baby should have black hair—pigtails, not ponytail—and green eyes, because leaves are green and Sophie Anne was coming from a tree so she was basically like a leaf.

Sophie Anne was treated with fertilizers and nutrients to help her grow. She was examined carefully by the finest plant doctor in the entire Honey Tree Forest. And soon Devin, Ava, and Sophie Anne were back in the ranger station, where Ava signed the adoption papers so she could take Sophie Anne home.

In the car on the ride down the quiet two-lane highway, Devin ignored the tinny rattling of the engine she couldn't afford to fix and focused instead on the rearview mirror and the way the sunlight danced its way through Ava's auburn hair as she cradled the doe-eyed doll in her lap. Ava was enchanted by Sophie Anne, like a cat by a bird outside the window—or like Devin had been seven years ago, her hair sweaty and stringy, cradling her own little worm of a daughter with Rick still there beside her.

"That's your baby girl now," Devin said to Ava. "Just like you're *my* baby girl."

Ava smiled. The world exhaled when she did.

The car rattled its way along the road.

Ava spent the rest of the day running around the old shotgun house with Sophie Anne in her arms, whispering and giggling and sometimes feeding her with a little teaspoon from the imagined contents of an empty mason jar. The doll was expensive, stupid expensive, the kind of thing Rick would have called a goddamn waste—the kind of thing he'd have clutched at too, another strap around the rubber band ball of resentment he kept bouncing around the back of his head, ready to let it loose the next time the electric company declared them overdue. But then it turned out Rick could drop things just fine when he wanted to. And if he'd seen Ava in the days and weeks and months after, then seen her now, today, he wouldn't have dared say a word.

So Devin sat at their little gray saucer of a kitchen table by the open window and cut coupons from a pennysaver with a pair of scissors she'd found in the drawer beneath the microwave the day she'd moved in, and Ava ran and laughed and smiled because that's what little girls are supposed to do.

When Devin slipped into Ava's room that evening, *My Little Pony* nightlight casting a soft orange glow that extended just barely to the white wooden bed tucked into the far left corner, Sophie Anne was sprawled out on the floor directly underneath Ava's dangling little fingers. Devin lifted the doll from the floor and placed it on the bed between Ava and the wall, then tucked them both in underneath the comforter. She leaned down, kissed Ava on the forehead, then retreated back into the hallway, where she left the door open just a crack and went to bed feeling better than she had for a very long while.

AVA ALWAYS SEEMED to drop Sophie Anne in the night, and somehow she would land farther and farther away: first a foot from the bed, then three, then nearly all the way to the nightlight, cast within its halo like a camper telling stories by fire. One night Devin even found Sophie Anne in the hallway, face-planted in the mauve fur of the carpet with her black pigtails splayed in either direction. Devin had retrieved her there and brought her back to Ava's room, and the next morning in the kitchen while she poured Ava's cereal she told her not to leave Sophie Anne in the middle of the hall like that.

"But I *didn't*!" said Ava.

"Then who did?"

Ava clutched Sophie Anne close and ate her store brand Lucky Charms knockoff. She didn't get the piece of junk plastic ring at the bottom of the box because toys are for girls who tell the truth.

Then Ava took the bus to school and Devin answered phones at the dermatology clinic, and then she picked up Ava at aftercare and brought them both home and paid the bills she could and ignored the bills she couldn't while Ava and her Honey Tree Baby ate pizza and watched cartoons on the rubber-bordered tablet that passed for a TV.

Sophie Anne was in the hallway again the night after that, and the one after. Early one morning Devin was pacing her way through another interminable bout of insomnia when she almost tripped over the doll leaning against the leg of the unsteady chair on the far side of the kitchen table. She nearly woke Ava right then and there, but instead she grabbed Sophie Anne's soft, squishy arm and brought the doll back once again past the nightlight and into Ava's bedroom, where she dropped it less than gracefully in the corner where the headboard met the gray-black scuff of the wall.

It was only a few days later that they couldn't find Sophie Anne at all.

Ava was close to tears pulling up the cushions of the old red sofa Rick had inherited from his uncle. She'd have missed the bus entirely had Devin not grabbed her rainbow-colored backpack, taken her hand, and pulled her through the door onto the walkway outside.

That's where they found Sophie Anne, sitting doubled over on the browned lawn underneath the window with its head in the grass like a string-severed puppet. The humidity of the morning had left dewdrops on the back of its flat felt neck, and Ava squealed as she darted past her mother to retrieve it. But Devin grabbed its dangling arms quickly and pulled it away from her.

"You can't just leave your doll outside like that," said Devin.

"I didn't!" said Ava.

"What if it rained and she got wet? What if somebody took her?"

"I didn't!"

"You need to be more careful!" Devin said. "She's your baby girl."

Ava looked like she was going to cry again. But before she could say anything Devin spotted the yellow-orange bus rolling its way to a stop at the corner of their narrow alleyway of a neighborhood. She heard the hiss of the cab descending upon its wheels.

"Go," said Devin. "You'll see her after school."

Ava turned and scampered over the cracks and weeds in the sidewalk, making it to the sliding door just as the greasy-haired boy from down the street hopped through. Devin watched as the door slid shut and the bus shoved its ungraceful body back into motion. Then she walked over to the car in the driveway, threw Sophie Anne into the passenger seat so the doll would be there when she picked Ava up from aftercare, and climbed into the driver's seat and went to work.

DEVIN SLEPT THAT night in fits and bursts and woke for the last time an hour before Ava would or needed to. Staring frustrated at the ceiling on the left side of the queen bed, the humidity seeping in like water through the windows of a sinking car, she twisted and turned, then shoved herself out from underneath the sheet and padded her way out of her bedroom into the hall. The house was quiet in the early hours, a quiet she hadn't yet adjusted to even though it had been months since the bedsprings creaked and groaned below her sweat-soaked husband. In response some nights she found herself seeking sound, nearly pressing her ears to the walls for the rumble of a distant motorcycle or a breeze rustling through the window to the coupons she'd left by the scissors on the table.

This morning she paced her way along the hallway, once, then twice. Afterwards she caught the whisper of her daughter's steady nighttime breathing. She followed it into the bedroom, the orange of the nightlight beginning to mix with the pastels of early dawn making their way through the window by the dresser. Ava slept peaceful and still, the comforter twisted into knots by her feet the same way they did by Devin's, on those nights when sleep came easy.

It took a moment to realize that Sophie Anne wasn't there.

Devin huffed. She left the room and started looking.

When she was through with the kitchen and the living room, and the laundry room, and even her own bedroom (though god knows why it would be in there), Devin found herself opening the front door and scanning the narrow plot of bare grass in front of her paint-peeling house. Nothing.

But there was something down the road.

In the dim luminescence of the sunrise it was difficult to see more than a little gray muddle in the distance, but as Devin walked closer, the asphalt rough against her pale naked feet, she could make out the green overalls and the thick black pigtails stretched past its neck. She could see the rounded fingers, the pinky of its left hand grazing a jagged black pebble.

When Devin reached Sophie Anne she stood above it for a moment, uncertain. Something jumped a little in her heart, like that wild moment between the first skip of the stone and its inevitable submission to the laws of liquids and gravity.

She nudged the doll, once, with the tip of her big toe. The doll rocked slightly, then fell back to the road.

Then she reached down, lifted Sophie Anne into her arms, and carried it back home.

Ava woke shortly after with Sophie Anne by her side.

Sophie Anne was beside Ava the next morning too, and the one after that. But one morning in the middle of October she was gone. Ava was nearly heartbroken all over again, ignoring the softening cereal on the kitchen table as she shoved her hands and head into every unexplored crevice she could find. Devin, feeling somehow unsteady, walked around the house front yard and back, and she scanned up and down the road as well, but she saw nothing but the other neighborhood kids meandering down the sidewalk toward the bus stop at the end of the block.

When she stepped inside again the tears had already started. Devin collected Ava's backpack, then knelt down and hugged her and kissed the top of her forehead.

"She'll turn up," Devin said. "Don't you worry."

Ava nodded, eyes wide and glassy, hair bouncing in a wave above her head. Devin walked with her out the door and watched her hurry to the bus stop, sniffling and wiping tears away as she went. She watched until after Ava was in the bus, and after the bus was gone, and then Devin searched again around the yard and Ava's room and anywhere else she could think of before she had to get in her car and go to work.

But something whispered at her as she drove. It was there when she took her seat behind the desk in the postage stamp of a waiting room and chatted with the early arriving patients. It was there as she handed out forms and scheduled and rescheduled appointments and follow-ups. It was there still, poking and prodding at the back of her neck, as she readjusted the plastic orange chairs and rearranged the magazines.

At lunchtime Devin abandoned her bagged lunch in the mini-fridge humming in the back corner behind the desk and left the office instead. She climbed into her car, turned the key in the ignition, and navigated onto the road that would take her to the narrow two-lane highway toward the Honey Tree Forest.

She drove in silence. The car rattled above the familiar road. The air was cool—the clouds had gathered since that morning, thick and monotonous as the car made its way through the sparse midday traffic. As she drove, Devin found her eyes scanning the grass and trees that bordered the road, but almost absently, her thoughts scattering around her head so fast and unspoken she didn't need to land on any of them if she didn't want to.

She had been on the road for twenty minutes when she spotted it in a patch of grass just a couple feet beyond where a guard rail should have been.

At a pace that very nearly resembled calm, Devin flipped on her signal and pulled over, slowly, onto the shoulder of the road. The car came to a stop a few feet shy of the patch of grass. Devin shifted the gear into park, then turned off the car. She checked her side mirror for approaching traffic and, finding none, opened the door, walked around the hood of the car, and stepped onto the grass.

Sophie Anne lay face-up on the ground before her.

Devin crouched down and lifted Sophie Anne from the grass. After a small white truck rumbled past, Devin climbed back into the driver's seat and placed Sophie Anne gently onto the passenger seat. Then she turned the engine again, shifted gears, signaled left, and U-turned back in the direction of work.

Again the drive was silent. Devin clutched tightly to the steering wheel, her eyes focused on the expanse of road in front of her. A hint of drizzle began to manifest on Devin's windshield. She switched on the wipers. They left a streak of muddy gray masking the trees beside the road.

Five minutes passed before Devin spoke.

"You don't live there," she said.

The words hung in the cool, stale air. Devin felt lightheaded. She stared down the road.

"You live with us now," she said. "That's your home. You belong to Ava."

A few more droplets landed on the windshield. Devin ignored them. Her left hand shook a little and she gripped the steering wheel tighter.

"Ava is your mother," said Devin. "You're never going back."

The wiper made another arc across the windshield. The wheels rolled heavy along the road. After a minute Devin let her eyes dart to the rearview mirror, where she saw the top of Sophie Anne's head lolling to the valleys and peaks of the asphalt beneath them. Her big green eyes hugged the nose of her felt face. Her pigtails bobbed.

Devin made sure the child locks were on before she left Sophie

Anne in the car in the parking lot outside the dermatology clinic. Later in the afternoon Ava squealed when she found Sophie Anne waiting for her in the passenger seat. She squeezed her tight and lectured her about not scaring her like that. At home Ava carried Sophie Anne all around the house while Devin sat at the kitchen table and cut more coupons retrieved from the last week's junk mail.

At night Devin walked around the house to make sure the doors were locked. She placed a chair in front of the back door in the kitchen. She shoved her mother's useless old ottoman between the front door and the wall. Then she shut and locked all the windows too. It was starting to get chilly at night.

THE NEXT FEW days Ava woke with Sophie Anne in bed beside her. The day after she was gone again, but Devin didn't have to look far to find her. She only had to leave her bedroom to see the front door hanging open, a cool breeze slipping past the dangling bronze chain of the lock and down the narrow hallway. The ottoman had been shoved away, not much but just enough for something small to slip through the crack.

Sophie Anne was on the sidewalk, face down. Devin retrieved her.

That night Devin knotted a shoelace around Sophie Anne's chubby right arm, so tightly it resembled the joint of a balloon elephant. She sat on Ava's bedside as she did it, Ava watching wide-eyed in her orange and pink pajamas.

"But won't it hurt?" said Ava, with concern.

"Not even a little," said Devin, dotting a finger on the bridge of Ava's nose. "That's the magic of the Honey Tree Babies. She's squishable." Then she lifted the other end of the shoelace. "This one you tie around the bedpost here. See? Like this." Devin demonstrated, looping the shoelace around the post by the open end of the bed, tying it securely beneath the white bulb at the top. "You can do this every night. And before you go to school, always be sure to tie the shoelace to something nice and heavy."

"What if she wants to explore when I'm not there?" said Ava.

"Well, we can't have her wandering off on her own," said Devin. "It's not safe without her mother there to protect her." Devin leaned down and kissed Ava on the forehead. "That's what we mothers do. We protect our baby girls."

Ava nodded solemnly.

Then Devin handed Sophie Anne to Ava. She double-checked the knot around the bedpost, then hugged Ava and kissed her and wished her goodnight. She stood and went to the doorway, her body feeling heavy as she turned off the light and closed the door shut behind her.

Devin went to bed. She dreamed about Rick.

In the morning Sophie Anne was still there.

Ava followed her mother's instructions dutifully after that. Every morning before she left for school, she tied the shoelace to the heavy chair by the kitchen table, where Sophie Anne sat as Ava ate her breakfast. Every night, she tied the shoelace to the post of the bed. Her knots were tight, and when they weren't Devin tightened them just to be sure. When Ava woke up and when Devin drove her home, Sophie Anne was always there waiting for her mother.

One Saturday morning in early November, Devin could feel the unseasonal chill clawing its way through the walls of her bedroom. The comforter was wrapped around her tightly. She hadn't slept. She wondered how often she ever did. She stared at the spicks and specks on the ceiling and thought how long it would take to count them all.

Suddenly a shriek pierced the morning air. Devin's heart nearly stopped. She lunged out of bed and into the hallway, then down and into the next room, where Ava stood atop her mattress, hair disheveled and eyes wide and hands cupped against her mouth.

Devin followed her eyes.

Sophie Anne sat against the dresser on the opposite wall of the bedroom, her head leaning back onto the drawer, her pigtails hanging a few inches above the carpet. Her face was cast upward, bathed in the twilight. The way the sun sparkled in her big green sewn-on eyes, she looked very nearly terrified.

It took Devin a moment to understand.

A tuft of white fluff poked from underneath the right sleeve of Sophie Anne's shirt.

Her arm dangled from the bedpost, the shoelace still knotted tightly to her wrist.

Tears welled in Ava's eyes.

Soon Sophie Anne was in Devin's bedroom. Devin had pulled out from the closet the sewing kit she once used to create and not only repair. While Ava watched YouTube videos through the twice-cracked screen protector of her tablet, Devin sat on the bed and weaved orange thread through the disjointed pieces of Sophie Anne's arm in undulating strokes so smooth they were almost graceful. The needle pierced the soft felt skin like Ava's disinterested finger through a slice of lukewarm French toast. Part of Devin wondered if it hurt. Part of her hoped it did.

When she finished, she set Sophie Anne atop the sewing kit and eyed the arm. She squeezed it, then bent it back and forth around the nearly invisible stitching. "Good as new," she muttered.

Sophie Anne stared up at the ceiling as Devin had only a short time before. She was a pudgy little thing. Inside her arm the stuffing was still torn, Devin supposed. Maybe it bent more easily now. Maybe she was better.

"I can always fix it," Devin said, almost to herself. "I can always sew it back together. Then I can rip it off and do it all over again."

The bedsprings creaked as Devin readjusted herself. She picked up Sophie Anne and placed her on the pillow, then put the thread and the sewing needle back into the kit. As she did she felt the familiar bubbling in her eyes and blinked it away just as fast.

"You think this is what I wanted?" said Devin. "You think this is what I wanted my life to be? Well, it's not." She closed the latches of the sewing kit and put it on her lap. "You don't always get to choose."

Sophie Anne lay face-up on the pillow. Her arm dangled somehow, even more than the rest of her.

"This is it," said Devin. It came out as a whisper.

Then she returned the sewing kit to the closet, retrieved Sophie Anne from the bed, and brought her into the living room where Ava squealed and squeezed her tight. She was intact. She was good as new.

SOPHIE ANNE WAS Ava's baby girl and Ava loved her. Ava carried her to Stacy's birthday party. She had Devin buy Sophie Anne a new dress for Christmas. It was a frilly emerald gown woven from the most magical leaves in all the Honey Tree Forest. The sales ranger said it would bring out the sparkle in her eyes. But the sun fell early in the wintertime and Devin couldn't see it.

In January Ava asked if Sophie Anne could sleep without the shoelace. Devin said they could try it.

Morning came and Sophie Anne was still there.

The dermatologist said there might be layoffs. Rick never answered his phone. Devin clipped coupons for laundry detergent and milk.

Around two o'clock one morning in February, Devin was lying awake and listening to sounds. The space heater hummed with heart more than heat. Ice crackled underneath the slow-moving treads of some misguided pickup.

If Devin stared at the ceiling long enough the specks would cross.

If Devin stared at the ceiling long enough it might be forever.

There was a clunk somewhere outside the bedroom.

Devin stiffened. Then she pushed herself out of bed, feeling acutely the chill outside as she cracked open the door to the hallway. The hall was empty.

But Ava's door was open, wider than Devin had left it. She was certain. She didn't see anything near the door though, so she turned left. Slowly, eyes sharp from hours spent staring upwards in the darkness, Devin stepped into the kitchen. She scanned past the chairs and the table toward the counter.

She found Sophie Anne on the floor beneath it. The scissors hanging open by her good arm where she had dropped them.

Cotton poking upward from her neck.

Her severed head lying upside-down beside.

Devin stared for a good long moment. Then she pulled a chair from underneath the heavy kitchen table and sat. Ava would be awake—not immediately, but soon enough. There was time though. She could go to her closet. She could get the sewing kit.

She didn't.

She felt the tears bubbling underneath her eyes.

She didn't stop them.

GHOSTS OF THE PANATAL

Daniel Braum

————•————

Ipanema Beach, Brazil — 2004

THE THREE-STORY BUILDING, indistinguishable from the others built into the sloping hills ringing the city, is the one Rio de Janeiro's unfaithful husbands and their guests know as "the Playground," their playground. In a room inside, the jungle room, a taxidermy jaguar head is mounted on a wall. The big cat once roamed the wilds of the Panatal, now it's lifeless stare gazes across the hideaway and through tinted windows to Ipanema Beach where revelers are worshipping the sun. The hillside and bustling hotel strip are the habitats of the rich. There is no middle class in Rio. The crime rate is astronomical. The new government camera system has cut it 90 percent. Still, the city is not a safe place, at all.

On a mountaintop in the distance, the statue Christ the Redeemer can be seen, monumental stone arms outstretched, silent and oblivious to everything below; the ubiquitous crime, the business men toasting with iced cachaça, the murderously hungry, the divine samba dancing, the rodizio feasts, the human trafficking all side by side together with every luxury and every human failing one can name. Beneath the jaguar head, New York businesswoman Esme DeMarco and a young Brazilian woman, who Esme's colleagues procured and paid to come, disrobe. The battle between the warmth from the themed room's fireplace and the chill of the AC plays out on their skin.

Esme and her brother, Natan, arrived unseen. In a chauffeured car that navigated the twists and turns of backstreets and tight alleyways to the ramp descending into the Playground's garage. An elevator took them, and Esme's three colleagues, up; the building designed for those like them to come and go unseen. Automated locks keep those inside in and those outside out. Esme thinks the entry is fun, something out of a Batman movie.

Esme's colleagues are in the Playground's other rooms, with women of their choosing. Lunch and discussion of their International Monetary Fund project was rushed short to maximize time. Natan is in the kitchen, where the servants are waiting to bring food and caipirinhas when summoned. An armed guard stands watching security camera feeds with professional stoicism.

Esme has already forgotten the woman's name. She does not know if she speaks English or Portuguese. She doesn't care. The young woman shudders when Esme reaches to touch her. She likes the way the fire reflects on the curve of the woman's calf. There's something wrong with her foot, Esme notices. The angle does not look . . . correct. The young woman places her hands on Esme's shoulders then slides them to her neck.

"Stop," Esme says. It is not her thing.

"Stop," she manages to spit; then finds she is gasping for air.

The young woman does not stop. Esme's vision is fading and the room becomes black, dark as the jaguar's lifeless, glass eyes.

American Airlines Flight 88. New York to Rio De Janeiro
(18 hours earlier)

"Excuse me, may I trouble you to switch seats?" Natan asks the woman next to him.

"That your wife up there?" the woman says.

Natan thinks the woman is beautiful and stylish. He notices her pronounced Adam's apple and masculine, well-manicured hands.

"No, not my wife. My sister," he says.

"Oh, I like your sister. I like that she dresses up for a flight."

"We, well she, has an . . . engagement, right from the plane."

"An engagement? Oh, *that* kind of business trip. I see."

"You could say that. I'm not along for the party though," Natan says.

"Such crocodile tears, my dear."

"I just got back in a relationship, one I've been fighting to keep. Don't know why I'm telling you this, even if I wasn't, that kind of party's not for me."

"You never partied with me, handsome."

"I'm sure you're up there with best."

"Up there? I am the best. I mean. I was. I saved my money. Started my salon in the Village. I do hair for runway shows too. It isn't much but it's *my* dream. In *my* studio, no one cares if you are a boy or a girl. It's all about the art. I swore I would never go back to Rio."

"Yet here you are."

"Here I am. My first and only time back. My mother. She's come down with . . . there's something about you doll, I never talk about my life."

"I get that a lot."

"Bet you do. You're not the only one with an eye for seeing things as they are. Your sister's a CEO or some shit but you, you're a pro. How much to kill my son of a bitch ex—"

"I get asked that, a lot, too. I'm a farmer now."

"A farmer?"

"A sunflower farmer."

"No such thing."

"Yet here I am," Natan says.

"I know men like you. I can spot you a *mile* away. You're a killer."

"150 acres in the Catskills, says you're wrong. As does a family of porcupines. And an old bear we all call Papa Honey. Who's been eating from the apple trees on my land probably since you were in diapers."

"A real farm? You grow shit?"

"The apples and blueberries have gone wild. I only have luck with sunflowers. I told you I'm here for my sister."

"I get it now," the woman says. "Some advice for you, handsome. Use protection—don't kiss. Absolutely *never* kiss on the lips."

"I'm not here for—"

"The advice is for your sister. Just telling you straight. Seems like your first time."

"You gonna switch seats, or what, my friend?"

"Or what. I'm comfortable already. But I like you. So one more thing. Beware of red-headed women."

"Um . . . thanks?"

"In my country it is safer just to flat out avoid them."

"Safer?" Natan asks.

"Kuru'pir."

"What?"

"You don't speak Old Tupi . . . "

"No."

"Didn't think so. Where I come from there is nothing but monkey shit and jaguar skin, and your own skin, know what I mean . . . "

Natan is about to reply when he sees the serious demeanor that has come over her.

"You are handsome and a charmer and I seem to like telling you things," she says. "You're a watch dog, I get it. So, in your . . . engagements . . . watch out for—"

Her voice cracks.

"—for the red hair, yes. If her feet are facing the wrong way, if you want to live, stop whatever you are doing, leave and run like hell."

"That's quite the . . . advice. You've got me all wrong though."

"Do I?"

The woman closes her eyes and turns her head. Natan notices her hair is red. Dyed though. Does that count? He glances at her feet just in case. For the rest of the flight he keeps an eye on Esme as she sleeps, as he promised her husband and promised himself he would. His sleep is fitful and burdened by the knowledge that the days are growing short that he can keep her out of trouble and snares of her own making.

Rio de Janeiro
(2 hours after landing)

ESME'S OLD FRIEND from graduate school, Elias Machado, lives in one of the lovely hillside homes with his kids and new fiancé. He is hosting Esme and Natan for their 48-hour trip celebrating his impending second marriage. Over the years, working on their various projects and investments, Esme and Elias have been to the great countries of the world; yet as far as Natan knows they've only seen it mechanically, with their architect eyes and technical minds. Elias has never been to the Amazon or the Panatal, the great natural wonders of his country, despite the project he and Esme are working on.

Esme and Elias have done all the things "right." They've succeeded on their smarts and strength and boot straps. They've built wealth and live in ways universally commended. What they share beyond their mutual love of numbers and logic and the precision of their trade is something they can't name and don't even know is a thing—an emptiness and inability to feel. Natan sees it. *He* knows it is a thing even if there isn't an English word for it. He's seen his sister struggle; seen her feed that emptiness with subterfuge, deception, and sex. He's afraid for her. He knows the empty things feed on you too. That there isn't much of her left. That is why he is here.

Elias Machado's servants take Natan and Esme's bags. Other servants hand them cool drinks before they are off again. Within minutes they and Elias and Elias' new fiancé are on the luxurious hotel strip where they rendezvous with their three business colleagues and their wives. There is a round of kisses and hellos then the men (plus Esme) and the women separate into two groups. As the wives enter the first boutique to begin their shopping, a large SUV with blacked-out windows turns the corner. Esme and the men and Natan pile in. The SUV speeds away. Past the coconut vendors, the volley ball players, and the telenovela film crew filming on the beach. The vehicle turns into an alley. It navigates the twists and turns and takes the ramp into the Playground's garage.

The two prostitutes taking their break in the Playground's kitchen are wearing only white towels. The guard insisted Natan wear only a towel too. He complied to avoid making a problem.

After snorting lines of cocaine and picking at a plate of spiced chicken, the women take turns making advances on him, which he refuses.

"It is our job," they say.

"This is my job, too," Natan replies.

"Are you gay?"

"I'm not gay."

"Are you married?"

"I'm not married."

Natan hears them decide in Portuguese that he is gay. They return to doing lines to the delight of the guard who watches them as if they are the most interesting television show. Behind him, on the screen, the camera feed shows Esme being choked by her naked plaything. Natan grabs a kitchen knife, secures his towel, and runs to the jungle room.

As Flight 88 speeds towards Brazil, Natan slips in and out of memories that become dreams as he falls into fitful bits of sleep. Natan's grandmother, Grandma Rivka had a cabana in the Catskills where he and Esme spent summers in their youth and later on in life. He sees Grandma Rivka tending to her field of sunflower seedlings one June when he was a young man, one of the last times he saw her.

"So fragile. So fleeting," Grandma Rivka says. "Your sister says why bother. I say, what a miracle seeds are. What a miracle this Earth is. These human bodies. Extraordinary cosmic miracles? Machines of divine will? What do you think, Natan?"

"I don't know."

Natan is at the farm to hide while trouble blows over. Grandma Rivka doesn't like it when he uses the farm, and her, this way. Yet she allows it.

"Your sister never comes."

"She doesn't . . . understand this . . . aspect of the world."

"You two will either become the worst of us or you will become great forces of good for humanity. I am counting on you to turn your sister around, Natan."

"How do you know, Grandma? Why shouldn't I just stay here and grow things, with you?"

"Would it matter if I said because I see it in the stars? Would it matter if I said I love Esme, I love you both. That I want to believe that there is a meaning to the world? And that meaning is us and what we do."

"It doesn't seem fair."

"What? What doesn't seem fair?"

"Life. Everything."

"Nowhere is it said that life is fair or is supposed to be fair. To think otherwise and to try to impose fairness on the world not only is a falsehood it is to invite sorrow."

"When you put it that way it makes me think, why do anything at all?"

"We do things because we want to. As for the rest, because we love each other. Now are you going to help your sister like I told you?"

"I will. It still sounds to me like there is no meaning."

"There is meaning enough, my boy, there has to be."

THE WOMAN ON THE PLANE next to Natan thinks of the small village in the Panatal where she was born as she drifts into sleep. There was something about the man next to her that inspired her to speak of the aboriginal language Old Tupi and all the things she left behind when she moved her life to Rio and then New York. Her life in Rio she does not allow herself to think of, not even in dreams.

How long has it been since she spoke of the red-haired things called the kuru'pir: the forest spirits of the Panatal. The things that can look like people except their feet are turned backwards. As a girl she once saw a kuru'pir use its back-turned feet to create a trail of footprints to lead a group of poachers deeper into the woods, to be killed.

As she grew up, the Amazon Rainforest River basin burned. Development threatened the Panatal at every turn. She learned the worst dangers no longer have to be present to do their harm. And she knows the kuru'pir have come to the cities. Doing the things and haunting the places she does not allow herself to think of. They have become good at disguising themselves. Why she felt she should warn this American man, she does not know. She decided she was too tired to say much more.

She slips in and out of a memory of a jaguar she saw as a child; the big cat gracefully entering the water and swimming across a gentle, flowing river. She falls into sleep and dreams of the forest spirit and the poachers and how it ended in blood and flames.

As NATAN IS RUNNING to the jungle room, a flash of self-pity washes over him. It is not fair that his fears have come to pass. He hears Grandma Rivka's words in his mind, that sorrow comes from trying to be an instrument of justice, and it dawns on him how many of his sorrows have been born this way.

In seconds he is in the room. Esme is being dragged across the floor and has gone blue. The naked woman has her by the neck in a chokehold. Natan sees her backwards-facing feet. Without thinking he is on them. With brute force he frees Esme from the woman-thing's grasp. His instincts come alive. The woman on the plane was right. He is a killer. He pushes Esme's former plaything against the window. Esme has dropped to the floor and is motionless.

"Go ahead, kill me," the woman-thing says. "It is what you do. It will not save her."

Esme is more than oxygen-starved. She has turned an unnatural sickly blue.

"A bargain," Natan says. "Take me. Trade me for her."

The word, the strange foreign word, the woman from the plane used, blooms in Natan's mind.

Kuru'pir.

"Take only you?" the kuru'pir says. "Not good enough."

"Do you value . . . your life?"

Natan hates the threat. He hates that he means to follow through on it.

"*You* and them," the kuru'pir says. "All four of them."

"My sister lives? And you take five of our lives? How is this fair?"

"Your life is spared. You will serve me. They will die."

"Why kill them?"

"You will kill them. Then you return with me to the Panatal."

"You want me to spend my life . . . in the Panatal?"

"You will give 20 of your years," the kuru'pir says. "It is a place of jaguars and flowers. You will kill. You will feel free."

Natan thrusts the kitchen knife into the kuru'pir's chest.

He drops to the floor and checks Esme's pulse and her breath.

The kuru'pir bursts into flames. Esme's colleagues and the guard rush into the room.

"Which one of you brought her?"

"How is she burning, she's nowhere near the fireplace. What the hell is going on?"

"It's him, the brother! I told you I didn't want him here."

"He saved your damn life. I saw it all on the camera, she was coming for us next."

"Is Esme going to live?"

"She has to live," Natan says.

He compresses her chest and breathes air into her blue lips.

"You have to live," he mutters as he tries to start her heart. "The price I paid. The price we paid. You are going to live and be the woman Grandma Rivka knew you could be."

A spurt of dark blood jets from Esme's mouth.

"You have to live," Natan cries.

The jaguar head does not hear his demands. Nor does the monumental statue visible on the mountain in the distance. If they have noticed these happenings they give no sign; just like the dwellers of the neighboring hillside buildings, and those fighting to survive in Rio's streets, and the sand-coated beachgoers reveling in the cloudless, sun-soaked Ipanema day, they remain oblivious to it all.

Hairberg

Sam Dawson

———◆———

GRAEME PULLED THE PLUG, briefly rinsed the razor under the hot tap. Set it aside. The water ran sluggishly down the plughole, so torpidly that it left an ugly film of foam and bristles stuck to the sink's ceramic sides as it went. Which meant that the pipe was getting clogged. He'd noticed the slowness a few days ago but hadn't quite put two and two together.

Now it was unmistakable. But easily remedied, so long as he had a plunger. Which he did, and to hand. He ran a little clean water into the sink, blocked its escape with the rubber plunger head, put the fingers of his other hand over the overflow and plunged. Quite vigorously.

It worked. It usually does. With a sound between vomiting and burping, the sink surrendered repeat gushes of dirty grey water unexpectedly full of two weeks' worth of his shaved bristles, all greasy with soap. He grabbed at as many of the small, unpleasantly squidgy clumps as he could and transferred them to the bin.

When the operation is that successful it can be paradoxically difficult to resist continuing: half repulsive, half addictive. So Graeme did, and finally found the real blockage. Hair. Wet, lank, clumped with soapfat. A long, smelly, dripping tangle, which clung to his fingers as he picked it out, unsure whether to consign it to bin or toilet. Yuk. Horrid, but at least the sink suddenly sucked water down the way it was meant to.

Given that his studio flat was meant to be a new conversion and he'd only moved in a fortnight ago, he should have been surprised. But he wasn't. The property developers were the newest kind, who had seized the chance afforded by government legislation to convert commercial buildings into shitty little box flats with no permission needed. All over the town you saw their work: former offices given a shoddy cladding job and ugly extra storeys which they laughably called "penthouses," all crammed with tiny, thinly-walled, prison cell-sized flats aimed at buy-to-letters and desperate first time buyers. And at Graeme, who fitted neither of those labels.

He was 33, just divorced, lucky to have a (so-far) secure job in IT. Bespectacled, a little shy, thinning on top. His wife had ended the marriage so she could more freely cavort with Steve, the office colleague of his that it turned out she'd been having an affair with for years. When the terms of the divorce were being agreed he did once timorously venture to ask his solicitor if, given these circumstances, he really did have to hand her the flat which he had mostly paid for, half his pension and a slice of everything he earned for the rest of his life. The solicitor had at first laughed at his joke, then looked at him as if he were mad when he realized it wasn't an attempt at humor, and Graeme had, as was his nature, let the matter drop.

So here he was, in a small box in a much larger one that had, until its conversion, been a YWCA hostel. Enjoying, if that were the word, a rare moment of time off from working all the overtime he could get in order to pay for both his new and old homes. Which he was spending sucking human detritus from the pipework. Standing over the sink in the tiny bathroom, his bum touched the shower cubicle (which it usually did unless he sucked in his stomach and stood as straight as a Guardsman). Hmm. Should he investigate that too? Might as well. It wouldn't cost any money.

He knelt. Fiddled with the shower plughole, which was plastic and, he found, designed to be twisted and then lifted out. Which it did once he had got the knack. It was coated with human grease and rancid soap, and stuffed with another thick wadge of cold, clammy, nasty-to-the-touch, nasty-to-the-nose, human hair. He binned it, and put the removable plughole in some bleach and water. Then looked into the pipe that its withdrawal had revealed. God, there was more. It was evident that the developers had reused or left in situ everything they could, just giving what had been built as cubicled hostel accommodation for young women a new paint job and entry phone and marketing it (using some truly imaginative photography) as "apartments for modern living."

He had to push his fingers uncomfortably far into the pipe to hook out the latest find. At first it resisted, but with hard tugging a whole rope of the stuff, doubtless from the heads of several women but now all matted together, came free. It practically wrapped itself around his wrist it was so lengthy and coldly adhesive. One-handed he managed to get a black bag from the kitchen area and transfer it to that, to be followed by the clotted contents of the bathroom bin. He left a trail of slimy drips and small curled flakes, which turned out to be toe and fingernail clippings washed down the plughole, only to be blocked by—and then to become part of—the obstructive hairberg.

Among them he noticed a large spider. Up close it revealed itself as a limply sodden false eyelash. He decided not to investigate the kitchen sink. He had had enough for one day.

Thinking about it, the block of flats was like an organism, he decided. The pipes were its circulatory system; the toilet system, which was, thankfully, not malfunctioning, its excretory one. In which case the former must be as clogged as the atherosclerotic arteries of an obese, cholesterol-loving, soon-to-be a heart attack victim. Yet the building went on regardless, its veins furred with the shedded remains of its occupants: skin, hair, nails, rheum, sebum, pus, tooth enamel, cerumen and mucus, everything but their bones really. Maybe it liked it that way.

He woke the next morning after a not terribly good night's sleep (the bed, like the room, was undersized), and took the two steps to the bathroom. As he washed he noted with approval the way that water was running away now. Noticed too a hair growing from beneath the fingernail on the middle finger of his left hand.

It'll be one of those mutant hairs, he thought. Like the one that had sprouted on his nose last year and had to be tweezed out, then three months later was back again. Something to do with getting older, he suspected; they desert your head, where you want them, and populate your ears and nose, where you don't. Don't ask him what the evolutionary advantage to *that* is.

Easy to deal with. Get tweezers from cabinet. Grip it. Pull. Which he did, and almost fainted with pain. It didn't come, it felt like it was as one with the sensitive skin below the fingernail. He took a deep breath and tried again. Same result. It was too deeply bedded in the flesh. He decided to let discretion be the better part, and, using a pair of nail scissors, simply cut it flush with the fingertip. Over the bin, not over the sink.

For several nights afterwards he dreamed that his flat had floorboards, and through the gaps between them, hair sprouted profusely, as it did from the plugholes and, danglingly, from the taps.

He was reminded of it at work when a client in his sixties came in. He was an academic in the geological sciences, one of those men who has settled comfortably into his age and into the same, lightly dandruffed suit, judiciously let out at the waist, that he purchased three decades before. Growing from the front of his nose he had three white hairs, so long that they had each formed a small curl. All the time Graeme talked with him he had to hide his fascination with them, look everywhere but at them, and resist the terrible urge to simply reach out, twist them around his fingers and pluck them out.

Which was probably the most interesting thing that happened in his life during that November. At home little changed. The extractor fans in the windowless bathroom and kitchenette failed. He, like the other tenants, discovered that the promised cable TV had never been connected, the aerial plugs were no more than decoration. But the developer had quickly moved on to their next project with various works left undone.

He was dimly aware of his neighbors, as they presumably were of him, but there was no real contact beyond a nod when putting out the recycling or holding a door for someone coming in or out. There were arguments over parking (each flat had one minimalist, allocated parking space) but he could afford no car and had enough sense not to complain when his slot was taken over by the famously foul-mouthed family who possessed a small posse of vehicles whose indiscriminate parking sparked regular rows he was happy to stay out of.

The most exciting—and more importantly, given his finances, free—event was yet to come. The office Christmas Party. From which he returned, but not alone.

Frances was an intern, a leather-jacketed bohemian with tats, piercings and a crew cut. She had picked him up—he wouldn't have had the confidence to do it—after being attracted by his introversion and diffidence, which contrasted nicely with that of some of the male sales reps, who had been pushily trying to chat her up.

She stayed the night, and it was OK, no disaster, but there was little magic to it. Recently graduated from university, she was living with her parents, so it seemed glamorous to her that he had his own place. Until she actually saw the pinched little studio flat, with its too-small bed. In the morning, when they woke and needed the toilet, they were both acutely aware of each other's too-close proximity, and the utter failure of the minuscule bathroom's cheap plasterboard walls to muffle sounds or smells.

Her parting was polite but final. She left him at his front door, insisting that he didn't need to see her downstairs. The window was open and a draught caught the door as he closed it, slamming it crashingly shut in a way that made it appear that he was desperate to see the back of her. He thought of following her to explain, but he didn't have the energy.

The encounter left him feeling guilty and vaguely unfaithful, though to whom he couldn't say. He wondered how much of herself she had left behind to add to the building's history of womanly occupation. Didn't they say a human sheds a million skin cells a day, not to mention the 100 hairs lost every time a woman washes her hair? Which would mean that a paper thin imprint of Frances had settled over the poky little flat's surfaces, joining his own dusted residue.

That night he didn't bother to undress for bed. The next day was Saturday and, listless, he slept late and when he woke just laid where he was. It was only a bursting bladder that finally drove him to step into the bathroom.

Afterwards he went to zip up. Then noticed the long hair that had partly emerged with the urine. Which he'd have to remove: the end of it was sticking out from his urethra. At the last moment he thought to kneel down on the floor, just in case. Then he took hold of the hair and gently began to pull.

This time he did faint.

But in the end he removed it, very slowly and very painfully. All 30 centimeters or so of it. A woman's hair, of the type he had come to know well. He told himself not to worry. This wasn't a malignant growth; instead, it had to be something he had somehow ingested and which had travelled through his body intact. But, when he found more hairs in his stools and another two more growing from his fingertips, a niggling, depressive part of him decided that it was a punishment. Probably for bringing an outsider into the flat.

It wasn't a mistake he was likely to repeat. The office shut for a week over Christmas, and Graeme found himself lapsing into a somnolent lethargy. He didn't have the strength to deal with his parents, who, though they had been polite to his now ex-wife, had always advised him against marrying her. To get out of having to see them on December 25th he invented a special duty rota under which he had to be the one on call in case any of the firm's big corporate clients had computer issues over the break. They probably didn't wholly believe him, but he found that he didn't care. He was happy just to be able to curl up on his bed for a week undisturbed, half watching films and TV on his laptop. Once or twice a day he would make toast or a frozen microwave meal and take it back to eat, supine, on his increasingly crumb-spattered bed.

There was no Christmas card from his ex-wife. He wondered if she would call instead to wish him season's greetings. She didn't.

On Christmas Eve he ran out of foodstuffs and had to contemplate going out to buy supplies. He felt he ought to really. But when he double-checked he found that he still had half of the bottle of wine which he and Frances had impishly liberated from the company's party, and an unopened box of cereal, although no milk. It would do. No need to make the journey to the supermarket after all. Eating a handful straight from the box, he went back to bed.

There was a point that evening when his laptop battery died, and he found himself watching nothing more than his reflection. Unshaven, unfed, lonely, with cornflake crumbs in his stubble. He cried, quietly, so that only the four walls could hear him.

Everyone knows that no one should be alone at Christmas.

When the church bells woke him the next morning, he wasn't.

The flat had heard his call, he realized. The building had provided.

The carpet from the bathroom was sodden. And next to him was a companion.

She was naked, except for a pair of contact lenses inadvertently washed down a sink months or years before. Her hair was long, wet and plentiful; her skin, millions of recovered flakes of it glued together by wastewater and human exudate, was perhaps a little grey, but then Graeme's complexion would hardly be described as rosy. If the paint on her finger and toenails didn't match that of their mates, at least they were cut short. Unlike his.

Tentatively, he reached out and, using a corner of the sheet, tried to dry her hair for her. Tried a little too hard. There was a wet, sucking noise and a waterlogged wedge of it came away in his hand, along with a lump of the damp, soapy flesh in which it had been anchored. (It reminded him vaguely of a steak tartare he had ordered once in a restaurant, not realizing that the dish is nothing more than raw mince; he had forced half of it down rather than disappoint the waiter.) Gently he squashed the missing piece back into her head and rearranged the dripping hair to cover the edges.

He squeezed her hand in apology, causing a trickle of dirty water to flow from under the fingernails, washing one of them away. He tried to replace it, but it was a compound, made from a collection of clippings, glued together with bodily secretions, and it crumbled to pieces. He flicked it away apologetically.

She didn't seem to mind. Instead, her mouth, outlined with the greased remnants of ten thousand oily, washed-away lipstick applications, opened slightly, in a seductive invitation that released a smell of drain gas. He saw the grey, damp-spotted tip of her tongue, waiting for the touch of his own.

By bringing Frances into the flat he had sinned, and then been punished. In the last weeks he had hit rock bottom, he knew. Then he had appealed for help. The building had listened. It had pulled its resources together, and constructed this companion especially for him.

The gift of company was both the building's answer to his plea, and its Christmas present to him, he understood.

He looked in wonder at the woman sharing his bed. *She* didn't care about the size of the flat. *She* felt right at home.

And he sank into her moist embrace.

THE CHANGE

Justin A. Burnett

———— ◆ ————

EVERYONE HAD ALREADY begun to whisper about the conversation by the time Harl saw it happening. Concord and Gabel were in the doorway at the front of the processing room. It was toward the end of the shift and the sunlight was diminishing, masking Concord and Gabel with shadows that rendered their gestures obscure. Gabel was crying, and Concord kept folding and unfolding his hands, as if he were explaining something of great importance. By the time Harl had stopped to watch, frozen midway to his desk holding a rack of specimens, Gabel was steadying herself against the wall with one hand, the other twisted desperately in the cuff of Concord's lab coat. Her breath came in rushed staccato bursts while his was calm, undetectable even, as if what he said was rehearsed.

Everyone knew about Gabel by then, but they weren't thinking about that now. The conversation momentarily eclipsed the general interest in her private scandals, even if, for no reason that anyone could recall, no one attempted to get close enough to eavesdrop. Just a few more feet and Harl himself would've been within earshot, a fact that plagued him later, as if his failure to intervene had resulted in something terrible.

But nothing terrible happened—quite the opposite. Gabel kept wiping away the tears and smiling, and everyone could tell that the smile was genuine and heartfelt and not at all the kind that would accompany tears of embarrassment or shame. If Concord's words produced a desired result, he betrayed no indication of the fact. His features, always stern through the workday, seemed more severe than ever, perhaps even angry. Gabel's tears softened nothing in him, but she shed them all the same, and happily.

At last, after what seemed an impossible stretch of time, Concord stopped speaking, straightened his lab coat, and returned to his desk. Gabel's gaze followed him dreamily from the doorway, and before the spell that had fallen across the room had time to dissolve, she receded into the shadows toward the front of the office. It was so quiet in the processing area that everyone heard the front door open then close behind her.

Over the next few days, when it became clear that Gabel wasn't returning to work, her absence began to reverberate throughout the pathology lab. For a short time, several employees insisted that Gabel was sorely missed. Twice, when Harl managed to carefully drift into the vicinity of a conversation, he overheard that Gabel no longer responded to phone calls or messages over social media. It was difficult for Harl to imagine that no one associated Gabel's vanishing with her conversation with Concord, but if any connection was made, it wasn't mentioned. Nor did anyone appear willing to question Concord himself. Harl could hardly blame them, for Concord seemed to grow ever more cold and remote, his dark scowl sealing him against the curiosity of his coworkers. That nothing regarding Gabel's absence was ever mentioned by the managing staff was more than Harl, who valued order and routine above all else, could bear.

Mercy was the only coworker Harl could trust, so it wasn't long before the unease Gabel's disappearance exerted over Harl forced him to invite her over for dinner. She accepted with no more non-chalance than usual, and Harl fell headlong into preparing his little apartment for her arrival.

Filled with the new terror of Mercy's visit, Harl was able to find some relief from Gabel's vanishing—indeed, the office already appeared ready to leave the matter behind, as if a preordained and absurdly short period of mourning, privy to everyone but Harl, had already come and gone. Harl even thought he heard Concord laughing one afternoon—a possibility too monstrous to leave to the evidence of his ears—and followed the sound to the break-room, arriving just in time to see the single bathroom door pulled closed with what seemed like unnecessary force.

Harl crept up to the door and pressed his ear against it. The laughing continued inside, though he could no longer tell if it was Concord's or someone else's. Multiple voices echoed in the cramped depths of the restroom, which suddenly seemed cavernous, stretch-ing into dimensions that far outstripped the capacity of the tiny suite. It was alarming that more than one—even more than two, it seemed, perhaps closer to four or five—of his coworkers were in the single-toilet bathroom at once. This was surely against the rules and wholly unprecedented. It was all more evidence of the disorder wrought by Concord's conversation with Gabel, madden-ing, but altogether forgotten with the snap of the lock just beyond Harl's ear, from which he fled the breakroom and into the darken-ing hallway. He heard the laughter once again, high, shrill, and menacing, only this time he was no longer certain it wasn't meant for him.

On the night of Mercy's visit, Harl decided to leave work early for one final round of preparation. Having been graced with a light load of specimens, the suite was nearly empty a full hour before the end of the shift. "Take it easy my man," his supervisor said as Harl headed to the breakroom for his lunchbox and coat. Harl turned to reply, but the supervisor was already looking elsewhere, a glimpse of worry like a quick shadow across his face. Harl followed his gaze just in time to watch Concord slink soundlessly from the processing area. The urge to follow him was brief, but so strong that Harl was forced to pause to gather his nerve before going his own way.

Once home, Harl's routine consisted of running his fingers along the surfaces of his furniture, not in search of dust, but to anchor himself vicariously through each object, as if he were a wayward balloon that tended to drift toward an unknown horizon when absent from the apartment's interior. All his furniture had come from boxes he had ordered online and assembled himself. They were nothing special, but he was proud of his home, which seemed in every way the counterpart to the office suite with the exposed drywall in the unused rooms in the back. There were times when he was drawn to these rooms, as if they held more than sheets of insulation and exposed wiring, but the comfort and intelligibility of the processing area always won out.

Mercy hadn't been at work, and Harl found a mixture of relief and unease in the thought that she was ill and wouldn't show up. Nevertheless, he had purchased a pack of hard seltzer on the way back—black cherry, the kind he knew she liked—and dutifully arranged it to where it was impossible to overlook upon opening the fridge. Harl then checked the furniture and, satisfied that he was himself and that nothing had come undone in his absence, sank into the couch.

It wasn't like Harl to sleep in undesignated areas of the apartment. The recent events must've weighed heavily on him, since exhaustion quickly overtook him even as he realized that he hadn't rehearsed a way to bring up the subject of Gabel and Concord to Mercy. Instead of alarm, he examined his oversight with a strange detachment, as if he were following someone through a wall of gray mist that condensed until he was no longer sure where he was. Soon, he was guided by nothing but the wandering dictates of his will, still calm and calculating despite the growing dimensions of emptiness enveloping him. It was good to be this way, for a moment—good to feel nothing beyond the soft lambent light dispersed across the mist.

But soon there was space again. Harl believed for a moment that he was in the bathroom at work. The light grew sharper and brighter and the walls around him were white and smooth like steel. In his mind, he called it the White Tower, and he was safe from the city within the White Tower. He was glad to be safe, even if he felt the tug of the city below, an insistence that at once took shape in his memory, like the breeze of someone passing close by when no one is there.

It was then that his sleep was interrupted by knocking. He shot upright, disoriented in a lingering whiteness that he tried to rub away with the heels of his hands. He rose, feeling his way blindly along the edges of the couch, ashamed of wasting the precious moments before Mercy's arrival.

By the time he opened the door, he could see that something was wrong. Mercy had brought an uninvited friend, a woman with strands of green dyed into her hair and who he didn't recognize from work. Before Harl could articulate his protest, he noticed something wrong with Mercy's face as well, a hard edge was there he hadn't seen before, a challenge in her eyes, and in waves he began to smell the alcohol on her breath as she shouldered past him into the apartment.

"Hey Harl," she said without introducing him to her friend. She glanced around the apartment for a moment, seeming lost until her gaze finally settled on him. She sneered then, and his heart began to race—he wanted nothing more than for them to go, leaving him to settle back into the dream he was already beginning to forget. Instead, he found himself pointing to the fridge when she asked if he had bought the seltzer. He burned with shame as she marched authoritatively across the room to retrieve it.

"Where's your bathroom again?" she asked, and before he could finish providing directions, Mercy was pulling her friend down the hall by the hand. Harl followed, watching as they took the door to the right rather than the left, vanishing into his bedroom and closing the door behind them. It was already locked by the time he reached it.

"Hey," he said, but it was no use. Already they were laughing, and when he knocked Mercy said "just a minute, Harl" in a voice so hostile he had no choice but to retreat to the living room. He began pacing in a spacious circle, stopping to touch each piece of furniture—the kitchen table with two chairs and no tablecloth, the small TV stand additionally supporting stacks of DVD cases, the small table at the entryway with the salt rock lamp that stayed unplugged—desperate to revive the sense of belonging that each item bestowed in the evenings. But the ritual was failing, as if Mercy and her friend had absorbed the magic of each thing and locked it with them in the bedroom. He realized suddenly that he had invited the disorder unspooling from the conversation between Concord and Gabel into his home. He shouldn't have done that. He should've left it contained in shadows of the half-finished suite. Harl couldn't believe he had made such an oversight.

There was nothing to do but wait, but already it seemed that an intolerable expanse of time had passed. What could they be doing? he wondered. He carefully crept to the door—the door to his own bedroom, although it no longer felt like it belonged to him—and pressed his ear against the wood, waiting in terror for sounds of destruction, sounds he was sure would annihilate him in an instant, leaving him dispersed like light across a thick canyon of fog. There was no laughing now, but voices, low and earnest. For the most part, they were indecipherable, but at last he caught a fragment of Mercy's, thick with the blunted edge of intoxication. "I have to believe she's *happy*, goddamn it. Whatever happened, she's *changed*." Harl was certain she was talking about Gabel.

THE FOLLOWING MORNING was one of the most difficult of Harl's life. Mercy and her friend had occupied the bedroom until the early hours. Harl found it impossible to fall asleep on the couch, so he sat there and waited, staring miserably at the empty square of the TV screen, which reflected a shadow version of his living room with his own slouched shoulders and unhappy face. For one terrible moment, Harl was convinced he was crouched in one of the unfinished rooms at the back of the laboratory.

When his bedroom door finally opened, Harl didn't dare to move from the couch. It took an extraordinarily long time for them to emerge from the hallway. Mercy's face was drawn and pitiful, tears streaming from her bloodshot eyes as her nameless friend guided her through the apartment. Mercy didn't look at Harl— she didn't look at anything at all. She was wholly enveloped in such a state of suffering that Harl forgot his own and rushed to get the door. Mercy's friend looked at Harl and said "sorry for everything" with what seemed to Harl an impressive sadness. He watched as she shuffled into the night, arms extended to support Mercy's unsteady step.

It was some time after they left that he entered his room. When he did, his worst fears failed to materialize. There was no mess outside of the empty box of hard seltzer on the bed with the empties packed efficiently back inside. Two indentions remained in the bedclothes where they had sat side by side facing the window, which was now a square of sheer night since the lights outside had long gone out. Nothing was amiss, and he paced the room several times before his anxiety began to settle. He imagined it would be impossible to sleep under the strange aura left behind by the pair, but again he was wrong. Exhaustion overcame him, and in moments he found himself descending a spiral staircase. He recognized the White Tower at once, although the further he wound into its depths, the more he found it in a state of incompletion. Large segments of wall gave way to darkness flecked with pale lights gleaming from windows and doorways of patchwork houses far below. Harl descended until he reached the ceiling of the mist illuminated by the distant lights, which looked like a mossy sea when he stared out across it towards the horizon.

The morning alarm came all too soon, but the green light lingered as he pulled on fresh clothes for work. He could still feel the tug of the city below the White Tower, which congealed in the clarity of morning around his last memory of Gabel, tears in her eyes and such a deep and sincere joy that it was like something he shouldn't have witnessed, an abject enigma he yearned to solve even if it cost him considerable comfort. With sudden determination, he decided to ask Mercy directly what she knew about Gabel. He felt she owed him that at least.

But she wasn't there. "Called in sick. Brown bottle flu, ho ho," Harl's supervisor explained in response to someone else's inquiry. Of course. Why hadn't he thought of that? Any sane person would've called in after such a night. There was no pity in this realization, but a deep weariness that bore down on Harl as the morning hours dragged on. Each minute passed as if it struggled to detach itself from something thick and gelatinous. Harl turned up his music, reproved himself for being distractible, and forced himself to focus singularly on the day's workload. It was with near superhuman effort that he finally pulled away from the itching impulse to cross the room and speak to Concord, who worked casually, almost carelessly, as if nothing was wrong in all the world.

Around noon, Harl awoke in the break room over an unopened can of V8 juice. He was alone. All was silent but for the steady hum of the analyzers in the room across the hall. He opened the timecard app on his phone to see if whatever fugue state had led him to the breakroom had allowed him the presence of mind to clock out for lunch. As he reviewed his time punches, a faint shimmer of laughter reached him. It was mean and careless, bitter with a sourness that seemed close rage—Concord's laughter, the laughter Harl had once followed to the bathroom door he now sat across from.

Harl followed it into the hallway. To his right the sun gleamed through the tall front windows of the suite. To the left, the direction from which the laughter drifted, were the unfinished rooms submerged in darkness. It seemed impossible to Harl that Concord's voice should be coming from the unused depths of the suite, despite rules against entering having never been articulated. It struck him as the height of sacrilege that someone had entered them, even someone like Concord.

He knew there would be no more resisting, and the first step towards the gaping black doorways in the back did not surprise him. As he walked down the hall, he waited for the inquiring voice of a coworker at his back, or the stern reproach of a supervisor. Neither came, and the sound of the analyzers diminished rapidly as he reached the end of the light.

Harl observed an alarming lack of fear in himself as he reached the first threshold. There was only a heaviness that seemed to press against him from inside, a strange stiffness that made him think of death, with which he was utterly unfamiliar. He had viewed relatives in their coffins before, their tidy features somehow unconvincing, as if they had been kneaded from dough. But these people were far from his thoughts now, irrelevant to the weight bearing down on him, urging him to the rear of the suite where the shadows were deepest and most forbidding. The laughter was no longer laughter, and Harl was no longer sure how he had mistaken the dry keening for laughter at all. It was a shrill, arid noise that seemed to reach him across a vast distance, but he followed it dutifully past gutted rooms with their wooden framework exposed and ceiling tiles scattered across the floor, black abysses full of pipes and wiring above.

The keening stopped as Harl entered the last room, which was no room at all, but a city street. His surroundings were now dark and unfamiliar. Over his shoulder, he could still see the ragged opening in the back of the office suite, a dim light growing dimmer as the heaviness swept him further away from the rear of the building. He couldn't imagine that the supervisors were unaware of the hole in the back of the suite, even if such an opening surely constituted a hazard to the integrity of a pathology laboratory. He felt that such a thing should offend his sensibilities, but it was far too difficult to rouse such feelings through his waking somnolence. Soon the suite had vanished, swallowed by rotting facades of storefronts whose many layers of peeling paint blended into a nauseating hue.

Somewhere in the towers of steam rising from the streets, Harl glimpsed what was certainly Concord's silhouette receding into the green glow dispersed uniformly throughout the fog. A renewed urgency filled Harl, who felt that this empty street constituted his sole opportunity for confrontation. He called out, but his voice was lost in the churning grumble of a nearby factory he hadn't noticed before. There was only the rapidly diminishing figure of Concord and the fog that threatened to swallow him forever. Harl charged down the street, so intent on his pursuit that he didn't see the green glowing city instead of the sky mirrored in the black surface of the puddles he splashed through.

Harl rounded a corner into the well-lit parking lot of an apartment complex just in time to see Concord slip into a residence. Pale green light duplicated across the gleaming surface of the vacant concrete emanated from the windows. Harl wondered at the absence of cars—such a large building and not a soul in sight! Yet it was also strangely familiar, Harl realized as he approached the door Concord had vanished behind. Like a dream surfacing quickly into reality, the crooked brass 116 and pot of plantless soil by the door hummed with strange menace. They were more than familiar. Harl was *home*.

He tried his key before pounding on the door, but neither worked. Harl scurried to the window he could barely see by standing on the far side of the hedges surrounding the wall. The blinds were drawn, revealing nothing but the cold green light.

He felt his way in the dark to the gate separating the parking lot from the courtyard. Through the iron bars, the windows surrounding the picnic table he knew to be buried somewhere in the blackness gleamed with a green glow identical to the one inside his own apartment. He knew his window facing the courtyard was open, since he left it that way to watch the tiny brown and gray birds congregate around the trash cans he could no longer see. Although prominent, the green light did nothing to illuminate the courtyard. Harl found himself avoiding the empty square once filled with patches of grass and litter, huddling closely to the brick wall leading to the rear of his domicile. It was impossible, but the sensation of immense depth overwhelmed him—one wrong step would spill him into the merciless lack into which the apartment windows wasted their sickened luminescence.

Indeed, the window blinds were open, affording Harl a clear look into his usurped home. He stood there for some time, formulating what he saw within, sheer unfamiliarity shocking his mind into disorganization. The image seemed to claw at his very sense of self, a jarring incomprehensibility under which the unity of all his experiences began to groan. Suddenly, at precisely the point beyond which he was certain to dissolve, his perspective shifted like a ship cast upright from the brink of destruction by a rogue wave.

"Hole," his mind told him, and a hole it was, a maw leaving the merest trace of a lip beneath the patterned print of the wallpaper. The green light thrummed from the hole itself, which was nevertheless the sheerest black, a pure darkness Harl found it difficult to stare into for any prolonged span of time. If the depths held anything at all—a watery underworld, a city filled with inhabitants impossible to imagine—it was hidden perfectly by the oblivion replacing the objects inside the apartment Harl had long tethered himself to. There was nothing but the hole and Concord, who scampered in and out of the blackness on all fours like an insect communing with a thrumming hive beneath. Harl lost himself in Concord's fitful scurrying and the terrible keening he associated distantly with laughter as the interior of the apartment began to shrink. From the window, Harl watched the glowing interior recede rapidly and did not notice the light dimming equally in all the windows surrounding him before winking out in perfect unison.

IT WAS MERCY who found Harl curled behind a heap of torn insulation in the furthest unfinished room. As she shook him awake, the incomprehension on his face alarmed her. Harl remained unresponsive to her inquiries and something resembling sympathy began to arise in Mercy, who had experienced her share of awakenings she couldn't account for. He smelled terrible, and she urged him to go home before the morning supervisors arrived.

Suddenly, a horrific clarity gripped Harl. He stopped Mercy in the hall before the breakroom. "I know where Gabel is," he began, and described what had happened to him.

Mercy's attempts to pull away ended quickly as words that Harl had not consciously sought poured from him. Her curiosity gave way to something mingled with awe and fear, and between his own articulations he heard her ask if it was real, if she hadn't dreamt it all along. They were no longer aware that they were blocking the breakroom, but the small gathering of employees made no move to push past them.

QUEEN BEE

Grace Lillie

———— ◆ ————

THE UNDERTAKER WAS to come on Tuesday. Of course it had to be Tuesday afternoon, during her weekly luncheon and tea with the ladies. She had phoned Bernadette to tell her the news, apologizing for the short notice and hoping the ladies would not miss her presence too much. But Bernadette responded as chipper as ever, saying Miss Rosie Trent would be joining the ladies. Mrs. Anderson would be missed, but at least there wouldn't be an empty seat at the table.

Mrs. Anderson was indignant as she hung up the phone. That infuriating Miss Trent was always popping up in places she shouldn't be. Ever since she moved to town last year she's been nothing but a nuisance, weaseling her way into her social group, trying to rework the fabric of the town to suit herself. Just last month she became the youngest member of the Women's Civic Improvement Club, against Mrs. Anderson's wishes, even though she was the one who founded the group. Everyone fawned over her, anticipating some new progressive ideas to improve the community, but Mrs. Anderson thought they were doing just fine and weren't supposed to be accepting new members till the fall anyway.

And now this. It seemed everything wrong with her life in the past year was tied in some way to Miss Trent. But there was no time to stew about it now. The undertaker was coming, and she must receive him with an appropriately dignified grief. No pettiness, no pouting, just poise and grace.

The doorbell chimed just as she finished powdering her nose. She greeted the undertaker, accepting his condolences and offering him a drink. They sat in the parlor, discussing and planning.

"A heart attack, Mrs. Anderson," he was saying. "I'm sure you were aware of his condition."

"Yes, the whole town was, with how he would go on about it."

"Well, your husband was quite the raconteur."

"Always had a story to tell, whether we wanted him to or not."

The undertaker sighed, reminiscing, and Mrs. Anderson poured some more scotch in his glass as he asked about open caskets and burial garments and funeral plans. He left two hours later with her husband's favorite suit and the obituary she had written to be put in the evening paper.

She poured herself some more scotch.

WEDNESDAY NIGHT WAS BRIDGE night. At the grocer's that afternoon, Mrs. Anderson ran into Miss Trent.

"Oh, Lucy, dear!" Miss Trent positively oozed sweetness and concern. "How are you holding up? Do you need anything?"

"I prefer Lucille, darling, or Mrs. Anderson." Lucy was the name of some blonde tart. "I'm doing just fine."

"Oh, you poor thing. So strong. I was just telling the other ladies yesterday over lunch, 'that Lucy Anderson is so strong.'"

"How was lunch?" She tried to sound casual, tempering her

curiosity and squeezing out as much politeness as she could muster through a gritted smile.

"Oh, the ladies were marvelous! And they wanted me to tell you that they understand you need your time to grieve, so don't you worry about Bridge tonight. You stay at home and rest, honey. Take some time to heal."

Mrs. Anderson was shocked. "They don't have to cancel Bridge night for me. We've not missed a week since Bernadette's grandson had chicken pox two years ago. I'm sure I—"

"Oh, it's not cancelled." Miss Trent made a placating gesture. "The ladies invited me to take your place for now, until you're ready."

Her shock turned to annoyance then to anger. Who does she think she is to decide such a thing? Mrs. Anderson felt ready enough for Bridge, but she smiled and said, "How nice. Do enjoy yourself, but I must be going."

"Of course. Give me a ring if you ever need anything." Her words were sweet, but her eyes looked venomous to Mrs. Anderson. Like a hive of delicious looking honey, but full of angry swarming bees.

Mrs. Anderson got home and poured herself a glass of brandy, seething over her conversation. How dare that woman? She's probably too young to even know how to play Bridge! Myrtle and Edith are sure to win, ruining a month-long streak. Bernadette would never have done such a thing on her own. She knows how important Bridge night is. What else is there to do on a Wednesday?

She took another long sip. Rest and heal. Hah. That man had it coming. Forty years of marriage was long enough, the last five of them filled with nothing but complaints about his heart and long-winded stories about nonsense and nothing. He was a fine companion and she would miss him, but she was hardly the grief-stricken widow Miss Trent made her out to be. And even so she would certainly rather enjoy the company of friends than slouch about at home. Bernadette knew her better than anyone, she should have known that.

It must have been that luncheon yesterday. Miss Trent probably worked her sickly sweet charms on those ladies, convincing them that Mrs. Anderson was some grieving mess, incapable of normal social activity. She probably arranged it so the undertaker had to come then, just so she could take the opportunity to ruin Bridge night. Heck, she probably killed her husband just to get into that luncheon.

Mrs. Anderson froze, glass half-raised. Could she have? No, of course not, that's too far. She's obnoxious, not malicious. But those eyes. Her smile never quite seems to go all the way to her eyes. There was something very unsettling about that woman. Mrs. Anderson shook her head and poured another glass of brandy. If she's stuck at home, she might as well do her best to enjoy it.

THURSDAY WAS UNSEASONABLY lovely. Mrs. Anderson decided it was a fine day for a walk. She pinned on her favorite hat and strolled over to Bernadette's house.

"Good morning, Lucille," Bernadette greeted her at the door. "How are you feeling?"

"Just fine, dear. I thought a stroll through the park would be nice, and I hoped you would be kind enough to join me."

"That would be lovely. Come in a moment and make yourself at home while I fetch my hat."

In the parlor, Mrs. Anderson made herself at home and poured herself a small glass of cabernet from the beverage cart.

"A little early, Lucille?" Bernadette returned.

"A bit of red wine in the morning is good for the heart."

"And brandy in the evening for digestion."

The two women laughed, and Mrs. Anderson poured Bernadette a glass.

"How was Bridge last night?" she asked, trying to mask her hurt feelings with an air of indifference. But Bernadette knew her too well.

"Now, now, don't be like that, darling. I wouldn't have dreamed of leaving you out—I know how much you love our weekly games— but Rosie made an excellent point at our luncheon. Robert only just passed, and with your meeting with the undertaker and planning the funeral, it seemed sensible to give you more time to rest."

Mrs. Anderson eyed her friend over her glass. It irked her that they seemed to be on a first-name basis so soon. But Bernadette was as kind as they come, no ulterior motive or hidden malice like Miss Trent. And she was so trusting and caring, it wasn't her fault she succumbed to Miss Trent's conniving.

"It's all right, dear. I understand. It was nice to have a quiet evening to myself," she lied. "But really, how was bridge? Were Myrtle and Edith unbearable?"

Bernadette smiled. "No more so than usual. They were infuriating at the start. You know how smug they can be. But you should have seen the look on their faces when we won the first hand. They insisted they let us win because it was Rosie's first time, but we just kept winning. They only won a handful of tricks the entire evening."

Mrs. Anderson nearly choked on her last sip of wine. That was not the answer she expected, and certainly not an answer she wanted to hear. Her delight in not losing their streak was overshadowed by her annoyance that Miss Trent was actually good at something. That she could be a suitable replacement bridge partner. What else could she be a suitable replacement for?

"All right, shall we go?" Bernadette had finished her wine as well. Mrs. Anderson's mood was sufficiently soured, but there was no way to politely decline after she had requested the company. So, they walked through the park, enjoying the early spring blooms and warm breeze. Before long, they were talking of other things and Mrs. Anderson completely forgot about Bridge and Miss Trent.

That is, until they nearly ran right into her.

"Dear me! I'm so terribly sorry!" she practically screamed in that high-pitched whine of hers.

"It's all right, dear," Bernadette said as Mrs. Anderson helped her regain her balance. Mrs. Trent had almost knocked them into the bushes, popping out so suddenly from a side trail. It was exactly the kind of ill-mannered lack of sense Mrs. Anderson expected from someone like her.

"Oh, Bernadette, you're too sweet." Miss Trent fawned over her with big doe eyes and a plastered on smile. "Hello, Lucy darling!" When she turned to greet Mrs. Anderson with that horrid nickname, she used a different smile.

"Hello, Miss Trent. You seem to be in a hurry, so we won't keep you." Mrs. Anderson took Bernadette by the arm and continued along as quickly as etiquette would allow. But Miss Trent trotted along behind them.

"I was in a hurry, Mrs. Anderson, but I was headed over to Bernadette's to see if she would like to walk with me. It is such a lovely morning, don't you think?" She cocked her head ever so slightly, like a pup seeking approval. Bernadette was taken in.

"Absolutely, dear. Please, join us." Miss Trent perked up at the invitation and squeezed in between Mrs. Anderson and Bernadette, linking arms with the older women. Mrs. Anderson rolled her eyes as Miss Trent started babbling on to Bernadette about the weather and flowers and silly nonsense, hardly seeming to breathe much less pause to let someone else speak for even a moment. After ten minutes she couldn't bear it any longer, and politely excused herself on the pretense of needing to rest.

But before she could extract her arm from Miss Trent's, Bernadette shrieked and pulled the walking party to an abrupt stop. Mrs. Anderson turned her head just in time to see a large beehive hit the ground in front of her. She jumped back as the bees began to swarm.

"Oh, the poor dears," said Miss Trent, not the least bit phased by the threatening sight ahead of them. "What a tragedy." She looked disappointed.

"Tragedy?" Mrs. Anderson had had enough of her nonsense. "It's a beehive, and it nearly fell on my head. Those awful little stinging insects can just build another one. In the meantime, we should go back and find another trail. I do not intend to get stung and spoil such a lovely day." As though her day hadn't been spoiled already by an awful little babbling pup. But Bernadette seemed distracted, looking thoughtfully at the bees, as though hypnotized by their swarming.

"Tragedy?" she murmured.

"Yes, Bernadette," Miss Trent turned after shooting Mrs. Anderson an annoyed look. She sounded wistful as she spoke. "They're such hard-working, delightful little creatures. They help the flowers grow, you know. It's such a shame that they lost their hive without purpose."

"I suppose you're right, I do so enjoy flowers." Bernadette cocked her head curiously, almost mimicking Miss Trent's earlier expression. "Do you know much about bees?"

Miss Trent's eyes lit up. "They are my absolute favorite animal, darling. They're so helpful! All the little worker bees do their very best to serve the queen."

"That would be nice," Mrs. Anderson chuckled. "I wouldn't mind having a few worker bees around to do my bidding." Miss Trent turned to her, the morning sun turning her brown eyes the color of honey.

"Oh, you wouldn't want to be a bee, Lucy dear. Most queens just sit around all day while others drone about. I'm sure that kind of life would bore you to death."

"I suppose so—"

"And some bees are quite sad, lonely queens without a hive of their own, constantly searching until they find one they like. And even then, the hive already has a queen, adding another difficulty to overcome."

As she spoke, something in her eyes darkened, and when she finished, their eyes remained locked. Mrs. Anderson suddenly felt afraid of the young woman in front of her, though she wouldn't have been able to say precisely why. But the moment ended when Miss Trent smiled her sickeningly sweet smile and turned back to Bernadette.

"Don't you worry too much about the poor bees, dear. I know a delightful young man who keeps bees just outside town, and I'm sure he would be happy to help with the hive. For now, we can go back a ways and take the trail that loops by a lovely daffodil patch. It's early in the season, but I think I saw a few starting to bloom. Lucy should go home and get some rest."

Bernadette nodded, still watching the honey bees swarm around their fallen hive, absentmindedly giving Mrs. Anderson a wave goodbye as she left.

MRS. ANDERSON POURED herself a glass of scotch. It was only lunch time, but she needed something to calm her nerves. That awful beehive nearly killed her, and Miss Trent was really getting under her skin. She had always been irritating, but there was something else. Something in her eyes that morning that was deeply unsettling. Something in the way Bernadette acted around her, too.

She looked around her parlor. It felt empty. Hollow. She missed Robert. He was irritating too, but he was a comforting presence. She could use one of his nonsensical stories to take her mind off things. But he was gone. His heart finally gave out. The funeral was tomorrow. For the first time that week, Mrs. Anderson cried.

HOURS LATER, THE BOTTLE of scotch was empty. Mrs. Anderson lounged in the parlor, resting, and there was a knock at the door. She didn't move, but the knocking just got louder and she heard a muffled voice call her name. She heaved herself off the chaise and answered the door.

Bernadette's arm was still up, mid-knock, and her eyes went wide with alarm when the door opened. "Lucille! Darling! Are you all right?"

Mrs. Anderson was confused until she turned to the mirror next to the door. Her face was puffy and red and streaked with makeup. Her hair was disheveled from her difficulty unpinning her hat. And it appeared from the large stain on her blouse that she had spilled some of her scotch.

She looked back at her friend, who still looked very worried. "Come in, Bernadette. Can I get you anything to drink?"

"No thank you, dear," she answered, brusquely walking in and throwing open the shades. Mrs. Anderson hadn't realized how dark it was in the parlor until the evening sunlight streamed in. She went back to the chaise while Bernadette picked up the empty bottle and tumbler off the floor. "Rosie was worried about you. After we met with her beekeeper friend and got the hive situation sorted, she said you had looked unwell this morning and suggested I check on you after dinner. It's a good thing she did."

Miss Trent again. Of course she wanted Bernadette to come over, to see her like this. She was equal parts embarrassed and furious, but still sluggish from the scotch. Bernadette handed her a glass of water.

"Did you have a pleasant afternoon with dear little Miss Trent and her friend?" She tried to sound pleasantly curious but must have let some of her annoyance slip.

"Don't talk like that, Lucille. I know you don't like her, but she's a sweet girl. And she's been very helpful these last few days."

"Helping me to the grave." If the conversation was going in that direction, Mrs. Anderson didn't have the energy to be civil.

"Now, now. She had nothing to do with your current state. You're grieving, and the beehive must have unsettled your nerves." Her scorn turned to concern. "I know you were fond of Robert, but I didn't think you'd take it this hard. We all knew his heart wasn't going to last him much longer."

Something snapped in Mrs. Anderson. She sat up too quickly, her head spinning. "But it was supposed to last longer than this! One minute he's here telling his ridiculous stories, and the next I get a phone call that he had a heart attack on the golf course! It's wrong. All of this is wrong." She slumped back onto the chaise and reached blindly for another bottle on the beverage cart before Bernadette rolled it out of her reach.

"Lucille, darling. I know this is hard. Imagine how hard it was on poor Rosie! Just out for a stroll, and suddenly seeing her friend's husband collapse? My Gerald said she ran as fast as an Olympian to get to the clubhouse phone and call the ambulance. It was a good thing she was there. She was telling us about it just the other day."

"What did she tell you? This is the first I'm hearing of it." Mrs. Anderson was shocked. She knew he was on the golf course and someone called for an ambulance, but she never asked who. That Miss Trent was the last person to see Robert alive was too much for her.

"Lucille, dear, I'm sure no one wanted to cause you any more grief than necessary," Bernadette said hesitantly.

"Tell me," Mrs. Anderson barked at her friend.

"Well," Bernadette sighed, "it was just awful. Rosie was walking on the trail between the woods and the golf course, and she heard a noise around the bend, a thud and some buzzing. We think Robert hit his ball into a beehive, and when he went down the hill to retrieve it the swarm was so frightening his poor old heart couldn't take it."

Bees again.

"And even with the shock of it, Rosie has still been so helpful, keeping us going through all this. I tell you, when I heard the news I was sure the town would fall apart. You've done so much for this community, you're like a queen here. We all love you so. But Rosie has taken on a lot of responsibility for someone so young."

Bernadette kept talking, but Mrs. Anderson wasn't listening. Another beehive. Her husband dying of fright while she was busy being the queen of the town. Miss Trent was there, just like she was at the luncheon, Bridge night, and the morning walk that almost killed Mrs. Anderson. It all fit.

"Lucy? Are you okay?" Bernadette interrupted her thoughts, and she spun at her friend, eyes wild.

"What did you call me?"

"Darling, what's wrong?"

"You said Lucy. You called me Lucy. Just like that woman. That wasp of a woman!" She was on her feet again.

"Lucille! Sit down! Where are you going?"

Mrs. Anderson didn't turn around. She kept walking towards the door. That woman wasn't going to get the best of her. She may have killed her husband and stolen her friend, but she would put an end to it.

She trudged along, her thoughts a whirling fog, the scotch still not worn off. Down the lane, onto the main road towards town, or maybe the other way? She couldn't remember. She found herself on a trail through the woods, perhaps a shortcut. Eventually it came out of the woods and around a bend at the base of a hill.

MRS. ANDERSON OPENED her eyes. Everything was hazy. Her head hurt, and there was a buzzing in her ears. She was laying in something sticky and wet. Leaning over her was a young blonde woman, her face full of concern but her eyes full of venom.

"Miss Trent," she sputtered, each syllable bringing pain. The woman smiled. But gone was the sweetness, the pretense of friendliness. This smile was one of malicious triumph.

"Oh Lucy, polite even to death. Your husband was that way, too. Everyone in this town is so polite. I do so love this town." Her voice crooned, like a lullaby, urging Mrs. Anderson to sleep. "Don't you worry, dearest. I'll take good care of it for you."

MALOCCLUSION

Dixon March

————◆————

THEY PASSED OVER the Colorado border, and the land turned flat and the sky gray and gravelike. Deb Tallie felt twitchy, like she'd missed a turn somewhere, like she was lost in some prairie purgatory where the dead go to sit forever and stare at nothing.

Beside her Barret groaned a cowish noise. "Christ, Tallie, look at this." Barret pulled his lip up to show an obscene pink inner mouth. His two front teeth, which had never been in amazing condition, were now shattered jagged knives. Worse than it was an hour ago. The teeth seemed to be in a slow collapse and had lost more shards along the crevices and cracks started by the bouncer's fist back in Holyhoke.

Tallie kept her eyes on the road. "I told you not to drink so much."

"I'm gonna eat a bullet this hurts so bad." His new lisp was more prevalent now that the swelling was down a bit from that morning. Barret drew up his knees in the passenger seat and continued to stare into the broken abyss around his tonsils. "If the eyes are

151

the windows to the soul, what's the mouth?"

She didn't answer. Her eyes flicked to the rearview mirror, to the two-lane ribbon of concrete and the distant purple ghosts of mountains. A black sedan had been following them for the last ten miles. She tried to talk herself into believing it was just a civilian sedan, one that had crept out from behind a billboard five miles back. It didn't work.

She imagined the sedan in movie scenes, the camera zoomed in and panned over the yellow letters on the door: S-H-E-R-R-I-F-F.

Then her mind-camera swooped to the Subaru she drove with its *go vegan* bumper sticker. In a cut-away shot, the camera peeked in past the driver's side bumper to show the black plastic-wrapped bricks tucked inside the wheel-well like Russian nesting dolls.

Tallie returned her focus to the drive ahead. Hands gripped death-tight at ten and two. On both sides were fallow fields of grass bowed by wind that came and went. It was like a haunted moor, and any minute now she expected some crumbling gothic manor would appear along the razor edge horizon and out from it would pour a crowd of hungry ghosts. She asked Barret, "What's our next exit?"

"Christ, how would I know." Barret lifted his lips again to stare at his damaged self in the mirror.

On the road, a green sign approached, its reflective coating sun-peeled and caked like a desert floor. A town's name barely readable but she thought it said *Twin Mounds*, three miles.

"Let's stop there," Barret said.

"That's not on route."

Barret touched a fingertip to one of his ruined teeth and howled. "Jesus, Dee, you can't leave me like this. I need something for the pain."

"There's Tylenol in my purse."

"Fuck Tylenol. We could change a tire."

"We are *not* changing a tire."

"Hey, Fisker will get his—so what if I take a gram off a brick? Not even a corner, a tenth, less. There's fucking four of them."

Tallie slid her hand into her bag to rest on the holster that contained the Springfield Hellcat. She imagined a medium shot of the Subaru's interior with Barret's brains splattered across the backseat. In a voice-over she heard herself break the news to her sister. *I'm sorry, Dina, but that dirtbag husband you love so much . . . No, it wasn't me.*

Then she heard the dialogue with Fisker, pictured the look on his long Danish grim reaper face when he asked, *Why is my Subaru splattered with your shit brother-in-law's brains?* The scenes tumbled through her head, a bad montage in a movie she wished she wasn't in.

Not for the first time, she regretted her decision to bail on that crap film school in the Bronx with its professors and their quid pro quo deals on their casting room couch. Fucking a few pruny douchebags seemed less of a sacrifice now, too many decades later, but either way she'd have ended her career spread-eagle and used up. Joining the army, she thought to herself, with no little bitterness, had been *such* a good response.

Tallie breathed deep and her heart refused to give her lungs space. "When we get to Westport, we are leaving this car in Fisker's garage and walking away. You are not getting me or Dina killed because you picked a fight in a bar."

"Do you not see my broken fucking teeth?"

She checked the rearview mirror. The right half of her face was white like a Halloween mask and the road behind them as straight as a coffin nail. The sedan was still there. It had gained.

"We can't stop," she murmured.

Barret poked a chunk of gum that gushed a fresh stream of red down his chin. "Jesus, Dee, it *hurts.*"

A sign bloomed up ahead to welcome travelers to the town. The name and population number was unreadable underneath a cloud of black scratches, as if they'd crossed out and rewritten it too many times. Tallie saw nothing of a real settlement, just a handful of crumpled farmhouses and a silo and a speed-trap where the limit dropped to 45. She pumped the brakes to ensure she adhered to that dictate and crept the Subaru to the right lane, stayed in it.

On the road behind her, she watched the sedan drop speed and reverse course, a maneuver that had it cut across both lanes in a wild U-turn. The back tires of the sedan kicked up dust as they intersected with the dry shoulder, knocked about the wildflowers there, then sped off. It was as if the officer of the law had vanished in a cloud of ninja smoke.

Tallie watched the sedan fly off in the opposite direction. She'd have paired it with a high-speed shot, some Yakity Sax in the background. She wondered what had the sheriff so eager to *nope* out of there so hard.

Barret lamented again while he stared into the pit of his mouth. "It's ruined."

"A door," Tallie said.

"What?"

The speed limit slowed further to twenty-five as the road entered a commercial district with wood frame buildings at least a hundred years old, battered and paint-peeled.

Tallie kept a keen watch on the speedometer. "If eyes are the windows to the soul, the mouth is a door."

"Wow. You shoulda been a fucking poet, Dee." Barret ejected a string of bloody saliva onto the dashboard.

THE HIGHWAY TURNED into a sleepy main street called Cadmus. In a slow cruise, Tallie drove past a handful of parked vehicles, decades old, smothered in rust with flat tires melted to the pavement. The wind carried a whisper of dead leaves and paper trash tumbleweeds, and most of the shop windows were dark, nameless, drawn blinds closed like eyelids.

In her mind she took it in with a wide establishing shot and pulled up sharply to catch a scatter of crows leaving a naked tree in the distance. The gray glassy sky gave no sign they were on earth.

Barret hooted for her to pull over at a drug store with a lifeless neon mortar-and-pestle sign in the window. Tallie parked and grumbled *no way* was anybody home.

"If this is a ghost town, we can take what we want." Barret left the Subaru and approached the store. The door swung open in his impolite fist and screeched in a song of dead hinges, and he paused to give Tallie a looter's smirk the second before he vanished inside.

She hovered on the curb, self-consciously alone, and checked the burner phone buried at the bottom of her handbag. The phone mutely declared *no bars.* Any minute, she assumed, the county sheriff in his black sedan would ramble up center street and tell them not to let the sun go down on them here.

She looked, but behind her the road was vacant.

With a few curses under her breath, Tallie followed Barret into the pharmacy. She found herself in a crowd of low aluminum shelves with bottles and boxes strewn about, shower caps and hand soap and Alka-Seltzer and witch hazel in glass with cork stoppers. Her eye caught on one particular shampoo that read *Gee Your Hair Smells Terrific* in a crusty label, and it rested in peace beside a display of Lifebouy bars and piles of aspirin turned as yellow as old teeth. Her bowels grumbled with a worry she couldn't put a name to.

Barret was already at the counter to agitate the call bell, *ding-ding-ding-ding.* Tallie met him there and squeezed his hand so he'd shut the hell up with that racket.

"This place is a graveyard." Tallie gave him back his hand. "It's making us late. We need to go."

Barret waved her off. "Maybe they still got pills in the back, some old Percosets or something."

"Fisker will be . . . *upset* if we're late."

"Fisker's always *upset*. Fucking Ikea psychopath." He hammered again at the bell. It clanked weakly at the assault.

"He's going to do us like he did your cousin if we're not highly punctual."

"Who, Artie?" Barret gave her a dumb grin that displayed his jagged front teeth. The effect was that of an addle-brained moonshiner. "Artie had it coming. It was only a couple of broken bones, anyway."

"One of which included his neck."

Barret continued to abuse the bell. "Hell-lo hell-lo! Are we alone here or what?"

To settle her blood pressure, Tallie turned her back to the counter, slipped her hand inside her handbag, and unclipped the Hellcat's holster. She surveyed for any blind spots from which an enemy might leap: a moldy staff door that stood half open; the silver beast of an ice machine gone quiet; a corner with several racks of snack chips like jersey barriers in front of a soda fountain counter. Tallie's heart wrestled against her lungs, and she attempted a deep breath, wondered if in her old age she finally should talk to a doctor about how stress no longer warmed her spirit but sent her organs in a tumble of bad feels. She grimaced at the idea of a doctor's clammy hands on her. At that moment, a leathery voice leapt out—"How may I help you fine folks?"

After a spin and only a minor heart attack, Tallie saw a round white woman in a pharmacist's coat behind the register.

Not just white but bluish white, white in a drained sense, a Caucasian bereft of all blood flow, and the starched stiff lab coat she wore bore only the faintest frayed threads at the collar. When the woman smiled, it was a grin so straight and square Tallie thought of a sideshow barker or a snake oil salesman, some plastic-happy face with a mouth full of perfect, morally upright fake teeth.

Barret seemed only a bit disappointed. "I was starting to think this place was abandoned."

"No, no," the woman said. "We're just a little old fashioned. And trying to conserve energy." She cast an eye to the dead fluorescents in the drop ceiling and gave a little shrug.

Before Barret stuck his foot in it Tallie jumped in. "My brother took a tumble, and his teeth unfortunately broke his fall. Do you have any of those temporary tooth cap kits that will get us back on the road?"

"I'll do you one better. There's a dentist just across the street, Dr. Kauwen, served the community for sixty years. A fine Samaritan. I'm sure he can work you in right away."

Barret clapped his hand to his heart. "You are a lifesaver, miss. We'll head on over."

"Your sister's welcome to rest here while you visit with Dr. Kauwen. That damage might take a bit of time to correct."

"Fa-an-tastic." Barret slapped Tallie between her shoulder blades. "She don't mind a wait."

Fury brightened Tallie's cheeks. "She *might* mind," Tallie said flatly. Then, she addressed the pharmacist: "I hope this won't be long. We have commitments."

The pharmacist's grin widened, and at that moment her teeth appeared to slide a hair, go softly crooked. A sliver of lurid pink gum shone underneath, like a glimpse of bride-thigh just before the big event, but then the woman sucked her lips together to tuck the teeth up into their rightful place.

Dentures, Tallie thought. Flippers or prosthetics, overlarge and jammed into the woman's mouth. The woman's smile slipped because her dentures barely held on.

"Dr. Kauwen will take as long as necessary," the pharmacist said with a bit of a slur. "He will make you whole."

THROUGH THE DRUG store windows, Tallie watched Barret scuttle across the dead street, to the shopfront pointed out by the pharmacist as Dr. Kauwen's, the one with the cracked window and a ghost of gold lettering left on the glass. With a twist of dread, Tallie wondered why she hadn't seen the dentist sign on the way in. The "Dr." and "DDS" letters were paint-chipped and dull, but they were legible. Beyond them the office was as dark and motionless as a stagnant pond.

When Barret was well and truly gone, the pharmacist appeared behind the fountain counter, by the big silver soda pulls that rose like vintage Loch Ness monsters. She summoned Tallie with a wave. Tallie moved around the barrier of chip racks to sit on a creaky stool, and there she watched the woman fix a chipped glass of cloudy gray water, as though it were a thing Tallie would put to her lips.

The woman's smile menaced her. "What brings you fine folks through town?"

"We're on vacation." Until that point, Tallie had kept her hand in her bag, but the dread in her gut churned again and she concluded it was a useless gesture, a thin bravado. To litter the route with bodies would piss Fisker off just as badly as if she ran off with all his product. Still, as soon as her fingertips left the bag, she felt naked, as though pressed onto the sweaty vinyl cushions of a casting room couch. No good choices available. "I'm exhausted from the drive. You'll forgive me if I'm bad at conversation?"

"Wholly understandable. You must have driven a ways. Few folks make it out here."

"How many people have you got in town? On the sign the population is scratched out."

"Is it now?" The woman blinked and made a small *hmph* noise in the back of her throat. "I imagine juvenile delinquents must have had a hand in such nonsense. We've had a shortage of good, Christian citizens since the fluoride debacle, that and the railroad pulling out."

"The fluoride debacle?"

The woman nodded grimly. "Sixty or so years back the state tried to come up in here and mandate that the water treatment facility turn on the fluoride, awhile after we'd voted to turn it off. It was doin' such damage to the brains of our young ones, you know, giving them neurological problems, lowering the IQ of the populous, what have you."

Tallie nodded, mouth shut tight.

The woman continued as if Tallie had agreed with her on such matters. "You know the state had their pencil necks out here to tell us what to do, even put some folks in jail. Our Christian men were dragged about the street. We even had ourselves a protest. Not so many died on that day as the Goodland Chronicle would have you believe, only a handful, and it was more of ours than theirs."

A weighty silence followed. Tallie didn't break it.

The woman sighed. "After the protest, we prayed and prayed to be delivered from such evil, and we prayed so hard that a solution arrived on our very doorstep in the form of Dr. Kauwen." The pharmacist turned her eyes heavenward.

Tallie's dread sharpened. "So *how many* people died during the protest?" She imagined a hectic scene, country yokel extras swarmed by clouds of tear gas and jack-booted thugs, their beehive hairdos melting in the fumes. Or maybe it was the yokels who formed the mob, chased the state bureaucrats down blind alleys and bludgeoned them to death with bats and wood planks. A number of scenarios played out in her mind with vibrant, choreographed gore.

The pharmacist refused to validate any of them. "How many needed to die for us to be free of government overreach?"

She kept on with the tale before Tallie could speak again. "Dr. Kauwen took it all the way to the county seat and gave them what to. The Goodland Chronicle said Dr. Kauwen was there when the county commissioner died in that twisted way, but of course that's not true. The media lies, you know. Dr. Kauwen saved us from the worst of terrible fates."

Tallie kept her face neutral. "The terrible fate of fluoride?"

The pharmacist gave a sage-like nod.

"But . . . " Tallie couldn't resist herself, the words tumbled out before she caught them. "Don't you think it was a conflict of interest for this guy? I mean, a dentist gets money the more cavities they fill. I'll bet the town had a lot of cavities with no more fluoride." Tallie chuckled. "People love to scam people."

A darkness crossed over the eyes of the pharmacist, like the shadow of a carnivorous bird against a pale sky.

The woman said, "We *prayed* for Dr. Kauwen, and the lord delivered peace unto us. If we were all to have sat under Dr. Kauwen's drill, it would be as God willed it." After a breathless pause, the pharmacist added, "As a guest in our house, you'd best not question such miracles."

"Okay, okay." Tallie softened her tone, showed her palms. "I'm sure the guy is great."

After a moment of dagger eyes, the pharmacist's smile returned. "I'm sure your brother is loving the fine care of Dr. Kauwen's touch right now."

The idea pulled Tallie's attention across the street. "I'd better go check on him."

"You'd best stay here." The pharmacist's smile did not waver.

Tallie stood slowly and backed away a step, as though in a retreat from an aggravated rattlesnake. "Thanks for the water."

With the woman's eyes on her, Tallie made her way back through the dead quiet of the drug store. Unease curled about in Tallie's gut as she scanned again the *Lifebouy* soaps and shampoos with their commentary on the scent of her hair. Something was off about the place. She could not escape the idea. When she reached the exit and glanced behind her, she caught the pharmacist's face and its broad artificial smile like a psychotic mannequin. Then it hit her. The off thing.

On the shelves there were products to clean every part of a human body, other than a mouth. No toothpaste, no toothbrush. Not a single box of floss.

Outside, Tallie scanned Cadmus Street and found it to be bathed in afternoon sun, quiet and vacant. No birds sang. No noise of life or citizenry. A whisper of wind chased garbage down the sidewalk, but apart from that she felt as though she walked upon the surface of another world long dead.

She jogged to the dentist's office and ducked inside quickly, and there in the gloom was a collection of chairs and end tables, a waiting room covered in grime and heaps of old magazines. On their pages, corseted models smiled with haircurler coifs. Tallie wondered if their hair smelled terrific. Dust motes drifted in the thin light from the window blinds, like sea creatures with nowhere to go, just waiting to be eaten by something bigger.

"Lou?" Tallie whispered.

No response. Tallie crossed the space on twitchy heels, towards the back where she made out the shape of a clinic door, the wood paint-peeled and splintered.

She tried again. "Lou, you there?"

"Dr. Kauwen is with a patient, miss."

Tallie veered about to see a woman there, as pale as the pharmacist, who wore a set of nursing scrubs so tight they might as well have been mummy wraps. She bore the same aggressively straight and boxy false teeth.

"You may wish to wait in the drug store, miss." The woman regarded Tallie with a look of flat, brainless hatred. "There's a soda fountain."

"That's my people in there." Tallie withdrew the Hellcat from her bag and held the weapon low, finger light on the trigger guard. "I'm going to go get him."

"The patient is under sedation. Dr. Kauwen needs to finish his work."

"Okay, fuck you, I'm not leaving without him."

With the receptionist's eye hot on her, Tallie advanced to the clinic room and kicked the door open. Beyond lay an unlit chamber with tin cabinets and shelves cluttered about in shadowed heaps, as though tossed in a storm, plastic grinning teeth and rusted needle picks scattered about haphazard. Any alternate exits were hidden in a heavy curtain of shadow. In the center a yellowed bulb illuminated a dental chair as if on stage, beside a cracked and blood-stained spit basin overfull with foul discharge, and it was there she found Barret.

He was sprawled out, hair stringy and sweat-dark against the mint green cushion, face obscured by the headrest. A dim whimper escaped him, echoed into the dark that pushed up against the edge of the light.

Tallie nudged Barret's shoulder. "Come on, Lou. Time to go." She crept around the chair and ignored the smell, an atrocious bowels-and-blood perfume she'd not experienced since her stint overseas. With held breath she came around to look Barret in the eye.

But first she looked him in the mouth.

In full, obscene view there was his tongue and his tonsils and his gums, bare and inflamed red. Stripped clean of teeth. Each tooth socket was empty and oozed gore. Not a tidy extraction by any means. Metal contraptions on either side of his face kept his jaws wrenched apart. New growths cut through the holes in his throat like infant needles. Foamy spittle seeped down his chin with each tremble he gave, each wordless moan, and his eyes pleaded at her, all pinprick pupils and exposed eyeball whites.

Tallie jerked her eyes away, as if she'd caught him in some lewd, bare naked spread. Too much of his insides for her. It felt porno-graphic. But then he bleated a cry and at the anguished sound, she regained her senses.

She turned back to search the appliance on his jaw for a release. "*Jeezus*, Barret . . . " But she didn't care for the way she'd said it, like she thought all this was his fault. "I'm sorry . . . "

The receptionist appeared at the door. "Dr. Kauwen will come back."

Tallie flicked a steel latch near Barret's neck and made him yelp a shapeless noise. She wrestled with the clasps and straps and kept the Hellcat directed at the receptionist in a one-handed grip she didn't care for. "How do I get this thing off him?"

The receptionist's dentures had slipped more and now in her mouth the teeth lay at a slope. They flopped awkwardly when she tried to speak. "Dr. Kauwen is coming."

"Back the fuck off!" In desperation, Tallie fired a round into the floor and the wood splintered near the receptionist's stained white shoe. The report echoed. The woman didn't flinch despite the near loss of her foot and stood there as limp as a boneless doll. Around the room, the shadows squirmed and seemed to draw about the noise.

Tallie had the sudden sense that the shot had only caught the attention of something large in the darkness, like it was not simple darkness there in the clinic room but eels that squirmed in oil. She regretted the hasty discharge of her firearm. With renewed adrenaline she struggled to wrench the contraption on Barret free, and he whimpered and spit blood at her efforts.

A thump came from somewhere in the eel-full shadows. Almost like a footstep.

"Dr. Kauwen is coming," said the receptionist.

"Shut. Up."

The receptionist's oversized dentures had slipped loose to give Tallie a glimpse of her bare gums. Strange ivory shapes trembled beneath.

Then came another footfall, slow and burdensome on the wood floor. It sounded as though a gorilla crept up, near a portal hidden in the gloom, but from exactly where Tallie could not determine. The echo was disembodied, the bootheel of a monster from a dream.

Resolved to not meet it, she ripped the contraption off Barret, hooked her finger around a loose point in the leather belts and Barret howled. Blood seeped. The metal clattered on the edge of the gory spitbasin and splashed into the redblack muck there. Barret moaned as a new footstep came from some nebulous point in the darkness, pursued by another.

"Dr. Kauwen is coming!" The receptionist's false teeth tumbled to the floor and shattered like eggshell.

Tallie took aim at the woman's center of mass but could not stare at anything but her dark void of mouth, the disorderly rows upon rows of wicked fangs that circled as far back as her throat, like the orifice of a wicked lamprey.

Another hammer step shook the tin cabinets, rattled the liquid in the basin. Tallie hauled Barret off the chair, hoisted him up under her free arm and unloaded two shots into the receptionist. The woman flailed backwards and collapsed. Her legs sprawled out in the doorway and Tallie dragged Barret over them.

The clinic room shook. The cabinets and the chair and all the dental detritus clattered about with each monstrous step, *wham-wham-wham . . .*

Tallie pulled Barret through the waiting room, his body a bag of dead meat, and she did not once look back. When they hit the front door, Barret vomited a bucket of red foam onto the doorstep. The light of day shone over them. Tallie in her beeline to the car found a crowd of townspeople now emerged at the entrances of their darkened shops, all bluish white faces and dentures crooked or slipped off entirely to lie on the sidewalk like Halloween toys. The people all wore the same face.

Tallie fired a round somewhere in their ranks. They paid it no mind. They shuffled forward, limp and boneless, their bared throat of fangs the only lively part of them, as though parasites filled their core and had no use for such things as arms and legs and spines. They all screeched in unison with a slur. "Dr. Kau-en! Dr. Kau-en!"

The concrete beneath Tallie's feet quaked from the approach of whatever invisible monster she'd narrowly missed inside the dentist office. Window glass shattered at her back and wood groaned as though pushed to the brink of collapse. Something did indeed approach, and she could not deny it. The mundane structure that hid it from the light of day could not weather its horrendous proportions. It had to be something big. Tallie knew she should not look behind her, but she did.

A long shadow covered her as she looked up, up. The whites of her eyes grew large, her pupils shrank. A guttural sound slipped from her contorted mouth, but it was not any recognizable word that could give name to the thing there. It was the speech of troglodyte ancestors who balked under the eye of unwholesome and hungry gods.

She might have stood there struck stone in terror had not her inner camera-eye zoomed out to the scene and thought, *high angle shot, make sure to get all the extras in the frame.* A zombie protest of townspeople, maybe some exploding cars, some fire hydrants shattered in a fountain of unfluoridated water. *Pure cinema gold,* she giggled madly to herself.

The moment of disassociation gave her enough sanity to wrench her eyes away from the dentist office and hobble to the Subaru with Barret under one arm. From out of the drug store charged the pharmacist with a lamprey mouth that sucked and thrashed, and Tallie fired what remained of her clip into the woman's face. The woman hit the left side bumper, streaked a smear of brackish blood on her way to the concrete. She'd almost reached the driver's side when Barret slipped from her grasp, too blood-slippery. When he crumpled to the ground, he took Tallie down with him.

Tallie's knees cracked sharply against the pavement. She sucked air, no room for curses in her tight-packed chest. Beside her Barret slumped on hands and knees, and a sick tremor ran through his body. She managed to get back on her feet with a hobble that suggested her knees would not ignore this slight, but terror chased the pain away and Tallie wrenched at his arm. He would not budge. Strings of blood hung from his lips like party streamers.

"Get up, goddammit, Lou!" Tallie scanned the street to see the townspeople had crept closer with their depthless mouths. She hauled Barret a few more steps. By the Subaru the pharmacist in her ruined blood-mash face flopped about broken and prepared to stand up again.

Tallie's attention fixed on the pharmacist with a quick panicked cross-reference to the emptiness of her clip. She thought to chuck the Hellcat at the woman full-force like some idiot in a movie, but before any bad decision could be made, a sharp pain rattled her, a dozen little stabs like a barracuda bite.

She barked a cry and saw Barret's mouth around her wrist.

He bit down with mindless aplomb and then unhinged his jaw to go in for another. Fangs burst forth from his abused gums, rows upon rows of new ivory razors like shark teeth. Wildly, she thought, *he kissed my sister with that mouth.* She tumbled away more by instinct than design and tripped on her own heels, and she thought surely she was dead now. Then she felt the warm bumper of the Subaru at her back.

Tallie made a frenzied search of the handbag and by some miracle found the keys before Barret stumbled broken to her to make good on his interrupted second bite. Her arm poured blood into the bottom of the bag, soaked all her crumpled tissues and made the key fob slippery and wet. In her fumble she managed to graze the unlock button, and the Subaru chirped. Tallie wrenched open the door and dove behind the wheel. The second the door latched shut Barret appeared at the window like a mad animal and slapped the glass with blood-marred palms. His ruined jaw flapped about, eel-like.

Behind the wheel, Tallie's hand trembled with the key fob, but she managed to dance it into the ignition. The engine turned and sang a beautiful song. She put the Subaru in reverse, and in reflex checked the rearview mirror. The glass was black. Not the shadows of the townspeople swarmed around the car but the event horizon of the dentist office and the thing that now stood there, towered, like a dead god. At the insistence of her lizard-brained ancestral memory, she wrenched her eyes from it. She thrust the stick-shift into first. The wheels spun up over the curb and launched the Subaru forward in a hop-jerk over the bodies of the townspeople. The tires smoked. Where she'd been, only black rubber burns remained on the pavement.

As she sped down Cadmus Street, she gave one last glance in the mirror, in some fickle hope she could return to save Barret. He was nowhere. Maybe in the crush of bodies on the curb that even now twitched and began to stand back up. In the clouds of white burnout, she caught the edges of the thing, the *Dr. Kauwen.* It clambered in sludgy pursuit, as if unaccustomed to the burden of light. It was hard for her not to giggle at the way it burst out of its ragged dentist coat.

A MILE OR SO out of town, the road behind her was clear and the blood loss started to feel real. Tallie pulled over. She trembled like a newborn puppy. Grabbed one of Barret's shirts from the back and wrapped it around the new holes in her arm. The shoulder she'd parked on tilted softly into a ditch filled with wildflowers, and with the angle she felt tipped over, dizzy, like all her thoughts might spill out of her in a swarm of agitated worms.

In the distance ahead, she spotted a whirl of dust behind a tall gray row of grass. The same black Sheriff's sedan appeared from a side road, as though on a long bypass. It sped towards her, a pin-prick that grew bigger and bigger.

Tallie hustled to cover the red blood seep with her jacket around her shoulders, middle-aged soccer mom style. The sedan flashed its lights, slowed and came to a stop behind the Subaru.

Her hands refused to lay quiet, so to keep them steady she tucked her bloodied one in a pocket while the other death-gripped the steering wheel.

The county cop lumbered slowly up to the driver's side window, still smeared with Barret's gore. When she rolled it down, it squeaked.

From behind mirrored glasses, he spoke to her with a tone akin to a two-by-four. "Is there an emergency, miss?"

"I just cut myself a little."

He said, "There's blood on your vehicle."

Tallie shrugged. "I cut myself a lot."

By the side window, the wildflowers wavered pink and yellow in the breeze. A cowbird flitted about.

"You're missing a passenger," the cop said.

The image of Barret's trap jaw came to her, his new rows of teeth. "He wanted to stay back in town."

"You *stopped* in the Mound?"

His eyebrows arched above the rim of his glasses. A moment of silence passed.

Then, he said, "Your passenger's not coming back." It wasn't a question.

Tallie confirmed it with a slow shake of her head.

The cop gazed at the speck of town behind them and reflectively she looked, too. Something shivered above the horizon like a heat mirage, a flutter of reality slightly ripped, as insubstantial as gauze.

Tallie pictured in her mind-camera a wide establishing shot of the town and the townspeople. They rambled about Cadmus Street limp and hungry, bemoaned by the loss of fresh blood, new enamel. She imagined Barret, disoriented, mouth wordlessly moving, full of blood just barely tasted.

Tallie thought, were she more noble, she'd return to the town with a few cans of kerosene and set the place ablaze, call it some mad attempt to avenge her sister. In truth as soon as it occurred to her she knew it was a fantasy. A happy ending seen only in movies. Really, she was going to tell Dina her husband died from his injuries from that bar fight in Holyhoke. Such was the risk of concussion. She'd say sorry she had to leave his body by the side of the road, for fear of Fisker's wrath. Whoops. Fisker might not care for it, but his grim reaper face held no horror for her now.

The cop examined her dully. "I take it you'll not come through this county again."

Tallie nodded.

He slapped the roof. "Drive safe." And then he lumbered off. His boots crunched softly in the shoulder, and she listened too long to them. Crunch, crunch, crunch . . .

When the sedan sped off, she attended to her arm once more, removed the jacket with a wince and flexed. A spurt of black blood ran thick as syrup from the wound, and she attempted to clean it with a bottle of water from the passenger side floor. The water rinsed the blood from her flesh and exposed the holes there. In the flow something came loose from the ragged edge of a bite mark, and she picked it out, grasped it between thumb and forefinger. Soon, she thought, her icy dissociation would melt and there would be screams. But for now it was a distant prospect. She sat for a while and stared at nothing. Behind her the town of Twin Mounds hummed beneath the flat grave sky, and she could not imagine the dark of night made its residents less agile.

"Roll the credits," she whispered. Then out the open window she threw the thing she'd picked from her wound: a single ivory fang.

Limber Lost

K. Wallace King

———— ♦ ————

IN THE YEAR before she returned to the land with the lake she'd sometimes wondered if she had never been alive at all. That she'd been born a ghost. She was prone to thoughts like this. She'd grown up in a house that was an exact copy of the model next door, a father gone before she could remember him, and a mother certain her lot in life was everyone's fault but her own. Her mother's bitterness lashed out at her daughter with a tongue like a velvet whip. It was hardly surprising Carole had been a shy little girl, inhabiting an imaginary world populated by elves in tree knots, fairies behind the plastic garden shed, trolls under the house. Who she was and who she was meant to be seemed as hard to grasp as running water. Even as old as she was now, Carole sometimes felt as see-through as a window, revealing only a room of neatly arranged furniture while she held her breath behind a closed door.

In the morning she made coffee in her little French press. She drank it standing by the kitchen sink looking out the window at the neighbor's sickly rosebush. Then to work. Work was transcribing accident reports until lunch eaten at her desk or at the mall sitting alone at a chrome table in the food court in the shopping mall. Carole drove home, hands clenched on the steering wheel, aware that at any moment one of the metal machines whizzing by could smash her to bits. Yellow lines seemed a silly symbol of safety.

Once she saw a deer on the shoulder of the 101 North. She wanted to stop, but couldn't, boxed in by cars going well over the speed limit. She took the next exit, her mind swamped with ridiculous plans to rescue the animal, but traffic was snarled and came to a halt. Through neighboring windshields angry faces cursed one another mutely through the glass. By the time Carole was heading south on the freeway again, she was afraid to look across the concrete barrier. Afraid to see if the deer was still there, frozen between forward and retreating.

At home, Carole's evenings passed watching television shows that although eventually cancelled, seemed to simply morph into identical shows with new actors and updated wardrobes. There were mornings when the full hot of the California sun blared through her curtains and hit her smack in the face. Panicked, she'd put her hand to her chest to check the puttering of her heart. When Carole discovered she was alive she got up and begin making coffee in the little French press.

One Saturday afternoon the mailman knocked on Carole's door and she'd signed for a certified letter. Pretty sure something mailed certified couldn't be good news, Carole put the letter on the kitchen counter. But each time she passed, the green and white *Certified* sticker on the envelope seemed to shout, open me! At last she opened the letter with a dull steak knife, slicing through the return address.

It was a letter from an attorney. Her great aunt had died and left Carole her farm. She had not seen nor spoken with her great aunt for years. Carole stared at the crisp white paper, at the no non-sense font announcing the name of the law firm, remembering the farm with the fairy tale Victorian house with a porch wreathed in gingerbread carving, and the pretty dark blue lake tucked among walnut and elm trees. Once when she was a child her mother had left Carole with her great aunt for a week.

It had been spring and Carole, little then, had walked barefoot with her aunt to pick wild strawberries through a field of purple flowers. Violets, Carole remembered. Her great aunt had pointed at the lake, winking in the sunlight. She'd told Carole something about the lake, but Carole couldn't remember what it was. Only that it made her smile.

That week stretched out in Carole's mind like a year once she returned with her mother to the city in the west. Returned to the dull dun colored tract house. She remembered the farm at first vividly, then like a dream, until finally the memory faded to an occasional silvery glimmer.

Carole called the attorney to make sure this wasn't some sick prank. Though who cared enough about her to bother, she couldn't imagine. But it was true. She was her great aunt's sole beneficiary. When Carole asked how her great aunt had died, the lawyer said a pipe had burst in the kitchen. Her great aunt must have slipped and fell. She had apparently been knocked unconscious, because according to the coroner, her great aunt had drowned in only a few inches of water.

Carole sat down on the edge of her old, stained couch remem-bering that floor. It was laid with ancient slate flagstones, unkind to anything dropped upon it, especially eighty-eight year old heads brittle as robin eggs.

Carole turned off the television and held the letter to her heart. She was startled when she heard herself laugh. Who would have thought she'd be so lucky? She tried to remember what her great aunt looked like, but all that came to her was a soft voice. What she remembered more clearly was the house, like a tall white box with lacy edges, and the lake, which in her childhood memory seemed almost as vast as a deep blue sea.

Over the next two days Carole packed everything she cared about, which was not a great deal, and shoved the boxes into the back of her car. She left all her nicked, mismatched furniture behind. It didn't occur to her until she was many miles away that she hadn't bothered to quit her job.

SHE DROVE WITHOUT realizing how fast she was going. Once east of the Rockies, dipping down into the Midwest, she began to smell honeysuckle and felt a soft dampness to her skin. She spotted robins and redwing blackbirds swirling over green fields. She'd forgotten all about these things, these scents, this moist air.

The farm was in an area that had long ago been called the Limberlost. No one was sure why it was called that, although there were stories of lost men or women ending in tragedy and heartbreak. The Limberlost had once been an enormous swampy bog. It had been a place with quicksand, rattlesnakes, turkey vultures, black bears and much more. The Native people understood it. However, the white man saw no use for land they couldn't farm, so they'd drained the Limberlost. The earth, rich with thousands of years of absorbing snakes, vegetation, and the occasional careless human, produced bountiful harvests of corn.

The lake on the farm was a leftover from the Limberlost. It was ringed with cattails and its shallows were filled with tadpoles and crawdads. The ground around it was spongy and smelled of sweet decay.

As Carole drew nearer to the farm, she began to feel something like excitement. Perhaps the feeling of wearing the wrong skin might disappear. It was a new beginning. She hummed along with a song on the radio in her Kia Sorento, remembering how tired she was of people asking her how she was then watching their eyes dim when she answered. She didn't think she could have stood another Friday night's tacos eaten alone while the tables around her filled with laughing couples. In her twenties she'd had only enough dates to count on the fingers of both hands. Each had ended with her feeling more awkward, more lonely. And last year, no one asked her out at all.

She arrived at the farm on a Tuesday and began to settle in. A day later she discovered there was a tenant farmer living in a trailer on the other side of the lake. Apparently, he rented acreage to plant corn from her great aunt. Continuing this arrangement was fine with Carole. She didn't know how to farm. She seldom saw the man that first spring.

The air was so fine that she slept with the windows wide open. She mowed the lawn with a clickety old fashioned mower, but beyond the sagging fence all grew wild. She took to the over-grown garden and put in tomatoes, carrots, onions, and squash. As the days passed, she found herself kneeling in the dirt, talking to stalks of rhubarb or singing to runner beans. She let her hair grow and it became streaked with sunlight. She grew tan and wiry and slept soundly in her great aunt's feather bed. When the morning sun warmed her bare skin (she had stopped wearing anything to bed, who was there to care), she woke smiling.

Carole also spent entire days exploring. She searched the attic and found daguerreotypes, ancient photographs of whom she assumed were long dead relatives. One, a picture of a young man with long dark hair that curled around his ears and gold rimmed eyeglasses, particularly caught her fancy. No matter how she turned the old pho-tograph, his dark eyes seemed to follow her behind the lenses of his glasses. She took the young man and a few other of her dead rela-tives and set them on the fireplace mantel in the living room.

One afternoon when Carole was exploring, she was distracted by a bee buzzing against the small closed attic window. She fumbled with the window latch to let it out, banging her shin on a traveling trunk she hadn't noticed before. When Carole opened it, beneath a pile of ancient newspapers and mismatched ladies gloves, she found a woman's velvet cape the color of garden moss, trimmed in brown velvet. It was very old but only slightly faded. There was also a little stack of envelopes tied with a thin pale ribbon. She opened one of the envelopes, but when she tried to pull out the tissue thin stationary inside, the paper crumbled to dust. She closed the trunk, but took the velvet cape to throw around her shoulders on cool evenings.

That same afternoon, Carole discovered books in a wooden crate in the root cellar. Old *Readers Digest Condensed* novels, a book on the how-to's of jams and jellies, some Agatha Christie paperbacks. When she moved a porcelain pickling crock, she discovered another book. *Tales of Wonder, Tales of Woe, Stories From the World of the Limberlost.* The book had been published in the late 1800's and sadly, some of the pages were impossible to separate due to moisture damage. Many of the photographs were blurred, or smeared, and Carole could smell mold on the binding. But there was one colored plate that for all the world looked just like the lake on the farm. It was big and deep blue and ringed with cattails and weeping willows.

Sitting on the chill cellar steps she read of cottonwood trees with hanging vines, of enormous moths, of bears and cougars. She read with fascination of the things exposed when they'd drained the swamp: a mastodon skull, the skeleton of a giant sloth, a long extinct peccary nearly completely intact, flesh and fur mummified by the boggy water. She read of deep cuts dug out of the earth by enormous glaciers around the globe, how they created black peat bogs and icy fjords, which was how the Limberlost came to be.

In the evenings Carole liked to sit in the old porch swing looking past the wild coneflowers, the black flag irises, at her very own glacial lake as it winked in sunlight or seemed to float like a ground hugging cloud in the rain.

One day Carole was at the local market and in front of her, pushing their shopping cart together, was a young couple. Carole smiled at the way the girl fluttered by the cereal boxes. The way the boy pretended he didn't care. The girl laughed as she pulled a box from the shelf. In the next aisle, the boy pulled the girl to him and kissed her passionately right in front of the frozen peas. *They're so perfect.*

She smiled as she passed them with her shopping cart, but they didn't notice her. Why would they? She was, as usual, unnoticeable.

Carole's smile remained frozen, unchanged as one painted on a doll, all the way back to the farm. When she walked into the house the lights were off. The house was cold. From the front window she watched a pair of anonymous taillights, red as feral eyes, disappear up on the county road. She turned on a lamp and the faces of the dead she'd placed on the mantle stared back at her. The young man with dark curling hair seemed somehow different. Was he faintly smiling before?

They're watching.

Carole walked to the mantle and turned the photos to the wall. Then left the room.

That was silly. Silly of you. Just pictures.

In the kitchen she made herself a sandwich. When a knife clattered to the slate floor, the metallic chink and the brief echo gave her a start. The sound made her hush herself, want to tiptoe. She turned on the radio. Pretended to be interested in the crop report.

That night in the feather bed she cried so long and hard she stopped up her nose. The next morning her face was fat, gray and puffy. At noon she was still sitting at the kitchen table, staring vacantly at a cup of cold tea, when the tenant farmer came to the door with three striped bass. He'd fished them from the lake.

Carole was surprised at how he talked and talked and even more surprised when she asked him to stay to supper. His name was Toby Cobb. She knew it from the check he'd written her for leasing the acres on the farm. Together they'd cleaned the fish, she'd fried them and they ate them up with fresh kale from the garden and an heirloom tomato salad. He talked and she listened. He was tall and if not good looking (his nose was too pug and he hadn't much in the way of a chin), he was fit and farmer tanned. He had long muscular legs and big feet he kept stored in heavy steel-toed construction boots.

They began to see a lot of each other. Toby would come by to find out if she needed anything in the morning and soon he started coming by in the evenings, too. They began to sleep together in the big bed with the moon shining through the window. Although it was strange—as much as he talked she never felt she got a real sense of who he was. And it seemed to her that the rhythm was not quite right when they were together. Carole could never picture Toby Cobb kissing her by the frozen foods.

She was sitting on the porch swing when she saw him running through the purple thistle and milkweed beyond the fence. Toby jumped up the steps to where Carole sat. He was trembling and dripping with lake water. She could smell the dark fishiness of it. He had a twig caught in his hair. His mouth gaped open then closed and he took a deep breath. "There's a body in the lake."

For a moment Carole had just watched him, watched the way his chest heaved, at the way the wet cloth of his shirt stuck to his shoulders, outlined his biceps. Toby wiped his hand on his wet jeans. He didn't look at her as he spoke, he kept looking back at the lake. He'd dived in after his silver pocketknife. "You know the one," he'd said. She'd nodded, although she didn't. Well, he hadn't even given it a thought, diving in after it. But the lake was deep, so surprising in its coldness, its thick, piney chill. Down, he'd dived. And, on the second try, he'd quickly, blindly, patted the black lake bottom and found himself clutching a hand. He knew it was a hand without seeing it, knew the awful, certain, feel of fingers.

While Toby phoned the police, Carole sat right where she was.

She rocked forward and back. She could see the lake sparkling in the distance. It looked silver in the afternoon light. Maybe, she thought, if there actually was a body in the lake, it ought to stay there. That thought was drowned out by Toby. "Wonder if I'll be interviewed on the news." He didn't notice that she didn't answer. Carole was watching the sheriff's car descend the gravel driveway toward the house.

That long afternoon Carole sat in the grass by the lake watching the diver go down and come up again. The body was stuck in the mud at the bottom of the lake. The bottom was too dark for the diver to see much. So they brought in a small crane. The diver pulled a harness down to the lake bottom while the sheriff talked to Toby.

At last the diver signaled with a thumbs up. Carole watched as the harness with the body broke the surface, water cascading from it violet and red in the last rays of the setting sun. The arms hung down on either side as it dangled in the air.

It looks so helpless.

A moment later the crane operator ground the gears and dropped the body unceremoniously beyond a clump of cattails.

While the diver shook water from his hair like a dog, the sheriff and the tenant farmer circled the body. For a moment, Carole hung back, but the faces of the men got the better of her. In the distance, Carole heard the church bells chime in town. A squirrel chittered. Two quarreling catbirds darted over the lake. The men shook their heads, muttering things about it not being right, odd, strange. It seemed to Carole the sheriff was frightened.

But of course. They'd pulled the body from the bottom of a dark glacial lake, from thick, rich mud fed by layers and layers of reeds. This had once been Limberlost. A place that kept things. Preserved them.

As the men stepped back, Carole kneeled beside the body. Tannins had stained the skin chocolate. High cheekbones and a long and elegant nose. The eyes were shut tightly, the sockets somewhat sunken, but the eyelashes were observably individual, the lips seemed to faintly smile, and the thickened snakes of his long hair spread on the bank in a muddy nimbus. His knee-high leather riding boots were still remarkably intact, as was the clothing, a saturated coat, a mottled, blackened vest. Trousers molded to what were clearly once athletic muscles. One hand was missing. There was nothing beyond the wrist but a stub of yellowed bone, yet the other, a nearly perfect mud brown hand, wore a ring on the third finger.

As she knelt beside the body, the sheriff notified the Coroner and the State Police. It was now dusk, sun fallen, fireflies blinked. The two men were absorbed in their speculations, they didn't notice when she slipped the ring off the finger. She did it quickly and efficiently, not even checking if they had seen her. She kept the ring cupped in her palm when the sheriff asked if she might make them all some coffee. Carole somehow managed to nod as she slipped the ring into the pocket of her jeans.

By the time she brought down thermoses of coffee the man from the lake was zipped up in a coroner's black bag, as if it were any other dead body. Then they took him away. Carole almost said, no, stop, leave him. The body was from her lake, after all. And it had been so well preserved because of where it had been for so many years. What would happen to it now? But she kept quiet and just watched as they drove away.

In the dark she couldn't stand the labored rhythm of the tenant farmer, so she pushed him away, far to the other side of the bed. In her hand she clenched the ring of the man from the lake. She ran her fingers over the filigree. She'd cleaned it and the stone was lustrous black onyx. In its center was a small red ruby or garnet— she wasn't sure which—cut in the shape of a tiny heart.

Carole saw the lake man's face just as she was falling asleep.

CAROLE WASN'T SURPRISED when Toby decided to try to reconcile with his ex-wife in Ohio. She was only mildly surprised to discover she didn't really care. At night her sleep was filled with wondrous dreams. In that first startled moment upon awakening, Carole often had a sensation of weightlessness, of buoyancy. But it never lasted. The moment she was fully awake, she was back in her body, heavy and earthbound.

Except for expeditions to the market, she saw no other human being in January or February. That winter was very cold. The water in the lake froze down to a depth of a solid foot. When she looked out the window she thought of Artic permafrost and things discovered under the ice.

Carole spent entire days in the kitchen, it was the warmest room in the house. The overhead light was on from one dawn till the next. She tried to read but couldn't concentrate for long. She'd find herself staring at the slate floor then disappear into a daydream. She had this recurring vision of herself staring down into the lake and seeing the man's tannin dyed face looking back. Carole had memorized every line and crevice of his face. She remembered the feel of his one hand. The skin thin and fragile. Like the tissue paper letters in the old trunk. The ring had slipped into her palm so easily, as though it were meant for her. She wore it on a piece of yarn around her neck.

One freezing foggy morning Carole could not get out of bed. She had a burning fever. She slept and dreamed. When she finally awoke, her sheets were drenched. Her fever had broken and the sun was out. A bird sang joyously, cotton puff clouds floated past the window.

Slowly she sat up, she was weak as a kitten. She cocked her head, thinking she heard someone below in the kitchen, walking on the stone floor. Yes, she did hear the sound of boots below. She leaned back on the pillow and sighed. Toby. He'd come back. He still had a key.

She wondered how long she had been sick, her body trembled when she sat up. She must have been very ill. She heard heavy boots walking through the living room, across the wide wood plank floor and pause at the bottom of the stairs.

Carole called out, but her voice was a whispery croak. She heard the boots move through the living room and across the stone slates of the kitchen. She felt a surge of relief, it was hard to be so alone in a big old house. She fell back to sleep with the winter sun winking through the bedroom curtains.

Later, she woke to twilight. She felt much better. She wrapped herself in the old quilt and clutching the bannister, slowly hobbled down the stairs. She saw that the light in the kitchen was off. She jiggled the light switch but the light remained off.

The kitchen was empty, there was no one there. The slate floor chilled her bare feet. In the fading dimness of the day, she could see the dirty dishes she'd left piled in the sink the night she became sick. Carole looked in the refrigerator and closed it quickly. Something had gone bad. How long had she been sick?

Gingerly, she climbed onto the kitchen table, reached up and untwisted the naked light bulb. She felt dizzy and swayed for a moment. She held the light bulb against her ear and shook it. The broken filament answered her. It must have just burned out or surely Toby would have changed the light bulb.

She made a pot of tea, turned the oven on to warm the kitchen. She waited for the tenant farmer to come back and fell asleep at the table. When she woke, still alone, the clock on the wall said it was well past midnight. Outside the kitchen window the world was black.

SHE WAS FINALLY well. Everything was. It was warming up, spring was coming. One afternoon, it was a beautiful day, Carole made a little picnic lunch and packed it in a brown paper bag. She hiked up to the lake. The air, hinting still of ice, pinked her cheeks. She smiled up at the leafless trees. Down on the ground she noticed tiny green heads among the dry leaves. Soon, violets.

She sat by the lake all afternoon until the wind picked up. It was growing dark as she walked home. There was one of those streaky rose and orangey sunsets. Small bats fluttered and swooped for insects. She twirled a knobby stick she'd found. She was whistling when she'd turned to look over her shoulder. She had that feeling that is unmistakable, the feeling of someone watching.

She pushed open the gate to the yard. Once again, she turned and this time, away in the distance, over by the lake, she saw something. A dark cut-out against the dimming sky. She quickly ran up the porch steps but, before she stepped inside, she looked back toward the lake. Was it closer? She locked the door.

Carole didn't sleep the whole night, that night. She kept peering out the bedroom window but there was no moon so she really couldn't see anything. In the morning, exhausted, she'd fallen asleep. She slept most of a long day of rain and when she woke, her blanket was sopping wet. She couldn't understand because she was certain she had closed the window beside her bed, yet there it stood wide open, the wind billowing the old lace curtains. She was chilled to the bone and ran a hot bath.

In the bath water, in the steam, she submerged herself and held her breath. She watched her long hair float. Down below in the kitchen, she heard the boots on the slate floor again. The water in the tub was so warm. She'd sprinkled lavender in the water and baby oil. It was restful, it was peaceful. She closed her eyes. On the staircase she heard footsteps and she smiled, inhaling the lavender.

When she woke she was alone in a tub of cold water.

THE AIR FILLED with scents of things ripening, sometimes rotting, in the late summer heat. Carole didn't go anywhere anymore, didn't want to leave the farm. What did she need anyway, from anywhere? She forgot to remember what day it was or week or month. She slept so much. She dreamed. She wore the velvet cape day in and day out despite the heat. Her long hair sprung from her

K. WALLACE KING | 183

head in humid tangled curls.

One day she was sitting by the lake. Twigs crackled and she'd turned. Through the trees, filled out with leaves, she saw a shadow moving toward her or perhaps away. She wasn't sure because it was not a solid thing. It was more of a shifting shape, an outline.

She got up, looking into the thick clump of silver maples and swamp oaks, sunlight splashing through the leaves. *Oh,* she said. She was aware of the powdery tufts of exploded dandelions tickling her bare shins as the breeze picked up. A bumblebee droned. A catbird called from a walnut tree. The wind rustled the leaves.

The lake shimmered as she approached. Passing cattails, as her feet sank deep into the mud, a solitary bullfrog thrummed in rhythm with her heart. Dragonflies skated across the lake's surface, gold and emerald, as the water, so dark it was almost black, met Carole's knees. First one foot was sucked free from the mud then the other. She felt the cold squish of it between her toes as she hummed a song she'd never known before. The heavy ring nested between her breasts, shifting with the movement of her body, the cold metal warmed by the heat of her. The green velvet cape fluttered behind her. The humid air whispered as it lifted her wild curling hair.

Now the lake gently slapped her thighs, then clasped her waist. It nuzzled her shoulders. When the lake sought her lips, she closed her eyes and parted them. All the hollow lunches at all the solitary tables were washed away.

Down went Carole, past startled fish. Down to the antediluvian bed of the once glacial lake with a smile that would be perfectly preserved.

GHOST GIRL

J. S. Kuiken

———◆———

LORENS WAS CHARMING, for a man. I've never had an eye for men, the way other girls do. I never understood why girls might hum in appreciation over a man's shoulders, or comment on his hands. I was always too busy noticing the shapes of girl's legs, the curve of their throats, or listening to their voices, warm and bright as firelight. I don't think men were meant to be warm and bright to me. They've always been like barren landscapes, scraped clean of leaf and blossom.

But Lorens did have a way about him. He sat me in his kitchen to interview, offering hot, fresh biscuits drooling with butter. I devoured them, shaky and famished from walking two days from the last village.

Lorens' cuffs and collar were starched and pressed, his cream colored cravat neatly tied, made of a shining material that seemed too soft and fine to be real. I wanted to touch it, because I couldn't imagine anything finer than a rabbit pelt.

"It seems you know how to work hard, between what you tell me and your obvious appetite."

He laced his fingers together. His hands and nails were so clean they looked delicate.

"What should I call you?" he asked.

"Katja," I said.

"Katja," he said, as if he'd said something much more lewd than just my name.

It made me uneasy. But I told myself it was this new place. This enormous farmhouse with more than one room, swept wooden floors, and no whistling cracks. I wasn't used to being around such a fine gentleman. It was normal for him to creep closer and closer as the interview continued.

He smelled of heather shaving soap.

"I think," he said, "we have room for you, since the last lower maid departed."

He smiled and all his teeth were so very white.

I DIDN'T MIND the work. Scrubbing soot from fireplaces, keeping the fires lit, scraping out pots and pans, dusting and sweeping. It was nice after surviving on my own, after Mama and Papa died. I always had enough to eat. I had a soft pallet up in the attic. The other lower maid who shared the attic grumbled about it being too cold and drafty. I thought it extravagant for only the two of us to have all that space. I even had my own uniform of fine linen. And every week Lorens paid me from his own hand, his palms pink and soft.

This other lower maid tended the garden. She left. Because I was so efficient and cheerful, the garden became mine.

Beneath all the folds and furrows, the soil was moist and soft. I sank my fingers into that black earth, breathing the scents of rosemary and thyme, the sticky sweetness of raspberries. The sun browned my skin with her kisses. It was a good summer, the best of my life to that point.

But like every season, that summer waned. The skies turned gray, and no matter how many layers I wore, or how many blankets I smuggled, it was chilly in that attic. Lorens hired a new lower maid to replace the old one. That's when the night visitations began.

HANNE WAS THE NEW lower maid's name. She had hair black as good soil, skin pale as salt.

The first time I heard the groan of the ladder which led up to the attic, I thought it might be mice, or even the wind. But a strange, ghostly shadow came out of the attic floor, and crept through the dark towards Hanne and me as we lay on our pallets. The shadow settled over Hanne.

"Sssh," it said, in Lorens' voice.

On nights when he visited, I told myself they were lovers. If I heard thrashing, or Hanne's muffled cries, those were the sounds of her pleasure and passion. But, whenever Lorens came, I curled up, remaining very quiet and very still.

I was selfish and afraid.

One morning I helped Hanne with her hair and I couldn't help noticing how she grimaced when she sat.

"It's nothing," she said.

I tried to hug her, but she pushed me away.

HANNE LEFT IN the middle of winter. She was found a few days later, frozen dead in the woods, and gnawed on by animals. The village midwife said she'd been with child.

With poor Hanne dead, I had the work of two. I kept busy so I wouldn't have to think about how I'd failed her. I also didn't want to think about how Lorens frightened me. Around him, I didn't speak unless I had to, and hurried about my work. At night, I lay still, listening for the creaking of the ladder.

"You're like a little mouse these days Katja," Lorens said.

I said nothing.

If he came for me, it would be too dangerous to leave in the midst of winter. Hanne had proven that. Even if I did leave, I didn't know where I'd go. So I stayed and told myself lies. I told myself it would be fine. I told myself he wouldn't hurt me so long as I didn't upset him.

When I heard him slithering up the ladder and saw his pale form coming, I closed my eyes. The smell of his heather soap choked me. I tried not to move or make any noise when he touched me and then was inside me. It was difficult not to cry, but I didn't.

I'd never slept with anyone. What he did confused me. I always thought it would be kinder. More like a dance, two people sharing. It didn't seem like it should hurt, or leave me feeling gutted.

"Good girl," he crooned in my ear.

It did hurt less in time.

I never enjoyed it.

Once, he brought a lamp. He said he wanted to "see" me. He didn't think I would see him. The expression on his face had nothing to do with lust, or any natural need. It was just his hand around my throat, forcing me to do what he wanted.

I DIDN'T KNOW I had caught. Though my bleeding stopped, it had always been erratic. I wasn't sick either. I was hungry all the time, and my belly and breasts swelled until I needed a whole new uniform. I'd already taken my old one out as much as possible. I simply thought I was growing because I ate so much.

When the Housekeeper measured me for a new uniform, she *tsked*.

"What?" I asked.

"We can make you a new uniform, Katja, but it won't make a difference."

"Why not?"

She frowned.

"You're with child," she said.

"I—no—"

I sat down hard on the floor. All the new weight on my body was too much.

When I was a little girl, I used to set snares in the winter, my small fingers fumbling and numb as the snow came down. Once I set a snare and a vixen got caught in it. I know this because she chewed her own leg off to escape when she couldn't bite through the frozen snare. I followed the stream of her red blood through the white snow and found her dead.

Sitting, I knew what that fox must have felt with that snare tightening around her.

The Housekeeper made a noise.

"What will you do?" she asked.

I shook my head. I didn't know.

I COULDN'T KILL my unborn daughter, though I did think of it. It was a crime in those days, and enough people had seen me by then it would have been suspicious. It was a little too late for herbal purgatives to work without making me too sick, or killing me. I could have sloughed the child, but bled to death.

I thought too of throwing myself through the attic door, of falling, tripping, beating my belly. I could kill myself there, too.

I finally decided to go to Lorens. In my happier fantasies I thought he might finally let me go. He would send me away with some money and I could disappear to a quiet place where I was not known and where he did not climb up the ladder for me. I could start again. I could tell people my husband died and then my child wouldn't have been a sin.

Perhaps my condition would even make Lorens kinder. He would become doting and excited about the child I carried. Maybe when he touched me, it wouldn't be so bad.

Still, I braced. That he might hit and beat me until I miscarried. Or maybe he would throw me out without money or food. Perhaps both.

The day I told Lorens, he sat at his desk, pen scratching away while he wrote. His fine fingers smudged with ink. It was the first time I'd seen his hands dirty.

"Sir?" I asked.

"Oh. Yes, Katja," he said. "You wished to speak with me?"

He sounded very bored. But there wasn't any use tip-toeing.

"Yes, sir. I am with child."

He had a very strange expression for a moment, one I could not place.

"If you keep it, I will have to end your employment," he said.

"Sir?"

"Girls in such a . . . condition . . . are bad for the reputation of the household. I won't throw you out in that state, but neither can you work here if you have it. And keep it," he said, emphasizing the last words.

"What do you mean?" I asked, because I couldn't quite believe what he was suggesting.

"You cannot keep it," he said. "You must—get rid of it."

He went back to writing as if we had been discussing nothing of importance, and not the murder of my infant daughter.

But it was so common in those days, especially when a girl fell pregnant with her master's bastard. This was before the King made a law to protect women, so they would stop killing their children. Before that, there were many stories about it.

In Lorens' household, the Housekeeper, Cook, myself, and any other maids, often gathered by the kitchen fires at night to drink weak tea and tell stories. There were the stories of the nøkken who drowned children, of course, then stories about wood spirits who seduced and killed men. But my favorite stories were the ones about the dead children. There was always a woman with a child she couldn't keep, either because she couldn't feed it, or she would have been shamed for having a child out of wedlock. In every story, this wretched woman gave birth and then killed the baby. In one tale she stuffed the body beneath the floorboards. In another she wrapped it in a stocking and buried it outside. But the child always came back to haunt her, to tell the truth so the woman's deeds would be laid bare and she'd be punished. Though those stories were grim, they satisfied me. I didn't like these stories so much after I caught.

So when Lorens suggested I kill my own daughter, I noticed how the iron in his fireplace glistened beautifully. I wondered if it would glisten all the more beautifully if I cracked his head open with it, painting the iron with blood and bone. I wasn't sure I would stop after the first few blows, and he was not worth being hanged for.

"You're dismissed Katja," Lorens said without any irritation when he noticed I was still there.

Instead I curtsied and left.

He stopped climbing the ladder after that.

IT CAME SLOWLY, finger-length by finger-length. My body did a remarkable thing and reshaped itself around this little life, steadily gaining more weight as spring bloomed into summer. The Housekeeper helped me with my clothes as I swelled. One day she said I looked bright as a candle-flame in midwinter.

Sometimes at night, alone in the attic, in the comforting darkness and silence, I would stroke my growing stomach, the child within, and hum songs for her. In the afternoons, as I bent over my work in the garden, I found myself explaining to her the different uses of certain herbs and plants, and what were the best ways to make carrots grow plump and sweet.

One night I dreamed about her. I wanted to name her Birgitta, after a saint. I dreamed about braiding her hair. It was smooth and dark as toasted flaxseed, just like mine. I held her close and breathed in her sweet, otherworldly scent.

I felt her squirm inside me the next morning, as I weeded around the mint plants. Dropping my spade, I sat, smiling.

"I love you, little one," I said.

The words, once said out loud, could not be unsaid, even if no-one else heard them.

WHEN BIRGITTA CAME, Lorens was gone. He was visiting another, larger farm, courting a woman people called the Widow. She'd inherited her husband's farm after he'd died, many years ago. She was too old to bear children, but Lorens didn't care about that. He wanted the land and the profit a larger farm might bring. More starched shirts and fine cravats. More maids to hire at the house.

So it was a relief Birgitta came while he was away. Otherwise, I would not have had any time with her.

The day she was born, the yellowed birch leaves turned red as fresh blood. I didn't think much of my early birth pangs. They were subtle and I always had aches and pains in those days. It was only after lunch that I felt my womb folding in on itself and I knew Birgitta was coming.

I told Cook, and she boiled water while the Housekeeper emptied her room for me.

Birgitta took her time. I spent most of the afternoon pacing in the Housekeeper's room before my waters came. The sun was listing to the west, the stars shining faintly in the east, when Birgitta finally decided to show herself.

I've never worked so hard for anything in my entire life. Every part of my body worked to help her into this world and burned with exhaustion and exhilaration.

"Where is she?" I asked as Cook gripped me from behind to keep me from collapsing. I heard a high, thin cry, piercing as needles.

192 | GHOST GIRL

Suddenly there she was—another person—my daughter, my Birgitta. The room seemed so much smaller and larger all at once.

Cook helped me into bed. I stank with sweat, birth fluids, blood.

The Housekeeper wiped Birgitta off and laid her in my arms. I sighed and clutched her close.

W<small>E COULDN'T BE</small> sure when Lorens would return. I barely slept that night, wondering what I would do, if I would be able to flee the next day before he arrived. When I did sleep, I would wake soon after and reach for Birgitta, so I could hold her.

I still cherish those moments. Those gasps of time.

Lorens returned in the morning, before I could run and while I was asleep. His tread in the hallway woke me.

"Why are the fireplaces so filthy?" he asked.

The Housekeeper sighed. I didn't hear her answer. Though my legs felt boneless, and I was raw with weariness, I got out of bed. I only thought about fleeing.

"I told her," Lorens said as the door opened.

I grabbed Birgitta and gripped her to me. She fussed as he stared at us.

"I told you to get rid of it—"

"You can't have her," I said, loud enough that he looked surprised.

"You'll have to work tomorrow," he said, before leaving.

The little room spun around me and I stood, swaying, holding my daughter. I was sure he'd return. I lay back in bed with Birgitta nestled against me.

Unfortunately, I slept soundly.

W<small>HEN I WOKE</small> it was night and there was no Birgitta, though, there was the lingering smell of heather shaving soap. I screamed down the hallway of that farmhouse, waking everyone. The Housekeeper and Cook could not calm me. I was rage, rage like knives. Rage like piercing Lorens through his heart. If he hadn't stayed in his room behind a locked door, like the coward he always was, I certainly would have killed him.

"Where is my Birgitta?" I howled, scratching and beating Loren's door until my fingers bled.

"She died in her sleep," the Housekeeper told me over and over.

I finally crumpled against the door, trembling and helpless.

Cook and the Housekeeper bore me back to bed, laying me down and wrapping me in blankets.

"I want to see her," I whispered.

"You need to rest," the Housekeeper said.

I didn't say anything. I was emptied, alone. There was nothing else; just the night, the dark.

IN THE DAYS after Birgitta's death, living was like walking through broken glass. The pain was so present I stopped feeling anything at all, except a yearning for silence which would be consuming as a snowstorm. I had fantasies of smuggling rope into the attic and preparing a noose. Of going to the village midwife and buying all her nightshade. I'd make a tea and drink it.

She died in her sleep, the Housekeeper said. She died in her sleep, Cook said. Lorens said nothing.

So, I really didn't notice when things began to go strangely.

The first morning that Lorens spat out his tea, saying the cream was sour, I didn't care. Cook tried it and said it was fine, but every time I poured cream for Lorens he said it was bad.

There was also the problem with the breads. No matter how much salt and yeast Cook added, Lorens' favorite breads came out flat and hard. He cracked a tooth on a slice. It should have delighted me.

I WAS PREPARING the garden beds for winter when I found her.

I went to the refuse heap for compost. There was a chamber bucket there, small, reeking of shit and piss. I pushed it out of my way, and it was too heavy to be empty. So I looked inside. Birgitta's tiny body. Stuffing the bucket.

I couldn't get her out, though I tried. Her flesh was very fragile after nine days. So I scraped a hole for her in the corner of the garden and buried her, bucket and all. I told her the bucket would keep her sheltered and safe.

I didn't even cry. I was cold and hard as the garden beds.

THAT NIGHT, I dreamed of her death.

I watched everything as if I were sitting in the corner of the Housekeeper's room. I saw myself asleep in bed. I saw Lorens enter the room quietly and take my Birgitta in his arms. She stirred and he *shushed* her. His face was pale and drawn as he placed Birgitta down in the bed. He put a pillow over her face and waited until she stilled.

He scooped her into the Housekeeper's chamber bucket and left. He told the Housekeeper to throw it out with the other refuse.

I don't know if I was comforted when I woke from that dream. Relieved, yes, enough that some of the ache in me lessened.

WINTER CAME, BURYING the woods and farmlands in snow, salting the windows and trees with ice. Lorens' bread remained flat, his milk and cream curdled.

He had a sudden and queer infestation of moths. They gnawed holes in his clothes, though they didn't leave any droppings or dust.

He also complained about noises in the night. Little fingernails scratching against wood. He thought it was mice, but the Housekeeper and I never found anything.

Then one night he heard a baby crying. He forced everyone in the household out of bed and went through our things, looking for a smuggled infant. He found nothing but our unwashed sheets. He went back to his room, slamming the door behind him. He stopped complaining about strange noises, but there were dark circles under his eyes, and he was curt with me if I was too loud putting a fresh log on his fire, or poured his cream too quickly.

No one else had bad cream or bread, holes in their clothes, or heard noises.

The day after winter solstice, a heap of snow appeared in the corner of the garden. I waded through thigh deep drifts, chilling myself to the marrow, and knocked the snow over. There, heather grew, a purple bruise against the white landscape. The flowers were so potent we smelled them in the house and attic. The Cook and Housekeeper enjoyed the scent, but Lorens whined that it gave him a headache.

He tried to come up the ladder that night. The first creaks made me want to rip my own skin off, if it meant I wouldn't feel him ever again. But the creaks were followed by a long pause. Then Lorens cursing, the ladder rattling. I crept to the door in the attic floor and peered down through it.

"What have you done?" Lorens snapped when he saw me. He tried climbing the ladder. He made it halfway before stopping and sliding back down.

"You greased it! With butter or fat!"

He looked ridiculous. His untrimmed mustache bristled furiously while he flapped around in his sweaty nightshirt. I went back to bed and fell asleep listening to him trying to get up, and failing.

In the morning he made the Housekeeper and Cook go up. They both could. Even one of Lorens' workmen from the village could. But he couldn't. He tried while the rest of us watched.

Everyone looked at him as if he were mad, but dared not say anything while he blustered and tried to appear dignified. I bit my lip so I wouldn't laugh.

NOT LONG AFTER, she came to visit me in the nights. My Birgitta. Before having her, I would have thought it folly, but after having her, I *know*. There are instincts I have, deep as blood and bone. I created her. I harbored her. I brought her forth. I would know her in any form in this world, or beyond the veil. Having given birth to her, ghosts did not seem so impossible.

So, I knew her. At first a tendril of black, unfurling in the night. She wound around, cocooning me.

She was full of noise. Not screaming or crying, as Lorens heard. No; for me she was full of song.

She sang the same songs I had sung when I carried her. And her smell—heather—filled the air, making it heavy.

I felt very small that first night she came, and afraid. Until strong little arms hugged me, and a tiny face pressed into my belly.

She nuzzled me and sighed contentment. The blackness she'd wrapped me in was warm and quiet.

"Hello little love," I whispered in that deep dark with her.

THOUGH THE SNOW and ice melted, and the trees budded, winter endured in me.

The heather spread from its corner, invading the neighboring beds. While I told Lorens I did my best to contain it, in the nights I sometimes snuck out and added extra compost to the heather beds. In the daylight I hummed over them and sprinkled ground chicken bones. Bees came early that spring, drawn by the flowers. I even saw flocks of birds which shouldn't have been there hopping around the garden, looking confused.

And though my pain lessened each day, the world, for me, was leached of taste, color, sounds, and smells. Eating food was like chewing and swallowing dust. The sunrises and sunsets blushed only with grays. Boiling water felt the same as freezing water. My ears were stuffed with fluff and I didn't hear the cooing doves. Even the earth remained icy to me when I broke the garden soil for spring planting.

The only thing I seemed to feel or hear was my daughter. Her heathery scent, her songs in the night, her comforting darkness engulfing me.

As for Lorens, well, he complained constantly about pains and headaches. He chewed his nails because he was nervous all the time.

Even so, he planned his engagement. The Widow was coming to visit, and he wanted to ask her hand.

I DID HEAR her carriage rumbling up to the house, cutting through my muted senses. I thought it might be thunder. Then the noise was so loud it hurt.

The household turned out to greet her. We'd all scrubbed ourselves and wore our cleanest smocks. Lorens was trying to be dashing in one of his finer suits and cravats. I hadn't gotten all the soot out from under my nails, but I didn't much care until the carriage door opened and she stepped out.

I thought she might be an old woman. I'd imagined some bent over creature with silver hair and a face full of deep seams. But her hair caught the sun and it was the same color as late autumn wheat. She was astonishingly tall to me, and the way she straightened her shoulders made her seem like a queen, not just the widow of a wealthy farmer.

Lorens, ever pretending to be a gentleman, tried helping her out of her carriage. He fairly threw himself at her, though she didn't seem to see him at all. But she looked right at me.

I tucked my filthy hands beneath my apron.

The lines around her mouth were handsome, and her eyes hazel, like stones in a river.

LORENS ACTUALLY GAVE up his room for her, moving into the Housekeeper's room, and forcing all the servants except Cook into the attic. I was afraid at first that Birgitta wouldn't visit me with others there. And if she did, would they hear and feel her too? But when she came, enfolding me in her dark and warmth, the others slept soundly. They didn't stir as her scent made the air in the attic hot and heavy. They didn't wake as her songs vibrated in the floor boards and roof beams. In fact, the Housekeeper complained about how cold it was, and how noisy the doves were.

The Widow's name was, fittingly, Astrid. It came from a word we used for the gods and the divine once.

I was assigned to help Astrid and her lady's maid, because I had been doing the same tasks for Lorens: emptying his chamber bucket, cleaning and stocking his fireplace, nurturing the fire when it went out, bringing him fresh water for his morning and evening ablutions, and whatever else he requested. With him it was all chores, something I did without thinking or being present. With Astrid though, it was very important her washing water was warm, not cold or scalding, and her chamber bucket was cleaned immediately in the mornings so she wouldn't have to endure the stench. I fretted over her fireplace, making sure there were always burning coals.

On the third morning of Astrid's visit, she asked me to do her hair. Her lady's maid sat wrangling Astrid's boots, buffing them to a shine. I took up a mahogany comb and tried not to shake like a fearful little girl. Her golden hair glided through my fingers, the softest and finest thing I had ever felt. The scent of lavender soap wafted from her. As I worked, I noticed she had a particular way of crossing and uncrossing her legs, her thighs whispering as they brushed together. I thought there was something wonderful about that, though I couldn't have said what.

"This is lovely Katja," she said when I finished.

Her voice was throaty. When she said my name I felt a particular heat low in my belly.

"I can . . . I can do it for you every morning," I said.

"I would like that," she said. She didn't look at herself in her mirror, a little hand-held thing, but at my reflection as I peered over her shoulder.

I couldn't imagine what she saw. All I saw was a mousy, simple girl who wasn't brave enough to protect her daughter, and to run from a man like Lorens. But I found myself thinking about what she might see.

On the fifth morning of Astrid's visit, when I brought washing water, she gasped.

"How do you manage to perfume this with heather every morning, Katja?" Astrid asked. "Dried heather doesn't smell this good. Is it an extract?"

"Oh. No. I don't. It's just well water."

"The smell is divine. It's like magic. If you believe in such heathenous things."

She winked and I smiled.

On the eighth morning, I spent a long time combing her hair. Too long, because we were late to breakfast. But I couldn't stop unraveling her braids just so I could see the soft white skin of her shoulders. I wanted to know how that skin would feel against my lips. I was still thinking about that at breakfast, so much so that I didn't hear Astrid ask about the little girl.

"Little girl?" Lorens said. There was a tremor in his hands as he cut his bacon.

"Of course. I hear a little girl singing lullabies in the night. You didn't tell me there was a child in the household."

"There isn't," Lorens said. He cleared his throat noisily.

I was shocked that she'd heard Birgitta, enough to drop and shatter a teacup.

"That will come out of your pay," Lorens said.

"I can buy a new set before the wedding," Astrid said, looking at me.

I picked up the shards, shifting through them as much as my own feelings. I was angry, yes, and jealous. How dare this strange woman hear *my* daughter? But then I was also relieved. I wasn't alone anymore.

During her stay, Astrid liked to sit outside while I worked in the garden. Or, what was left of the garden by then. The heather had conquered all but a few beds, strangling the thyme and mint, crowding out the carrots. Right before Astrid came, Lorens had me pull it all up. It had taken me most of the day. But the next morning the heather had all grown back, exactly as if I'd never touched it. Lorens had a fit and accused me of not doing my work properly, so I pulled it all up again just to spite him. It grew back.

Astrid, however, said she enjoyed the heather. She sat quietly, relaxed while she watched me work.

Her presence scalded me, like the sun. When she sat outside and watched me, I became very aware of the earth's softness: how readily she yielded to me, her dark crevasses parting. I could hear my own breathing, and Astrid's, over the song of birds and the wind through the trees. I moved, rhythmically, sweat beading my breasts and back. When I finished, I stood, shaking and elated, fingers sticky with soil.

Astrid always smiled at me when I was done.

"Where did all the heather come from?" she asked one day.

"It started in the winter," I said. "After my daughter died. I buried her over there." I pointed to where the heather grew thickest.

I didn't really want to tell anyone. It felt like tearing a thorn out of my skin to try and explain it. But with Astrid it seemed safe. She looked at me after my admission without pity or contempt, but understanding.

"I lost a child once, right after my husband died. It was a long time ago, though."

"Oh," I said. "I'm sorry." And then: "How . . . did you go on?"

Sometimes I wondered if I would ever leave this place: my daughter and her visitations, Lorens, this garden where my child was buried.

Astrid thought for a moment.

"I rose in the mornings, even when I didn't want to. I ate when I wasn't hungry. I worked but I don't remember it. I just did what I had to. After a time . . . " She folded her hands. "I haven't stopped loving that child, or mourning. But in time, it was easier."

I almost snorted at that. I thought it was impossible, that things would never be easier. But she didn't mean any harm. So I went back to my work.

"You seem young to be wed and having children."

"I've never wed," I said. "It was last fall, right before my seventeenth winter, when I had her. And when she died."

As soon as I said the words I was ashamed. I sounded like such a simple, stupid girl, and a whore at that, having a child out of marriage.

Astrid looked at me for a long moment.

"What about the baby's father?" she asked softly.

I bowed my head and shrugged. How could I even explain? He'd forced me and I hadn't even fought him off. If I said anything surely she would see how weak I was. I'd rather she think I was just a whore.

Astrid stiffened.

"I'm sorry to hear about your daughter," she said, and went into the house.

THAT AFTERNOON ASTRID rejected Lorens' offer of marriage, and said she was returning home the next day. Dinner was tense. Lorens snapped at me about his cream, though it had been sour for months. Astrid frowned when he did, the lines around her mouth deepening.

I said nothing. I didn't look at anyone. I decided I would serve dinner like I usually did, and then crawl up to my pallet in the attic. I hoped Birgitta would come to me and wrap me in her warm, dark embrace. She'd been quieter for some days, and then absent others. I'd surprised myself by not missing her more than I did. Yet that night I yearned for her.

But Astrid asked for me after supper. I went to her room, a rock of fear and nervousness in my stomach.

"I'm leaving early in the morning. Will you braid my hair one last time?" she asked.

She wore a green dressing gown. I could see the curves of her through that gown, even the shape of her breasts. I fumbled with combing and braiding her hair. Her lavender smell was overwhelming and so very hot, and close. It took me longer than usual to finish with her hair, but she didn't say anything. Only smiled at me in the mirror.

"I forgot to ask your daughter's name."

"What?"

"Earlier, in the garden. What was her name?"

"Birgitta," I said.

"Birgitta," she murmured.

"You're not leaving because of me?" I whispered.

Astrid stood.

"Yes and no," she said. "I'm leaving because I couldn't marry a man like Lorens. He is false in many ways. But they also tell a lot of stories about him in town. About how he treats his maids."

She looked at me.

"Are those stories true, Katja?"

"What stories?"

"I think you know."

She gazed at me so gently I didn't know what to say for a moment. I fidgeted with the hem of my apron.

"Yes. They are true."

Her expression hardened. I was surprised she heard me at all.

"Is that what happened to you and your daughter?"

"I didn't want to," I said, finally. "He forced me and I caught. But I wanted my daughter. To keep her. He told me I couldn't. When she was born he . . . he took her away from me. He killed her."

The words, though quietly spoken, echoed in the small space between us. I felt dizzy. I felt something like—triumph. I had placed my shame and sorrow onto him. Instead of keeping it within myself, a bleak fire which I'd been nursing even though it burned me.

The blame was no longer mine, but his.

Astrid's expression softened. She took my face in her hands.

"Come with me."

"As your . . . maid?"

Even in that moment I couldn't fathom anything else.

"No. As my—friend. If you like."

I wanted to say "yes" so badly it hurt. But it was all too much for me. My victory in giving Lorens the blame, her caring and compassion. The way she looked at me as if I was not weak, stupid, or a whore. This struck me harder than any scornful blow.

I heard Birgitta cry, up in the attic. I could tell Astrid heard her too, and her expression became very sad.

"I can't," I said.

Astrid took her hands from my face.

ASTRID LEFT ON May Day morning. I wanted to bury myself in the garden and not think of her leaving, but Lorens said I needed to hem his trousers. He'd lost so much weight since the middle of winter that his May Day trousers didn't fit.

He was pathetic. There were dark circles carved beneath his eyes, and his hair was wild, nails chewed bloody. He reeked of sweat and the whiskey he drank to calm his nerves.

"I don't remember the last time I slept," he whined as I crouched to pin his trousers.

I almost told him he might sleep easier if he didn't rape women and kill babies, but I wanted to be done quickly.

I was so viciously angry with him that I shook. I shook so badly I didn't notice, at first, the pins curling, and pierced my thumb with one.

"You're very clumsy this morning Katja," he said. And then: "It's been some time since I visited you."

He touched himself through his trousers.

My rage was white and blinding as lightning. I stood, spitting out the pins, which curled into nearly perfect circles. I heard Birgitta howling. Lorens did too, because he fell backwards, cringing. His wrists and ankles were yanked to the wall, as though he were bound by iron bands.

Birgitta spoke to me then. She told me all the things we could do to Lorens now, all the things we had dreamed of. Where I should stick those unbent pins. What I could cut off first, using his favorite pocket knife. What beautiful noises he would make as I looped one of his fine cravats around his throat and draw it tauter and tauter. How lovely his innards would look, pulled out a finger length at a time while he was still alive to feel every tug.

Lorens began to cry, for he heard her, too.

But then I thought of Astrid. Of her warm skin and her smoky laugh. I thought of working in the garden while she watched. I thought of what it would be like to lay beside her—to lay beside someone who truly cared about me—and feeling our bodies moving together.

There was a low sound, like the last growls of thunder as a storm clears. The remaining pins stopped curling, and Lorens sagged to the floor in a shuddering heap.

He called for me as I left. I ignored him. I went to the attic and gathered what few things I had. I said goodbye to Cook and the Housekeeper.

I stopped in the garden, and inhaled the sweet scent of the heather one more time. I thought of cutting a few stems and taking them with me. Perhaps I could press and dry the flowers, keeping them. But they would surely lose their smell in time, their color and vividness fading until they were nothing but frail shadows.

Instead I knelt on the ground and told my daughter I loved her, always. Then I said goodbye to her, before I stood and walked to the road, and away.

I'D HEAR THE STORIES later, from people who passed through Lorens' village. The May Day feast stories. My favorite stories.

The village folk gathered in the meadow behind Lorens' house for the meal. After the tables were cleared, the dance began, and everyone was in good spirits. But the smell of the heather was unbearable. The priest's eyes watered. Lorens looked like he had a rash. Others coughed and sneezed all afternoon.

The music for the first dance played. This is when the little girl's voice was heard, bright as spring sunlight. At first people thought it was one of the village children singing, but it wasn't. The smell of heather became the smell of shit and rotting flesh. The little girl sang about how her father, the farmer Lorens, had smothered her while her mother slept and couldn't defend her. The village folk had heard all manner of unsavory tales from the farmhouse for years, and yet they couldn't believe what this voice claimed. Until she sang sweetly that he'd thrown her body in a bucket and had her tossed into the refuse. Her bones were buried in the garden.

The celebration ended. Lorens sent everyone home. In the morning he was found dangling from the roof-beams in his attic, strung up by his own cravat. The priest said it was suicide, and Lorens was damned. So he was buried outside church grounds, in an unmarked grave. People don't remember him, except when they tell stories about the dead girl, a ghost girl, who once haunted the farmhouse.

AS FOR ME—I walked down the winding road, between Lorens' village and another. I didn't know exactly where I was going, nor did I care. I let my feet and my joy carry me.

After two days, I came to the next village. It had a very large farmhouse, larger than Lorens', and ivy grew on the side. I didn't know for sure, but I walked up to the green door of the house and knocked.

A maid answered and called for her mistress.

Astrid came to the door. She wore blue and it made her hair all the more radiant. I bent towards her as a flower bends towards the sun.

"Katja. This is a surprise," she said.

"Good or bad?" I found myself teasing.

"Good," Astrid smiled. "Would you like to come in?"

Her words were warm as a long, lingering kiss.

This Night I Will Have My Revenge on the Cold Clay in Which We Lie

LC von Hessen

————◆————

This night my tendons and fingernails shall root below the earth, wrenching aside cracks in pavement and plaster, tapping the strength of lost foundations and forgotten bones.

I shall take my revenge on the barbers and fishmongers, on the crest of the Fourth Horseman, on the planted flag. The black web that chokes and constricts. The liminal hymn of possession.

This night I will have my revenge on the little man, and let neither flesh nor fae constrain me.

IN THE WAKE of the epidemic, certain small businesses within the city were known to host clandestine gatherings after hours. This was meant to help recompense the revenues lost when their shop windows gathered dust, their entryways were boarded up, their coffers lay fallow, by official decree. For the guests, this served as a tentative return to social debauch after so long hiding from Pestilence. Among these festivities was a secret sex party held in the lower level of a discount department store.

She was invited to this party by the little man.

Now, he didn't have any iteration of genetic dwarfism: he was not that sort of little man. Nor was this a slight on his endowment, which she had neither seen nor experienced. He was indeed short, but simple shortness would not have earned him the sobriquet of *little,* and he did not rightly strike her as a *small* man. He had the mien of a sinister doll, with his hair parted just so, his wax-pale complexion, his dress shirts and waistcoats, an unblinking witness in a doll-sized chair on an old woman's white shag carpet. He was handsome, at least by her standards: the gently Byronic air of a man with dark secrets of eros slinking around in his cranial folds, yet scaled down a bit, so his head ended at the tip of her nose— though as her own height was slightly above average by ladies' standards, he was not *as* little as one might assume. He did not know she thought of him as *the little man*, though he wouldn't mind being called such, at least not by her. A sly smile of delight that she, Celestine, had a private name for him at all.

But yes, the little man. He might even have been hosting this party: she hadn't dared ask, as the mere prospect of attending, let alone *touching* another person, perhaps even her acquaintance, *the little man*, was thrilling enough.

The pair of them slipped into the discount department store some time after dusk, a quiet retreat into a side entrance, down the stairs to the lower level. She was not sure whether this party was sanctioned by the higher-ups, a pock-faced CEO waving an indifferent assent to young people's diversions in a fog of cigar smoke, or perhaps an enterprising floor manager or cashier who had finagled the keys after dark.

She, Celestine, wore a pale blue sundress, the better to blend in with the diffuse blue-grey shadows cast by after-hours floodlights across the cheap linens and linoleum tiles. A silver pendant, a token of her patron goddess, glimmered through sheaves of strawberry-blonde hair wafting about her sternum.

He, the little man, wore his black velvet waistcoat. The white sleeves of his dress shirt were ruched up to the elbow, revealing the scattered lines of dark hair on his forearms, the insistent blue snaking of his veins. He clasped his hands together and peered about for a proper place to speak with Celestine in relative privacy.

A company of milk-pale mannequins, their heads lopped off clean and bloodless, patrolled the floor as hip-cocked Templars of Commerce with sales tags dangling from their mushroom-stalk necks like announcements of stockaded criminals' misdeeds. Pairs and thirds, a few in costume, huddled in dim corners, conversing in museum whispers. A man spoke of his return to the factory where, at the cafeteria table, his fellow workers silently passed a cake from hand to hand: literally, with bits of cake scooped out by one's bare hands, ungloved, unwashed, unsanitized, frosting beneath one's nails, crumbs brushed away from unguarded lips. A woman recalled the ambulance sirens that had passed so frequently outside her windows that the sound was often caught in her head like an advertisement jingle. A woman said she'd thought of working as a glass machine girl in a pachinko parlor, sitting in a box like a mechanical fortune teller and seeing only her reflection in the mirror as anonymous hands and various organs probed her legs and apertures for as long as their tokens could buy, and could imagine whomever she wanted without breathing the same foul air. A man had left his office shortly before the shutdown to see a derelict on the sidewalk with diseased organs spread out on the pavement before her, perhaps or perhaps not her own, as a High Denialist sermon blared in the nearby park. A woman had heard of that sermon, seen the photographs of its patrons fallen down dead as they stood.

Celestine wrenched her attentions back to her host. The little man, so he explained, derived from a line of impoverished chandlers. In time, they had tried to increase their fortunes with a line of wax candles fashioned into intricate shapes. Perhaps she knew of that ingenious mold of the Virgin Mary with eyes that wept waxen tears the further the candle burnt.

"Oh," she said, "did your people make that?"

"No," he said, "but it did inspire them."

Perhaps, he intimated, he could sell models of anatomical hearts and Hands of Glory to the occult supply shop at which she worked as a stockist, a job she had been fortunate enough to keep since the shop had been operating mail-order during quarantine. But, she tried to explain, Hand of Glory, *main-de-gloire*, was just a corruption of *mandragore*, the mandrake root, and did not mean an actual hand. At any rate, the shop was already well-stocked with veneficia.

One branch of his people, the little man continued, had broken from the family trade and partaken in a certain hubristic voyage to the Antarctic, had perished on a southerly island and been disinterred some 200 years later displaying his well-preserved breeches and wig and hard-gritted teeth, an expression the little man now demonstrated for her. He had first seen the infamous photograph as a child in a book about mummies, paired with a paragraph questioning whether hair and nails continued to grow after death, all without knowing this cadaver was his distantly-great grandfather.

Celestine, who knew more of maritime history than the little man assumed, considered that if the man in question were truly an impoverished chandler without prior sailing experience, he could not have advanced to an officer's rank by the time of his premature death and thus would not have been buried in an officer's trappings. Some obscure joke, perhaps, at the ancestral little man's expense, at his bravado and vainglory.

Furthermore, she recalled a great admiral who had died at sea and was preserved in a cask of rum for the voyage home; an emperor-general whose body was immersed in honey for the long procession back to his domain. Yet the ancestral little man did not come home. Like a noosed, bound, repeatedly-stabbed mummy tossed into the bog as a leathery sacrifice, a warning to the curious.

"It does," he said, "get very cold in the ground." The little man's pale knuckles brushed hers and his lips twitched upward. A rosy bloom spread through her skull and veins.

Ah yes, she thought. This *is why I'm here.*

An impatient knock on glass meant he had, unfortunately, to depart from her side for a bit so he could let someone else in. A strain of communal lust in the quiet air was beginning to stir. A nipple pinched behind three layers of cloth. Sluglike glistening of engorged tongues. A hand cupping and squeezing a denim bulge. The vibratory hum of a nearby throat. Anticipatory arousal.

Celestine was encouraged by the prospect of impending coitus *with the little man,* yet bothered by the tiny pricklings at the very top of her inner thighs. She ducked behind a pallet of earth-toned tablecloths and retrieved a razor from her bag. With a slick of spittle on her palm serving as lather, she lifted her skirt and hurriedly began to shave. She had last shaved yesterday morning and the little chopped hairs were already pushing through the surface like an obstinate crop of weeds.

This act was mainly to prevent stubble burn, which had indeed happened with another man in her past, a **very bad** man, a varlet in fact, with his irrational rage at being unable to turn her heart and pin down her mind; at any rate, that man's last visit had led to three days straight without shaving, and consequently a raw chewed-out splotch was ground into his frenulum by her pubic stubble during an especially vigorous round. He had shown it to her, lifting up his flaccid cock in the aftermath of the act, with a look of pride in his cocaine saint's eyes. That chafed instrument, she thought now, had been all he was good for. And had she not been inside a discount department store, she would have spat at his memory.

So long it had been, so long, the populace bound up indoors like pupae waiting to unfurl. So long since she had charted a new expanse of living flesh, practically revirginized by extended quarantine. The corporeal experience of sex was a living memory turned to dust, scattered to the winds alongside the agents of Pestilence.

"Come, come," said the little man, and led her by the elbow to a discreet door off the children's aisle. It was here, he explained, that he rented his private workshop.

Like most sculptors' studios, the little man's workshop was beset with an array of orderly clutter. Stray appendages of wax dummies hung on butchers' hooks above the walls to either side, dangling above a cement floor littered with sawdust shavings. Odors of hot metal emitting from lumpy molds for experimental candles. Anvil and vise. Compass and square. Antique wooden chairs busted up for spare parts, spindles splayed like broken ribs. The little man, smiling softly, bid Celestine wait a spell while he tended to a large pot of burbling wax on a cast-iron stove at the back of the room.

She stood, hands folded, beside a large work table in the middle of the studio. One of the little man's creations dominated most of its surface: a crudely human figure, female, its substance resembling not so much beeswax as the sickly yellow of raw fat. The figure's supine frame was propped up by the angles of its disproportionately thick arms, its legs bowed around a child-sized human chair in a sexless U shape. Its lips were pursed and carmine-red, its wax skull bedecked with a shabby dark wig.

Most curiously, the angles and curves of its limbs were inset with hair. Not like a naturalistic growth of human hair, but strung across the gaps like an Aeolian harp. And yes, this was definitely hair, not wire or catgut. Celestine peered closer: strawberry blonde. She involuntarily touched her own hair in that exact same hue, fingers brushing against the body-warmed heat of the silver token of her patron goddess.

And in a flash of insight, she knew.

The little man was controlling her with black magic.

(And just *how many* awful men must have used black magic on her before, those execrable pinpricks lodged in her cerebrum over the years! So many arrows shooting through her daydreams on strings of queerly formidable lust: addictive and wrenching, entirely inexplicable in their sheer intensity. *How*, until now, had she been unable to see the truth?)

Stray strands of her own hair plucked from a restaurant booth, at a café table, on the occult supply shop's counter, (*in the sickroom*) (*at the funeral*) and secreted away to his workshop. And what other personal concerns had he managed to gather? Flakes of dander, used tampons, third-degree relics? All worked into his wax. And parading her before his foul little strings as if she would never know: the absolute *gall*. A cold-burning anger flushed through her body, a tremble of rage in her fingertips.

She yanked the hairs out of the sculpture. The hard wax instantly cracked in their wake.

She looked at the little man, looked and *saw*. The little man with his weak, stubbly chin like a half-descended testicle. His hair, receding unflatteringly at the temples as though a pair of horns were due to sprout. Delicate thin lips now came across as puckered and mealy-mouthed. A very commonplace little man.

And she had thought of— With *him*—!

But the little man, too, saw Celestine. Saw her damage to his puerile totem.

His no-longer-handsome features now twisted with spite, head lowered like a charging bull, hand upraised in a sinistral splay.

"So you've ruined my fun, Celestine," said the little man. "So I can still ruin yours."

And, deepening his voice to an oubliette pitch, he pronounced the incantation.

Celestine ran. She ran past the wax dummies now squirming on their hooks. She ran past the guests of the secret sex party, all their false skins sloughing off, mumbling their orders in her wake. She ran past the line of guests in suits and heels waiting for entry outside below a cage of scaffolding: they were, one and all, plague dead covered in wax. They had come to him, to the little man, for the wax cure, coating their skins to preserve the flesh, to keep soul and body entwined. And now wax veins unfurled from wax skins, wax phalanges emerged from wax torsos, tendrils and tentacles and bristling anemone-fronds probing and stretching and seeking Celestine. Such was his influence, his force in the world.

Yet, for all this, he wanted more.

How dare you, little man.

HOW DARE YOU.

Mother, my Mother, set me alight.

And Celestine burned silver-violet. Arms raised and eyes rolled back, she melted the world, melted it all with the force of her rage, with every step on the blacktop, every step under the scythe-hook moon, under the streetlights hoisting security cameras that wobbled in the slightest breeze.

She surveyed stray bones and clots of hair in the tallow that flooded the streets, that poured into the gutters and bashed at the grilles of basement windows. And it occurred to her for the first time that *the little man invited me here knowing I did not survive, that none had survived, the city streets empty since the Pestilence had claimed us all, sitting in our rats' nests with our box fans and air conditioning to forestall the rot, the cold clay in which we burrowed for so long.*

THE WARDROBE

Gordon Brown

————◆•————

THERE'S A WARDROBE that Lydia remembers. Some hideous, hand-carved monstrosity in a guest room. A guest room in some distant relative's house. A house she only stayed in for one night. One night when a funeral sucked her scattered family together like starlight to a black hole.

Even now, after all these years, she recalls it with near-perfect clarity. She was six, maybe, or possibly eight. Old enough and young enough to be stowed someplace out of the way. They put her on the second floor. The very last room at the end of the hall. The hall that seemed longer walking one direction than the other.

Lydia remembers bone-colored curtains that danced just for her. A four-poster bed that made her feel like a princess. A lamp that refused to light no matter how savagely she jerked the chain. A ship trapped in a bottle. A black-and-white photo of girls her own age. And, of course, the wardrobe. There was no missing that.

It swallowed the wall. It crouched on clawfoot legs. It rattled and held fast when Lydia stood on her tiptoes and tugged at the handle.

Locked.

To this day, Lydia is certain it was locked. No matter how hard she twisted, how violently she pulled, those enormous black doors stayed shut. That's the reason she was so surprised. So surprised when she woke in the dead of that dark night. That dark night when the wind held its breath. When she saw the wardrobe's jaws had opened.

IT MIGHT'VE BEEN a dream. Something that bubbled up from the wishing part of her mind. Something stitched together with stolen stories. Ones where little girls follow white rabbits down holes or squirm their way through mirrors. Ones where they climb ladders to enchanted treehouses. Ones where they're carried off by tornadoes.

There are always castles in those stories. Talking animals. Kingdoms in need of their long-lost queen.

Which is why Lydia remembers not being afraid. Not afraid when she lowered herself down from the fairytale bed. Barefoot on that wide, dusty floor. Fingers finding grips in the grooves cut deep in the wardrobe drawers. She remembers how easy it was.

She braced herself for the reek of mothballs. She held her arms out in front of her, groping for boxes of shoes, heavy coats on hangers. But there was nothing inside the wardrobe. Not even, it seemed, the wardrobe itself. Nothing beneath her feet as she inched toward the back, and no back either. Just deep-sea darkness, the feeling of falling, for miles and miles, and there, in the distance, an opening, a light.

A venomous, green light.

HOW DID IT WORK for those other children? The stories, when they finally came back to this world? Did they remember it all? The years they spent there? Did they lift their heads and whisper *oh, I've had such a curious dream?*

It couldn't have been so easy.

Lydia remembers waking up again in the four-poster bed. The wardrobe doors closed. A key in the lock. One that hadn't been there the evening before. She remembers going downstairs. The smell of coffee. The weak winter light. People filing in and out all day, telling her mother they were sorry, so sorry for her loss. And for a terrible moment, sitting on some comfortless couch in the parlor, Lydia felt so very strange. And then, so very frightened. And then, so completely certain that at any moment, a man with a brown forked-beard and sad, gray eyes and long, branching antlers was about to step towards her through the door.

That, at least, was the explanation she gave for why she started screaming.

There were other incursions in the years that followed. Memories washing up on the shores of consciousness. Names. Images. Snatches of song, wild and eerie. Some that she sang to herself in the library. Some that slithered around in her head for hours.

WHEN LYDIA WAS ELEVEN, she tugged towels off the rack in the bathroom. She draped them across the mirror. Same for the one in the hallway. The regally-framed one in her bedroom too.

She said she couldn't stand it. There was something wrong with her face. It wasn't the way it should be. It belonged to someone else.

WHEN LYDIA WAS THIRTEEN: another meeting. Her parents. Her teachers. A woman from the state with a soft, crawling voice who brought her into another room and promised to only ask a few questions. Why had Lydia bitten that other girl? Why had she tried to scratch those boys' eyes? Where had she learned words like *exsanguinate* and *force-feed*? Did she know what they meant?

Lydia sat blank as ever when she listened to her parents through the floor that night. Arguing again. If she seemed to be getting better. If she seemed to be getting worse. If all little girls are blood-thirsty monsters.

WHEN LYDIA WAS FOURTEEN: sleepwalking. Found by her parents at the top of the stairs, swaying against an invisible breeze, snarling commands in a harsh, low voice that wasn't hers.

At breakfast the next morning: *what were you dreaming about? I can't remember,* she lies.

Forms loom out of the mist. Petrified trees in endless columns. Doglike things with leathery wings. Stairs climbing every direction. Ash that fell like snow. A man with antlers sprouting from his head, stalking her through the twilight with such a sad look in his eyes.

WHEN LYDIA WAS SIXTEEN, it felt right. But only because her mother had mixed up the candles on her birthday cake so they wrote out sixty-one.

Lydia didn't sleepwalk anymore. She had pills for that. Chalky, disappointment-blue ones that dried out her mouth. Sent trembles through her fingers. Filled her intestines with concrete.

WHEN LYDIA WAS SEVENTEEN, she was drunk again. Drunk again and lying in the backseat of a friend's car, clutching a plastic bag full of sick, trying to keep it from sloshing against her elegant, blood-colored dress. Through the blur of rain on the windshield, she saw the stoplight turn green, venomous green, against a sky black as centipedes. And she remembered. Remembered the pinprick of light at the back of the wardrobe. Beckoning. Swelling. Bleeding arsenic over a rocky shoreline and the silhouettes of beached monsters.

On a cliff in the distance: the needle spires of a castle. On a rock to her right: a velvet-furred rabbit. Enormous. Cautious. Twitching his nose at her. Starting to ask: *Are you here to . . .*

The car lurched forward through the intersection. Lydia plunged her head into the plastic bag and started to vomit again.

WHEN LYDIA WAS EIGHTEEN, she was in her freshman year, in the first week of the semester, at the first party in her dorm. Nothing but a bunch of giggling girls crowded into a too-small room, crouching on the edges of stolen chairs, draped across boyfriends' laps.

Lights out. Horror film on the monitor perched atop a desk. Something Italian. Seasick lighting washing over the lead actresses' breasts. Creepy, green light that reminds her. Naked flesh that reminds her. Knives plunging in and out of men chained to altars that remind her. Ridiculous, deafening, gushing sounds every time the blade goes in.

It doesn't actually sound like that, she says. Not knowing why. Not able to stop herself.

Everyone stares, not sure if they should laugh. They finally do, but only after someone says *OK, Psycho* and the mood is ruined.

LYDIA KNOWS IT'S not her fault. All the therapists agree, and it's the only thing they agree on. Whatever happened, if something happened, happened *to* her, not *because* of her. The world is a terrible place. Bad things happen because they can.

Crossing the quad, the grass gives way to a carpet of cinders. She blinks once and it's gone.

Coming back from class, she hears footsteps behind her. A shadow at the edge of a streetlamp. The sickly halo of light shattered by the tips of antlers over gray eyes, a forked beard. She runs and no one follows.

In Intro to Psych, she digs her nails into her palms. She reminds herself to breathe as the words on the whiteboard rearrange themselves. Her professor wrings his velvet-fur paws, twitches his nose at her, starts to ask: *are you here to help . . .*

LYDIA WAKES ONCE more in the dead of the night. Pulled from dreams by a sound. An incessant, heavy whirring, somewhere in the room. Something beating against the window. No. Inside. There. Right there.

Only her phone, vibrating on top of her dresser. Trembling with urgency. A text from her mother.

I'm so sorry.

Please call when you can.

Your Great-Aunt Melinda just passed.

AFTER ANOTHER BLACK-HOLE funeral. After a dismal wake. After the flow of strangers and half-forgotten faces finally ebbs, leaving the home of some nameless cousin hollowed out and aching. Then it's Lydia's turn. Lydia's turn to drive over to Aunt Melinda's apartment. Pick through her jewelry. Three pieces per grandniece.

An uncle-in-law meets her at the foot of the stairs. Lets her in with his keys. Says he's stepping out for a smoke but to text if she needs him.

The apartment's stripped bare. Hardly anything left but the smell, the bookcases, the couches and tables too heavy to move. More in the back. There, in the bedroom. A lamp that won't light. Ships trapped in bottles. A four-poster bed.

And yes. Crouched in the corner. The wardrobe. Black. Claw-footed. A key waiting patiently in the lock.

And Lydia says: *if nothing actually happened, you have nothing to be afraid of.* And Lydia says: *if something did happen,* but doesn't let herself finish. She has her fingers on the handle. She turns it slowly. She steps inside.

A LIGHT.

No stars. No moon. Just an orb of venomous green light. An orb of venomous green light she knows better than to mistake for a sun, burning low over the rocky shoreline. Bones of enormous creatures, picked clean, juts out of the waves. Ahead of her: temple columns. No. Crematorium chimneys. No. The petrified forest, tumoring out toward a nonexistent horizon.

On a cliff in the distance: the needle spires of the castle. Beside her: motion. An inky shape against the deeper darkness. Long, velvet ears. A nervous, twitching nose. Dark eyes studying her.

The rabbit asks: *are you here to help us?*

But a look. An unmistakable look of recognition crosses his face.

It's you, he whispers, *it's you.*

He's running. Scampering through the gloom, kicking up ash, vanishing down the ridge and into the cathedral of fossilized trees. All the while: wailing, shrieking.

She's back! She's back! She's back!

Screams spiral out of the forest. Figures pour out of the shadows. Human. Animal. In-between. Fleeing deeper into the wasteland as Lydia takes her first steps forward.

IT DOESN'T TAKE long. The feeling comes back. The old ease that made everything here so simple. Her tongue catches the taste of the flat, bitter air. Her feet find familiar paths that carry her through the stone pillars toward the castle on the cliff. She reaches the stairs carved into the face of the rock. Flights that chase each other. Steps that fold in on themselves. But she ascends without effort. It's all coming back.

The summit. The gatehouse. The grand hall, roof ripped off, baring its heart to the sky.

She pauses—only for a moment—when she sees a face staring at her from the shadows. Forked beard. Sad, gray eyes. Antlers blossoming from his temples. But it's only a head. Only a head mounted on a stake, driven hard between the shattered flagstones. Still so disapproving, so disappointed, so hurt and betrayed after all these—how long has it been?

Lydia laughs. A sharp, nothing laugh. She slouches across the ruins and drops into the black throne at the throat of the hall. Bathed in green light. Whispering to it, in a voice all her own, how good it feels to be back.

It Goes Without Saying

Patrick Barb

———— ◆ ————

THREE WEEKS AFTER Halloween, Dad still wears the scarecrow costume.

Since the night of October 31st, a potato sack fright mask has covered his face and he hasn't said a word to any of us. He still goes to work every day (if any of his co-workers have raised concerns, they haven't trickled back to us) and drives his truck home around six o'clock every evening. About fifteen or twenty minutes later, depending on traffic, we hear his footsteps in the foyer. If I stop and listen, I can track him to the kitchen. Still wearing his costume, he sits at the head of the kitchen table and waits for the rest of us to join him for dinner.

Of course, he doesn't eat anything. He'd have to pull up the mask and show his mouth. Then we'd watch him bite, chew, and swallow. We'd hear it. So, we haven't seen Dad eat in a while. Not me, not Mom, not Marianne.

The first day of November, Mom joked Dad got filled up on candy from the glass dish he puts out for trick-or-treaters every year. She laughed so hard at her joke, and her laughter was catching. I laughed. Even Marianne laughed. Marianne laughed so hard, I swear, tears ran down her cheeks.

Then, we looked across the table at Dad, still in his costume, still wearing his mask, silent as a statue. The laughter dried up fast.

Marianne excused herself. Pushed her chair in and rushed to my room.

She's been sleeping on my floor since Halloween.

Now, with more days behind us, no one's up for joking about Dad, his costume, or not hearing his voice for so long. Mom sleeps on the living room couch and keeps the TV on all day.

"Can you turn it down, Mom?" Marianne asks from my bedroom.

I like having my twin sister spending time with me again. Having her around the house means no more dealing with the excuses and lies, no more helping cover up why she was out all night or who she was with.

It takes a minute for Mom's answer to reach us. "No. Don't feel like it."

The TV stays on.

I peeked in Marianne's old room the other day and found her cellphone under a pile of clothes. Had a bunch of missed calls and texts from Craig.

I consider asking her about Craig again. Craig the Senior. The Craig, Mom and Dad, but *especially* Dad, forbid Marianne from seeing. Craig who we all kind of knew she'd kept seeing anyways.

But the last time I asked, she slapped the hell out of me. It was the morning after Halloween. Not wanting to repeat that experience, I've kept my mouth shut.

Marianne's in my bedroom doing her school work—catching up on six weeks of Freshman English reading. Mom's in the kitchen making her third Manhattan of the night. I know because she's switched to pronouncing the word "ver-MOUTH" in an awful British accent.

She'll switch to wine soon.

No exhaustive search of the house is needed to locate Dad. No need to check Mom and Dad's room or the living room, Dad's study, or the garage—all the places he used to hang out. I know where I'll find him.

He's on the front porch, laying down flat on his back beside the glass serving bowl, still filled with candy weeks after Halloween.

I'm careful when I push the front door open and watch my step out onto the porch. When this whole thing started and we hadn't adjusted to the change, I pushed the door open too hard once while Dad was laying down, and . . .

I still get a little queasy thinking about the sound of the bottom corner of the door hitting Dad on the side of his head. Of course, he didn't say a word. No gasp or cry of pain, nothing. I closed the door and left him out there.

After I hit him, he still sat in his spot at the kitchen table the next day. Like nothing happened. Still not eating, still not talking, and still wearing the old costume.

"Hey, Dad. Not too many trick-or-treaters around for candy and surprise scares, huh?"

I bend down and reach into the bowl. I'm not religious or anything, but I pray Dad will reach over and grab my hand, stop me from taking a sweet.

I want him to say, "No, Mark. That candy's not for you."

But he doesn't. He doesn't say anything, and I take another Blueberry Blast Jolly Rancher. I untwist the wrapper and pop the candy in my mouth.

I lean against the porch railing, looking at our front yard and beyond. Our house is the one with Halloween decorations still up. Most folks have moved onto wreaths and candles, peppermints, and hand-painted snowman crafts. Our house is the one with stretched-out cotton-ball cobwebs in dusty corners and plastic bats, rubber spiders, hay bales, and pumpkins.

Down on the cement walkway leading up to our front porch, the smashed remnants of our family's four pumpkins await disposal. "One orange gourd for the four-d of us!" Every year at the pumpkin patch, Dad insists we repeat his cornball line, while he gets some tattooed carnie-looking dude who helps weigh pumpkins at check-out to take our picture. This past October was no different. Even if the schtick was growing a little old, I went along with the routine. I said the words and smiled. Mom did too.

But not Marianne. She wouldn't hold up her pumpkin or even look at the camera. She kept her eyes glued to her phone screen.

"Young lady, how many times do I have to ask you to put your phone away?"

Dad started calling Marianne "Young Lady" after he'd heard from Mom, who'd heard from one of her mom friends in the neighborhood, that Marianne was smoking menthols behind the YMCA with this senior boy named Craig Shafter instead of heading straight home after school.

"*Young Lady, don't . . .*"

"*Listen here, Young Lady . . .*"

Whenever he got going with the "Young Lady's," Marianne would whisper back, "Okay, Old Man," low enough so only I'd hear.

I laughed every time.

Now, I take the steps down from the porch to get a better look at the smashed pumpkins on the walkway. Even before his change, Dad was the only one who went in and out through the front door. The rest of us leave from the back or through the garage. As a result, we've all kind of missed the mess out here.

The orange and corpse yellow chunks with jagged hints of triangle eyes and triangle-toothed grins represent all that's left of the faces the three of us—me, Mom, and Dad—spent the night before Halloween carving. Working in the kitchen, we took turns with the plastic scoop and orange plastic-handled carving knife.

Marianne stayed in her room. She decorated her pumpkin with a black permanent marker, writing "FUCK YOU DAD" across the skin.

And what did Dad say to her about what she'd written on the pumpkin? "This isn't you. It's Craig."

That didn't help. *At all.* It was quiet in the kitchen for a good two minutes after Marianne screamed and stormed off. Then Dad took a swig from his mug and said, "Oh well, more cider for me."

Funny how Marianne's pumpkin survived what I assume was a bit of Halloween vandalism. It wasn't smashed, only moved down onto the lawn. Like someone picked it up and set it aside, away from the massacre of its contemporaries.

But it's far from unscathed. Not by a long shot. It looks like Marianne managed to get some carving done after all. Huge gashes mar one side.

Stray leaves crunch on the sidewalk. The sound comes from down by the McCormacks' house. They used to come over for dinner every Friday night. Their two boys are a few years younger than me and Marianne, but I never minded them. We'd geek out about anime and comics and monster movies. Marianne used to join in. Until she stopped.

Back at the beginning of October, I overheard her on the phone with Craig, saying she "knew that bitch Mrs. McCormack told Mom about us."

Speak of the devil . . .

Street lamps flicker to life, and my eyes adjust to see who's waiting on the half-lit sidewalk. I'd know the tall, lanky senior and his near permanent head tilt—making him look like he sees the world crooked and wrong—anywhere, anytime.

"Craig."

I whisper his name. But it's quiet enough outside that the sound carries.

He steps closer. He's got one hand in the pocket of his duster. His fingers clasp something poking out from the top. A flashlight? "Mike!" he says. Like we're old friends.

To tell the truth, it's the most he's ever said to me. I take a step back, retreating from the lawn. "It's Mark."

"Cool."

I know he doesn't mean it.

One of his thick-soled Doc Martens crunches in a pile of leaves left unbagged on our lawn. "Marianne, home?" he asks.

I shrug.

He takes another step.

"Cool." He means it even less now.

He steps on another leaf pile. A stumbling step follows. "Whoa!"

It rained on Halloween night. The top layer of leaves dried in the days following. But not the layers underneath. Craig slips and lands on his ass.

I wonder if all the stories I heard about Craig from the Mc-Cormack boys (that they'd heard from their mom who plays bridge with our assistant principal, so *she'd* know) were true. Like, the ones about him beating up freshmen kids until one of them had to go to the hospital, or about him using biology dissection instruments on some special needs girl's support bunny, or about the stuff they found smeared across the teacher's lounge wall and the words he'd written with it.

Marianne, whenever she'd talk about him, would say over and over again, "He's changed. He's not like that anymore."

Based on the way Craig looks at me, I lean toward thinking most, if not all, the rumors are true. But his angry, scrunched-up, tick-tick-ticking timebomb face isn't what holds my attention.

Standing this close, the orange glow of the porch lights melts away the early evening shadows. The handle sticking out of Craig's pocket doesn't belong to a flashlight. There's a rubber grip, sure, but it descends into a worn leather pouch, shaped like a tanned crescent moon. I think I see jagged metal teeth like a jack o' lantern's smile, but it's probably a trick of the light. Shuffling backward this whole time, without realizing it, I feel the bottom porch step press against the back of my legs.

Craig's watching his step this time. "She won't answer my calls, my texts, my emails. I wanna talk to her, okay?"

I don't shrug. I don't say anything.

He's on the walkway now.

I feel light-headed. The nearest street lamp hums, radiating a pale white light. Like moonlight.

Except moonlight's not even moonlight, yeah? It's the light of the sun reflecting, while it shines on a different part of the world. *Moonlight. Sunlight. Red flashing lights. Blue flashing lights. Red and blue flashing lights.*

I close my eyes. I don't know what I'm thinking. I don't know where the screaming inside my head comes from.

"Are you listening to—"

Craig doesn't finish his question. A creaking sound comes from behind me, from up on the porch. I dare to open one eye and peek down at my watch.

Looks like time got away from me.

Dad's getting up. Like he's gotten up off the porch every night— right at this exact time—since Halloween. I know his timing down to the millisecond. I'm the one who's clocked it. I'm the one who's watched and seen what Dad does.

I'm also the one who's figured out what's so special about the time. *8:30 pm.* It's the official end time for trick-or-treating in town. Some years back, when Marianne and I were little, they'd turn on the tornado warning system at the fire station. On those dark and blustery Halloweens, the wailing alone made you weak in the knees, made you want to drop your plastic pumpkin filled with Snickers and Tootsie Rolls and Kit-Kat bars, and run along home. They stopped doing it after parents complained. Mom did for sure. But not Dad. "A scare on Halloween's good for the soul," he'd say.

Even without the alarms, everyone's internalized that end time— *8:30 pm*. We don't even have to hear it, everyone *knows*.

It's 8:30 . . . 8:32 now. Dad bends down and picks up the candy bowl. Another night of no takers, except for me. I turn from the walkway and Craig. I take the porch steps up, fast as I can. Fear makes for a good motivator.

I turn back around. Craig's retreated to the edge of the lawn. His heels rock back off the curb and down to the black asphalt of the street. He cups his hands around his mouth, ready to make some big announcement.

Dad's standing beside me. Or maybe it's more correct to say, I'm standing beside Dad. Either way, we stand together.

Come on, Dad. Say something. Tell this creep to get lost. Tell him to scram. Tell him whatever you're supposed to say when your kid's afraid and you want to reassure them you'll keep them safe without saying those exact words.

But he can't hear my thoughts.

Not that he ever could.

"Hey! Marianne!" Craig yells so loud, I figure he'll rouse our cul-de-sac neighbors. I hope that'll bring the McCormacks out or the Carpenters on the other side of our house. Or even the Delgados at the end of the block.

"I know you're inside, Marianne! I know you can hear me! I hope you haven't said anything to anyone! I hope you've been quiet like I told you! You better be!"

Now, I cup my hands around my mouth, ready to shout something back. But before I can, the front door opens from inside. Marianne's hand wraps around my wrist. She pulls me through the doorway and into the foyer. Dad follows behind. Same as he's done every night since Halloween. Same routine over and over. All done without uttering a word.

Once we're inside, Marianne shoves the door closed. She spins me around so we're face to face. Dad shuffles by in his old flannel shirt that smells like mothballs and overalls stiff from more wear than their usual once-a-year usage. My twin arches her back, pulling herself toward me and away from Dad as he passes. She'd kept her distance from him even before Halloween. But it's reached a whole new level since then. If Dad minds, well, he sure doesn't say anything about it.

"What the hell were you doing out there?" Her whisper has a strident nails-on-chalkboard tone, like the first words you speak after a good long cry.

I don't know how she can think I don't notice. The bags under her eyes, the crumpled tissues in every room she leaves, the feverish red coloring spread around her nose and eyes. I don't know why Marianne thinks she can hide her tears from me after all this time.

"Your boyfriend's out there."

"He's *not* my boyfriend anymore."

"Anymore" carries more weight than weeks, months even, of abandoned, forsaken, and never-even-started attempts at conversation. It's almost a remedy to our first day of high school back in September, with me heading out to the bus stop and Marianne joining as far as the corner, where she was out of sight of our house, before whispering, "Don't say anything to Dad," then running down the street a little way to hop in the back of Craig's pick-up.

Of course, since Halloween, I *have* told Dad about the bus stop and a whole lot more. It's easy to tell him things now. Even if he's stopped talking, I don't think he's stopped listening.

"What's going on with you guys? What's Craig talking about? Are you in trouble?" I ask these questions, and even I hear how much I'm starting to sound like Dad. Not the more recent version of Dad from before his silent incarnation though. Not the one who punched a hole in the bathroom wall after Marianne came home wasted from a "sleepover" that was a cover story for a field party over by the old Kellerman place. I sound like the old Dad, the one who always made us laugh and who had a box of "special" band-aids, with Superman and Wonder Woman on them, reserved for the scrapes and cuts we'd get running wild around the cul-de-sac on hot summer nights.

Marianne watches the door. I know she's looking for someone tall and tilted with something sharp in his pocket waiting on the other side. We stand together. Quiet.

"Ohhh hey, handsum . . . "

The quiet never lasts long.

Mom's developed a routine of her own over these last weeks. She hasn't had it going as long as Dad's silent Halloween costume-wearing act, but she's going for the same level of consistency.

Here's how it goes: by now, she's left the living room and ambushed Dad. Dad's easy to find. Mom'll use one hand to grab him by the straps of his overalls, pulling him close so they're nose to mask. Here, in the present, Mom's slurring her words and walking forward, pushing Dad in front of her, maneuvering him down the hallway. Her other hand drags a nearly empty bottle of wine behind her, beating a rat-a-tat-tat rhythm against the wall with every single swaying step she takes.

"Oh, hello, dear. You're looking lovely thisss evening." She's speaking Dad's part now. She puts on this same dual performance every night.

"You shtill have a old Halloween costume . . . whoa, watch tha' vase. 'Yesh babe.' Donchu think yer whole laying down like a schcarecrow and leaping up to frighten kids when they take the candy from the dish act is gettin' stale? 'Hey . . . ' almosh there ' . . . who you callin' old, lady? Beshides the twins love it.' No, no they don't, you silly man. The twins doan—they don't love it!"

It's hard to tell with the lights off, but it sounds like they're getting closer and closer to the kitchen.

Marianne's hand on mine brings reality crashing down around

me. She hasn't stopped staring at the front door. She squeezes my hand. Once. Twice. Then, she holds the third squeeze, until I can't take the pain anymore. "Ouch!"

My heart gets slingshot up my throat with that last squeeze. Marianne hasn't used our old signals in a long time. Even before she'd run headfirst into her "fresh start" with Craig and his truck, Craig under the streetlamp, Craig with something in his pocket, she'd rejected the inside jokes, made-up words, and shared stories retold via raised eyebrow between the two of us.

Three squeezes and hold at the end. "Help."

But help with what?

WHAM. WHAM. WHAM.

The thunderous hammering of teenage fists against the door tells me everything I need to know.

At the sound, Marianne wraps her arms around my shoulders, pulls me close, and hugs me tight. Like she's giving one of the bearhugs Dad used to dish out when we were little. But there's no joy in her embrace. Only fear and desperation. I keep one hand free to flip on the light switch in the foyer.

"Damn kidsh! Going around the cul-de-sac doing Halloween pranksh. Don't think we didn't hear 'bout what you carved on the Delgadoshes—Del—Delgados door. Disgusting!"

Back in the kitchen, Mom doesn't sound like she'll provide much in the way of help. And Dad . . .

I can't think about them. There's more than enough for Marianne and me to handle right now. I take the lead, stepping toward our front door that's rattling on its hinges from all the knocking.

Enough of this.

Tell the truth, I don't know where the confidence, courage, whatever the hell you want to call it, comes from. I'm tired. Not from today but from all days. All the days leading up to this day, this night.

I'm here. I'm not locked away in my room playing video games with the sound cranked full blast. I'm not filling my ears with music, chatting gamers, and the boom-boom-boom of laser cannons roasting digital zombies, everything so loud I can't hear someone crying, can't hear screaming, can't hear frantic phone calls and screeching sirens. None of that this time.

Marianne grabs my hand again, pulling me from the door. Unsteady on heels, she stumbles backward.

I steady her. Red lines and burst blisters cover her feet. The straps of her fancy footwear dig in deep. *Has she been wearing these shoes since Halloween?*

I remember Halloween. I remember looking out my window while a new game loaded, watching Marianne sneak out the backdoor to join Craig who waited in the woods behind the cul-de-sac. She wore the black leather duster he'd loaned her and wobbled across our brown autumnal backyard. She'd looked closer to any real scarecrow than Dad ever had.

I wonder what kind of penance she's paying by leaving on those heels.

"Don't go out there," she says. I listen. Because she's my sister, and I love her. I trust her, and I love her.

But her words can't stop me parting the long, dark curtains in our front window to peer out onto the porch.

I could kick myself for turning the lights on. They make it harder to see what's outside. At first, all I see is my reflection. Then I see Marianne behind me. *God, how long has she looked so sick? So thin? Have I seen her eat anything lately? Even a piece of candy?*

My eyes adjust. Lucky me, there's no sign of Craig on or near the porch. Only the shattered remnants of our pumpkins. It looks like Marianne's pumpkin has joined ours in ruin. It looks like someone's put their boot down through the top.

"Should we call for help?" I ask.

Some things you never expect to say, some things you never want to say. Those words don't sound cool or "right" or whatever, in the moments when they're uttered. They sound surreal and ridiculous, as if we're five years old again, dressed in Mom and Dad's church clothes, playing "Good Guys and Bad Girls."

Marianne starts to answer. "I told him not to . . . "

"Look at you my shcary scarecrow. Don't got nothing to say, huh? C'mon, take this mask off . . . "

But Dad won't take it off. He hasn't since Halloween. And so Mom grabs and pulls at the mask, all by herself. Despite her efforts, the mask will stay in place. So, Mom mashes her lips, stained blue from wine, against the potato sack covering. She covers its bottom half in inky blue lipstick marks.

Done for now, Mom shoves Dad away. She screams, "You're not my husband! You're not him! Dammit. Damn you! You're not fair!"

This nightly ritual—it's the only thing they share anymore.

Glass breaks. The sound comes from the back of the house, near Mom and Dad.

Something—someone—big and heavy pushes hard, slamming their whole body against our backdoor. Mom asks a question and I hear her weeks-long bender getting sucked right out of her. "What are you doing here, young man?"

Boots stomp and glass shards scrape across the tile floor of the kitchen. Marianne pulls me toward the sound. Or I pull her. Doesn't matter. The point is, we go together, despite every adrenaline-spiked instinct telling us to do the contrary. We go because it's Mom and Dad.

And Craig's in the kitchen.

Of course.

He punched out the backdoor window to get in, but cut his hand in the process. He bleeds into the grooved indentations separating floor tiles. Thick drops splatter like warm raspberry jam.

Blood's not the only thing making me and Marianne stop short of entering the kitchen. There's also the black-handled hunting knife Craig holds in his hand.

"Hey, babe," he says, moving toward us. Something's wrong here, more wrong than a ghosted teenage lover. I need to do something, so I pull Marianne behind me. The fact she lets me do it shows how wrong things really are.

I've got a clear view into the kitchen now. Mom leans against one of the walls, and it looks like it's taking all the strength she has left to keep upright. Her bottle of wine remains in her hand. Eyes wide open, she's a frightened animal smelling predators around every corner. Craig's eyes are wide too, but not the same way. There's something else behind his too-big eyes and too-big smile.

His smile. So big. It's like he's holding onto it, making it stay put under his nose and above his chin. It makes his whole face look like another mask.

And then, there's Dad. He's standing in front of the fridge, right by Craig and that big knife of his with its dirty blade. There's something on the knife, a darker red than rust. Dad reaches into the fridge for turkey slices, wheat bread, tomatoes, and lettuce. Making another sandwich he'll never eat. Most mornings, either Marianne or I come by and sweep the uneaten sandwich off the table and into the trash. We try to do it before Mom comes in, hungover and angry at the world. If she sees it, she'll scream at us, "Don't touch that! That's your father's!"

But Dad doesn't care about the sandwich. Even now, I don't think he knows the sandwich is there. He doesn't act like he knows his wife, his son, and his daughter are here. And as he slams the fridge door closed, he doesn't even seem aware of Craig right beside him.

The rest of us are very aware.

Lucky for him Craig's attention is also elsewhere.

My sister's ex-whatever looks at me and then leans to the side to peer at Marianne standing behind me. Then, back at me. He rubs his fists under his eyes. Acting like he can't tell us apart. He doesn't let go of his blood-stained knife and comes close to slicing the wrist on his opposite hand. Finished with his pantomime, he stares at me. "I forget how much the two of you look alike. Like seeing double. You the same . . . everywhere?"

"You need to leave, Craig. *Now.*" Marianne finds her voice again. It's her "I was born a full minute before you, so you'll always be the baby" voice. "Mom, call the cops. Mom?"

But Mom's not in any shape to make the call. She's staring at her wine bottle, studying her reflection in the curved glass. "Mom!"

Craig moves fast. He swings the knife at Mom, using it more as a bludgeon than a blade. He connects, slapping the bottle from her hands. Mom's reaction, a simple, short "Oh," sounds painfully inadequate to the situation.

The bottle falls and shatters against the tiles. Chunks of green glass spray out. Caught in the line of fire, Mom takes several direct hits. Tiny cuts erupt across her arms, her legs, even on her face.

Marianne and I move as one. We both know what to do. There are two of us. And one of him. *Has to be enough, right?*

Craig swings his knife in crisscrossing arcs. We make it inside the kitchen, but that's about as far as he lets us get. "Uh uh," he says, wearing that fake smile again. "Been thinking about you, babe. Haven't heard from you. Miss our talks. Miss all the things we did when we weren't talking. Not hearing from you after everything, makes me wonder who you *are* talking to. And what you might be saying to 'em."

His rambling monologue gives me a chance to take a long, clear look at him. He doesn't look good. Underneath the duster, I'm pretty sure he's still wearing the clothes he had on when he met Marianne behind the house on Halloween night.

I can't remember if I've seen him at school since then either. I can't remember seeing anyone at school though. Too many sleepless nights tracking Dad's reenactments of a normal life, so everything's blurred together.

I remember men with mustaches and too-short ties, sitting behind wooden desks, and asking questions. Sounds like school, right?

"Did you notice anyone suspicious near your house or around the neighborhood that evening?" "Did you hear anything from the front porch?" "Can you confirm your sister's whereabouts around . . . "

Strange questions for *Algebra I*, I admit.

I wonder what those question-askers would ask Craig if given the chance. Would they ask him about his clothes, about those other stains colored similarly to the ones on our floor and his knife?

His dirty, disheveled appearance is in stark contrast to Marianne's. She's done laundry night after night. Over and over. She washes her hands until her knuckles get dried out and cracked, bleeding onto the porcelain and down the drain. Then, she washes them some more. Before we accepted that getting Dad to change was a lost cause, she'd try to get me to take his costume off, so she could wash it. "It's disgusting. It's *wrong*. Why won't he take it off?" she'd say.

"Hey, Craig, look. Whatever's going on here. I think this is a big misunderstanding. Let's calm down and talk this out, okay?"

I wonder if everyone else hears how terrified I am.

The legs of the chair at the head of the kitchen table scrape against gumball-sized shards of glass. Dad flops down in his seat. Everyone looks in his direction.

For a moment, he's the scarecrow, all stuffing and nothing else. Craig's keeping his distance. God, he's more frightened of a middle-aged man wearing an old Halloween costume to scare trick-or-treaters than I'd expect. I don't know why.

It's Dad. Dad and his dumb costume.

But Marianne looks frightened too. And it's not the knife-wielding ex doing it to her. It's Dad again.

Then, Dad does something different. He puts both hands under his mask and lifts. The lights go out. On one second. Off the next. We're all in the dark.

But we all hear something.

What we hear doesn't match the expected noises. No heavy breathing. No glass crunching underfoot. No sounds of a house settling around five unsettled individuals trapped together in the kitchen.

No, it sounds like we're outdoors. Owls cry out. Children screech and laugh. Parents shout out warnings. "That's enough! It's almost curfew time and a storm's coming! One last house and then it's bedtime! And no candy before bed, mister! No, no, keep your princess dress on!"

And more, footsteps on creaking porch steps. I know those steps and I know those creaks. "Can't believe you carved that on the Delgados' door. And the McCormacks'll freak when they see their sandbo—Jesus Christ!"

It's Marianne. But not the Marianne I've rediscovered over these last few weeks. It's the old Marianne. The one I didn't want to know. She screams like she's the one dying.

A meaty impact and the crack of breaking bones like a starter pistol firing. Pouring rain provides the perfect backing track.

"Oh my God! Oh my God! What did you do? What did you do?" There's Marianne again.

"What do you mean? Why'd he have to jump up and scare me like that?" There's Craig. Not the Craig here with us in the kitchen, though there are hints of him in the speaker's inflections. It's a different Craig, a from-before Craig, same as Marianne.

"Daddy? Daddy?"

"That's your dad?"

"Help me! Get some, I dunno . . . towels . . . something. Dad?"

A raspy cough, phlegmy and thick on the exhale—there's Dad.

"He jumped up. Jesus! I thought he was a stupid Halloween prop. God, he didn't even look real. He scared me. The knife slipped. God damn. Goddammit!"

"Daddy? Daddy, stay with me, okay? Daddy? Why won't this mask come off? Craig? Help me!"

The familiar creaking of our porch steps echoes off the kitchen walls, out the busted door, and into the night.

"Uh uh. No way. No way. Look."

"No, no, no, no. Daddy . . . I . . . "

"Marianne, listen. Look. There's no one out here. They're all back from tricks and treats. Getting out of the rain. I'll go. You go around back. Walk inside, and come back out here through the house. There's time. Get your Mom or your brother Mike or whatever to call 9-1-1. There's time."

"He's not breathing. Oh, Jesus."

"Go. Now. Go, don't say a word to anyone about this. It'll work out. It'll be like it never happened."

Craig speaks again. Here and now, with all of us and everything we know. "Mari—."

He doesn't finish. The lights come back on. Mom holds the neck of her wine bottle. We don't see the broken, jagged end moving past Craig's lips and down his throat. Whatever words he had for my sister will go unspoken. His palms slap the glass-covered tile, and he crumples to the floor.

I've heard enough from him. I've heard enough forever.

I find Marianne.

She pulls Dad up from the table. His mask is back down. His face covered. He's quiet. She takes his arms and wraps them around her shivering body.

"I'm sorry. I'm sorry. I'm sorry. I'm sorry."

Mom and I don't say a word. But we join them. Mom steps over Craig to get there.

And then we're all together, squeezing tighter and tighter. Tighter still. Holding it. First Marianne, then Mom, then me.

"I'm sorry."

And then, "I miss you."

We let go. The costume falls to the floor. As empty as it's always been since Halloween night.

I look at Marianne. I look at Mom. I want to say something. I *should* say something.

But I'll be damned if I can find the words.

ABOUT THE CONTRIBUTORS

STEVE RASNIC TEM is a past winner of the Bram Stoker, World Fantasy, and British Fantasy Awards. His novel *Ubo* (Solaris Books), a finalist for the Bram Stoker Award, is a dark science fictional tale about violence and its origins, featuring such historical viewpoint characters as Jack the Ripper, Stalin, and Heinrich Himmler. He has published almost 500 short stories in his 40+ year career. Some of his best are collected in *Thanatrauma* and *Figures Unseen* from Valancourt Books. His home on the web is www.stevetem.com.

CHRISTI NOGLE's debut novel, *Beulah*, is out now from Cemetery Gates Media and her collections *The Best of Our Past, the Worst of Our Future, Promise*, and *One Eye Opened in That Other Place* are coming in 2023 and 2024 from Flame Tree Press. Her short stories have appeared in over fifty publications including *PseudoPod*, *Vastarien*, and *Dark Matter Magazine* along with anthologies such as *Nightscript* III, IV, and VI and Flame Tree's *American Gothic and Chilling Crime Stories*. Christi lives in Boise, Idaho with her partner Jim and their gorgeous dogs. Follow her at christinogle.com or on Twitter @christinogle

LUCIANO MARANO is an author, photographer, and journalist. His written and photographic reporting has earned a number of industry awards, including his twice being named a Feature Writer of the Year by the Washington Newspaper Publishers Association. *Hidebound*, the first installment in a trilogy of werewolf novellas, The Ambush Moon Cycle, is now available from Raven Tale Publishing. His short fiction has appeared in *Year's Best Hardcore Horror Vol. 3*, *Monsters, Movies & Mayhem* (winner: Colorado Book Award), *Crash Code* (nominee: Splatterpunk Award), *Breaking Bizarro*, and *The Nightside Codex*, as well as *PseudoPod*, *Horror Hill*, and *Chilling Tales for Dark Nights*, among others. Originally from rural western Pennsylvania, he now resides near Seattle. Find him online at www.luciano-marano.com and on Instagram @ghosttowngossip.

JOSHUA REX is an American author of speculative fiction, and an historian who holds an M.A. from Bowling Green State University. He was born in Sandusky, Ohio and grew up in both the Midwest and New England. He is the author of the novel *A Mighty Word* (Rotary Press), the novella *The Inamorta* (forthcoming from Weird House Press), and the collections *The Descent and Other Strange Stories* (Weird House Press) and *What's Coming for You* (Rotary Press). His short fiction has appeared with *Nightscript*, *Pseudopod*, *Tales to Terrify*, and others. He is the host of the podcast The Night Parlor, where he interviews authors, artists, historians, and musicians. He lives in Providence, Rhode Island.

JO KAPLAN is the author of *It Will Just Be Us* and *When the Night Bells Ring*. Her short stories have appeared in *Fireside Quarterly, Black Static, Nightmare Magazine, Vastarien, Haunted Nights* edited by Ellen Datlow and Lisa Morton, *Miscreations* edited by Doug Murano and Michael Bailey, and elsewhere (sometimes as Joanna Parypinski). Currently, she is the co-chair of the HWA LA chapter and teaches English and creative writing at Glendale Community College. Find more at Jo-Kaplan.com.

M.C. ST. JOHN is a writer living in Chicago. He is the author of the short story collection *Other Music*. His stories have appeared, as if by luck or magic, in *Burial Day Books, Dark Ink Books, Nightscript, Flame Tree Publishing*, and *Wyldblood Press*. He is also a member of the Great Lakes Association of Horror Writers, serving as co-editor for the horror anthology *Recurring Nightmares*. See what he's writing next at www.mcstjohn.com.

JOHN GARLAND WELLS is a writer, poet and performer in Asheville, NC. In addition to his debut collection *Maxie Collins Dreams of Wretched Colors* being released in 2021, Wells tours the country performing original spoken word with his band Bad Ties.

HARRISON DEMCHICK is a developmental editor who has worked on more than eighty published books. As an author, he's written the literary horror novel *The Listeners* (Bancroft Press, 2012) and short stories including "Magicland" (Phantom Drift, 2019), "Tailgating" (Tales to Terrify, 2020), and "The Yesterday House" (Aurealis, 2020). As a screenwriter, his first film, *Ape Canyon*, won Best Feature at the 2020 Adrian International Film Festival and launched to streaming services in Spring 2021.

DANIEL BRAUM writes "strange tales" in the tradition of Robert Aickman. His stories, set in locations around the globe, explore the tension between the psychological and supernatural. His third collection *Underworld Dreams* contains "How to Stay Afloat When Drowning," which also appears in *Best Horror of the Year Volume 12* edited by Ellen Datlow. His first collection *The Night Marchers and Other Strange Tales* and his first novella *The Serpent's Shadow* are being reissued as trade paperbacks by Cemetery Dance Publications in May 2023. His first novel *Servant of the Eighth Wind* is coming soon from Lethe Press. Braum hosts the Night Time Logic series and the New York Ghost Story Festival. Find him on his YouTube channel DanielBraum, and at https://bloodandstardust.wordpress.com

SAM DAWSON has been quietly writing (and sometimes illustrating) stories for 25 years now. By trade a journalist, his collection, *Pariah & Others Stories*, was published last year by Supernatural Tales.

JUSTIN A. BURNETT is the author of *The Puppet King and Other Atonements*. He's also the Executive Editor of Silent Motorist Media, a small press responsible for the creation of the anthologies *Mannequin: Tales of Wood Made Flesh*, named best multi-author anthology of 2019 by Rue Morgue magazine, *The Nightside Codex*, and *Hymns of Abomination: Secret Songs of Leeds*, a tribute to the work of Matthew M. Bartlett. He's currently writing a novel while living in Austin, Texas, with his partner and children.

GRACE LILLIE is an author of countless to-do lists, hundreds of pages of D&D campaign notes, one scientific research paper, and now her first published work of fiction. She lives in Columbus, OH, where she works as a mechanical engineer to fund her ever-increasing collection of books and craft supplies.

DIXON MARCH is a reader and writer of weird fiction. At no point has she hosted a midnight radio talk show and/or intercepted dark messages from the stars. There are rumors she operates out of Omaha, Nebraska, US. Make no attempt to contact this person at dixonmarch.wordpress.com.

K. WALLACE KING is a writer currently living in Los Angeles.

J. S. KUIKEN is the author of short stories, essays, poems, plays, and novellas. His work has been published in an assortment of places, including *Foglifter*, *Bosie Magazine*, |tap|, and *Cactus Heart*. He earned his MA in Creative Writing from the University of East Anglia and was a 2013 Lambda Literary Fellow. When he's not writing, he's busy taking naps with his cat and having deep thoughts about how dreamy Dream of the Endless is. You can find him online at jskuiken.com.

LC VON HESSEN is a writer of horror, weird fiction, and various unpleasantness, as well as a noise musician, occasional actor, and former Morbid Anatomy Museum docent. Their work has previously appeared in such publications as *The Book of Queer Saints*, *Your Body is Not Your Body*, *Stories of the Eye*, *Vastarien*, previous volumes of *Nightscript*, and the ebook collection *Spiritus Ex Machina*. An ex-Mid-westerner, von Hessen lives in Brooklyn with a talkative orange cat.

GORDON BROWN grew up in the deserts of Syria and now lives in the deserts of Nevada. Since arriving in the New World, his work has appeared in *McSweeney's Internet Tendency*, *The Hunger Mountain Review*, *Tales to Terrify*, and more. He spends his time writing feverishly and looking after his cats, of which he has none.

PATRICK BARB is an author of weird, dark, and horrifying tales, currently living (and trying not to freeze to death) in Saint Paul, Minnesota. He is the author of *Helicopter Parenting in the Age of Drone Warfare* (Spooky House Press), *Gargantua-na's Ghost* (Grey Matter Press), and *The Nut House* (currently serialized in Cosmic Horror Monthly). His debut dark fiction collection *Pre-Approved for Haunting* is coming from Keylight Books in October 2023. In addition, he is an Active Member of the HWA and a Full Member of the SFWA. Visit him at patrickbarb.com or follow him at twitter.com/pbarb.

C.M. MULLER lives in St. Paul, Minnesota with his wife and two sons—and, of course, all those quaint and curious volumes of forgotten lore. He is related to the Norwegian writer Jonas Lie and draws much inspiration from that scrivener of old. His tales have appeared in *Shadows & Tall Trees*, *Vastarien*, *Supernatural Tales*, and a host of other venues. *Hidden Folk*, his debut story collection, was released in 2018.

———— • ————

For more information about NIGHTSCRIPT, please visit:

www.chthonicmatter.wordpress.com/nightscript

Made in the USA
Monee, IL
20 September 2022

ffc5d962-e93e-43b0-bc08-ba95058d5559R01